LOVE & INK

JD HAWKINS

Copyright © 2018 by JD Hawkins

All rights reserved.

No part of this book may be reproduced in any form or by any electronic or mechanical means, including information storage and retrieval systems, without written permission from the author, except for the use of brief quotations in a book review.

Want to keep up to date with JD? Sign up for his VIP list!

This book is dedicated to all the amazing tattoo artists who allow us to wear our dreams on our skins. Thank you for the inspiration, the love and the pure dedication to the art.

1

ASH

Today's the day. I know exactly what I want, where I'm going to do it, and who I want to do it to me.

The tattoo shop casts an edgy, looming presence over the sunny morning street in south Echo Park. Its dark colors dramatic against the corporate signage and clean windows of the coffee shops and vintage clothing stores beside it. Detailed images of skulls and roses cover the windows, hiding what's behind them, like the dark brooding scowl of a bad kid daring you to engage with him. I can feel my pulse kick up a few notches the closer I get.

Even as I pull up outside to park, I see one tatted-up person enter, another black-clad person leave. Mandala Ink isn't the biggest tattoo spot in Los Angeles—it might not even be the busiest—but it's by a long margin the best. Maybe even in the whole of California. To get a tattoo anywhere else is to settle for less, everyone knows that. Even me, and I've never even gotten one before—but I did months of online research and scoured thousands of pictures of tattoo art before deciding on this artist and this studio. With a waiting list six months long and a strict no walk-ins policy that applies to even the biggest rock stars and film celebrities, it feels almost like a blessing that I'm gonna get my tattoo here. Six months wasn't enough to change my mind, but it's done little to ease my nerves now that I'm finally right outside the place.

I get out of the car, pay the meter, and walk purposefully toward that dark door. A little nervous about pushing it open, but even more worried that if I hesitate I'll turn around and drive away. My adrenaline is singing. I'm finally really doing this.

I push open the door and enter, the buzz of a tattoo needle humming in my ears and the smell of disinfectant noticeable as I step inside. If the exterior was slightly intimidating, the inside is overwhelming. It's bigger than I imagined. The walls are covered with gorgeous, intricate artwork, from ceiling to floor. Patterns that can hypnotize, faces so beautiful they seem almost real, creatures and characters and crosses so vivid they dance as you look at them. There's a vintage sofa, a Bauhaus design that could be a museum piece, artful enough to make you want to look at it rather than sit on it. In front of it is a low, carved Asian-style coffee table, littered with art books. A glass counter splits the room in half, and behind the counter there's a curtain with an Indian pattern in purple and red. Inside, this place is nothing like I imagined, and yet it's perfect all the same.

A big guy stands behind the counter, talking animatedly with a female customer. I watch as he extends an arm, wide enough to see the entire wingspan of the dragon inked on it, and punches the fist of the customer, sending the spiky-haired young woman on her way.

The customer gone, the big guy turns his sparkling eyes to me. The top of his head's as bald as a baby, the bottom has a red beard long enough to braid. Is this him? *Schurkenwolf*? I know a few different artists work at the shop, but the main draw is Schurkenwolf, the owner—and the person I've scheduled my appointment with. Most famous tattoo artists use a nickname, but with a moniker that's German for "rogue wolf," I came here with no clue what to expect of the man himself...except that he's probably from Germany.

"Hey there," he says, in a musical southern accent that is in no way German and immediately dashes all my assumptions. "Welcome. What can I help you with today?"

"Are you—Schurkenwolf?" I ask, intimidated despite his friendly manner.

"Nope." He laughs. "I'm Ginger."

"Ginger! You're the one who does all the micro tattoos I saw on the shop's Instagram. I love your detail work on those," I blurt.

The big man actually blushes. "Thank you. You know we don't take walk-ins as a rule, but I'm happy to offer a brief consultation, and then we can go from there, if you're—"

"Oh, um, I've already emailed with you guys, actually," I say, stepping forward a little nervously, like I'm in a line-up. "I booked a tattoo with Schurkenwolf, around eleven today?"

He taps at a keyboard and squints at the screen in front of him. "Ashley Carter?"

My stomach lurches and I let out a nervous laugh. "That's me."

His smile grows even warmer. "Perfect. Go ahead and have a seat. Be right with you." He gestures at the sitting area and then disappears behind a curtain into the back of the shop.

I wait a while, flipping through some of the art books and losing myself in the elegant shading of a jungle cat's fur on a poster to the side. There are mumbled exchanges I can barely hear beyond the curtain, and then a voice grabs my attention.

"So you're Ashley?"

The voice is strong. Confidently slow and projected with the kind of deep tones that can only come from a tough body.

"Yeah," I say, finding it hard to pull my eyes away from the wall now. "But you can call me..."

I stop myself when I turn around, suddenly frozen to the spot. A wave of shock flushing all sense of reality out of my body.

He's big, shoulders broad enough to act as a battering ram, jaw strong enough to take one. Beneath his thick, dark hair he narrows his eyes into an icy-blue glare. A look of incredulous recognition.

"*Ash?*" he says.

"*Teo?*" I reply, in such a low whisper he probably couldn't hear me three feet away.

Still, I don't quite believe it. Not until he gives me that half-smile I never thought I'd see again, and it becomes undeniable. It's *him.*

He's filled out a little in the seven years since I last saw him, his smooth, boyish good looks gone rugged with time, the defined curve of his muscles adding some shape to that height. His arms sleeved with black and grey tattoos, a menagerie of geometric shapes, animals and flowers, hypnotic patterns joining them together. The memory that I carried around of him for seven years, of that brooding boy with his tight jeans and shaggy hair, who'd wait for me to get on the back of his bike so he could rev me away, gets violently torn up in my mind like a bad photograph. I can't stop staring at the gorgeous man he's become.

My mouth goes dry and I panic a little. These few moments that I have to consider so many memories and so much emotion feel like an eternity, but somehow still too short to find my bearings. I'd need weeks—maybe months—to handle the shock of seeing him again. To figure out whether I should feel angry, hurt, forgiving...or nothing at all. Instead, all I've got is the time it takes to breathe deeply and struggle to put on a nonchalant smile.

"How have you been?" he asks, moving close to the counter and putting those arms on it. He sounds totally neutral, totally laid-back. I know that seeing me must be a shock to him, too. But I have no idea how he feels about it.

I fight to come up with some kind of casual verbal response. What do you say to the guy who you loved with the devout passion only a teenager loving for the first time can muster? A boy who was your secret, who you kissed by the light of the moon, to the music of owls? To the boy who climbed in your window at two in the morning and stayed just long enough to leave you with a stolen flower, the lingering aftertaste of his lips, and the feeling that all the dramatic romances you'd read about in books weren't just true, but severely undersold?

A boy who skipped town without telling you on prom night, the night you were going to show the world you didn't care about them enough to keep your love a secret anymore?

I wonder if he's experiencing as much turmoil as I am, if he feels like his insides are being chewed up as well. If he is, he's not showing it. There's no softness in his eyes, no hint of recognition, nothing of what is owed to the girl he crushed.

Part of me wants to scream, to slap Teo in a futile attempt to hurt him as much as he hurt me. But the other part of me wants to grab him and hold him against me, tight enough to stop the wounds that bled for seven years without him. I'm so overwhelmed and want to do so much at once that I end up doing nothing.

"I'm fine. You?" is all I manage to say.

"Good," he says firmly.

"So you're—you're Schurkenwolf?"

"In the flesh," he says with an easy grin. "So what are you having done today?"

"Oh. Right." Automatically, I reach for my bag and pull out the old photo, sliding it across the glass counter to him. His expression softens.

"Your mom, huh? A memorial tattoo."

I nod. "Just her face. I'd like it on my inner arm. Bicep," I say, brain struggling to make the words sound like a proper sentence.

Teo picks up the photo and studies it with the calculating detachment of a mechanic looking at an engine. I wonder if he remembers the picture, remembers seeing it framed in silver on my nightstand all those years ago.

He casually places a pad of art paper on the counter beside the photo and uncaps an architect pen. Then he leans over the pad, deep in concentration as he sketches out what the tattoo will look like. I'd heard about this before, the way the flash for Mandala tattoos are usually sketched out right in front of the customer, instead of planned weeks or months in advance. I'd heard some people say they did this to save time, or maybe to keep things more organic, and I'd heard others say the fact that Mandala tattoos are so 'in the moment' made them even more incredible. Either way, the tattoo is the last thing on my mind right now.

I stare at him, less self-conscious now that his attention is entirely taken by the art. I take a step closer toward the counter, as if to look at what he's drawing, but really just to be nearer to him. He still smells the same, a mixture of bike grease and sweetness that's been baking in the sun. His hair is shorter now, but still that thick, never-tangled mass I could never resist playing with. In his tight black tank I can see the tattoos that cover his exposed muscles. I find buried in the patterns and scripts the motorcycle handlebars tattoo—the only one he had when I knew him—the one I used to trace with my finger back and forth, over and over...

Teo stands up to his full, overbearing height and spins the pad around so I can see the face.

"What do you think? Something like this? It'll have more depth and dimension when I do the shading, but this should give you an idea."

I only glance at the sketch—I'm in no state to perform art criticism.

"Looks great," I say, all polite smile and customer satisfaction.

Teo gestures to the curtain and leads me behind it, where the chairs and equipment are set up. With the professional demeanor of a doctor he pulls out some latex gloves and puts them on, talking at me over his shoulder as he sets out rubbing alcohol, ink, and packages of new needles. My heart is racing, a million thoughts and memories still flooding my mind.

"Take off your shirt and have a seat."

Once again I freeze as about a dozen emotions fight it out somewhere in the battlegrounds between my head, my heart, and my gut. Is he really going to not say anything? Is he really going to treat me like I'm some random girl who walked in off the street, and not the girl he swore his very soul to?

More to the point, am *I* really going to do this? Am I about to sit for hours in this strange state of unasked questions, unresolved angers, while Teo draws my deceased mother on me? I haven't felt this vulnerable, this confused, this paralyzed since that night, listening to the muffled music and laughter of other couples while I stood outside in my prom dress staring at the empty road as the night darkened, telling myself he'd show up any minute and waiting until the parking lot had emptied at the end of the night before finally calling a cab to bring me home.

I bring a hand to the lapel of my plaid shirt and start unbuttoning it slowly, hands acting of their own accord though I keep telling them to stop. He glances back, and I see his eyes flicker downward from my eyes to the bare skin, the thin strap of my bra visible. Despite everything else, I blush a little, remembering different times now. Remembering how it felt to be naked with him, on top of him, those same eyes covering my body like a slow kiss. He turns back to the equipment but I just stand there, feeling flustered and overwhelmed, noticing my ever-quickening heartbeat. But it has nothing to do with the tattoo.

Teo turns to me again and this time shoots me a confused look, as if wondering why it's taking so long. Suddenly he gets that half-grin again.

"You nervous?" he says.

"You know what?" I say, as I pull my shirt around me more tightly. "I think I am. I think I'm not...really ready for this, I guess. Sorry. Think I'm gonna bail."

I've already turned, pushing back through the curtain before Teo can say anything else. When I'm at the door I hear him call behind me.

"Hey Ash. Wait."

I turn to see him standing at the curtain, face still hard as ever, expression still unreadable, but a little softness in his eyes now that could just be my imagination.

"It's been...nice seeing you again," he says. "And if you change your mind, you wanna come back, just email Ginger and we'll get you in here right away."

This time I manage to keep it together. I purse my lips in an ambiguous gesture of acknowledgment, and leave.

2

TEO

Who needs a psychotherapist when you have a dog? One that doesn't need to ask questions to know how you're feeling, and only needs to lick your face to make you feel better. As if sensing the dark memories that are beginning to encroach at the corners of my thoughts, Duke whimpers at me, drags his leash around the house, leaps into my lap whenever I sit down.

It's hard to do the whole 'moodily twisting yourself up over the past' thing when you've got a mongrel pawing at the back door. So here I am, sweating my way up Runyon Canyon while Duke overtakes me, gets distracted sniffing around in the greenery, then realizes he's been left behind, and repeats.

I sprint up the dirt trail, fast enough that even Duke gives me confused looks. I push myself, forcing my muscles to hurt, my lungs to reach bursting point, so that I can't think, can't remember...

Ash. A face I thought I'd never see again. A face I'd consigned to dreams and unfinished thoughts. Seven years to tell myself it didn't matter. Seven years to convince myself it was the right thing. Seven years to bury those memories and move on. Seven years to forget. Less than seven seconds to bring it all back, as fresh and as raw as the day it happened.

Love & Ink 9

Did she even remember? She'd always been hard to read. A locked box of slow-burning emotions. As cool, collected and casual as someone who always knows something you don't.

She looked good. Those dark eyes as fierce as ever, that long blonde hair now short and layered, framing the perfect sweep of her face in vivid angles. A beauty so powerful it reminded me of all the good times as much as the bad...

I stop finally, panting hard, hands on hips. The L.A. sprawl stretching out in front of me.

"Duke!" I call out. I whistle with the little breath I can muster. "Duke, buddy. Where are you?"

I shield my eyes and look back down the path, taking a few steps until I see him. He's rolling around in the dirt, panting as much as I am while a girl squats beside him to playfully rub at his thick fur.

I smile and start moving toward them. The girl's got her back to me, hair pulled back in a short ponytail, but I can still tell she's hot, all nutcracker thighs in her three-quarter length yoga pants, grabbable hips and biteable ass.

Maybe that's what I need to clear the demons swirling in my mind, a little physical therapy administered by an athletic blonde who likes dogs. Shit, maybe the reason seeing Ash has me this fucked up is that I've been working so hard that I haven't been laid in a while. Maybe even Duke knows that and this is his way of helping.

I draw close, the sun still in my eyes, the two of them still playing in the dirt.

"You made a friend there, Duke?" I say.

The girl ruffles him one more time and says, "Beautiful dog."

She stands up slow, and I get ready to give her the eyes, the smile. She turns to face me, and both of our smiles drop like they're illegal.

It's her.

For a few seconds we hold each other's gaze like animals on each other's territory. Then the tension breaks the only way it can—with both of us laughing incredulously.

"Holy shit," she says, shaking her head.

"Two times in two days. You're either really good or really bad at stalking me."

She laughs and it sounds just like it used to, maybe a little stronger, a little more confident. Fluttery, like a bird springing into the air. I take a second to appreciate the way the sun glistens on the sweat of her shoulder, how her skin glows with the redness of pumped muscles. Suddenly I'm back in that humid summer, when we rode out to a lake, went skinny-dipping in the midday sun. We fucked right there on the rocks, bodies wet with sweat and water, hot and flustered, thirsty for each other. I swallow down my dry mouth and suddenly wish I could take her back there, no questions asked, no complicated history behind us.

"I've never seen you up here before," I say. "And I come run here pretty often."

She shrugs. "I just moved to this part of town last week."

"No shit."

"Yeah," she says. "I got promoted at work, so I could finally afford a place that doesn't feel like a converted closet."

I laugh a little, enjoying the way she relaxes in front of me, the sound of her voice bringing back all kinds of thoughts.

"What do you do now?" I ask.

"I'm a producer," she says, nodding. "You ever heard of *Hollywood Night*?" I shake my head. "Figures," she grins, "you're not exactly the demographic. It's a kind of celebrity gossip show. You know, 'this pop star got a nipple piercing,' 'this actor is dating this model'... It's not exactly the most artistically stimulating work, but ratings are good and so is the money. I can't complain."

"That's good," I say.

Ash looks askew at me.

"You still do that?" she says through a dimpled smile.

"Do what?"

"Say 'that's good' when you're trying to be polite but don't know how."

I laugh and look at Duke, who's sitting watching us with his tongue out like he's got front row seats to a play about old friends.

"Hey listen," I say. "About yesterday, at the shop—"

Ash waves it away.

"Sorry for bailing."

"I get it," I say, hoping she doesn't read too much into it. "First tattoos can be intimidating. I meant it, though, about if you decide to come back. We'll squeeze you in."

"Thanks." Ash smiles, and there's a slightly guilty silence between us, as if we've just brushed something under the carpet and agreed to keep it there. The silence goes on a little too long, and I search my mind for something to say. Something other than the things neither of us wants to address. Something other than goodbye—I'm not done drinking her in yet.

"Oh," I say suddenly, remembering. "You remember a girl named Isabel that we used to hang out with? From art class?" I say.

Ash wrinkles her nose up in thought.

"Isabel... Wait...braces? Coke-bottle glasses? Always wore that ripped pink cardigan? She was a band geek, but she was great. Really funny."

Through a laugh, I say, "Yeah, that's the one."

"Of course I remember her! She went to Europe, right? Right after high school. I was so excited for her, but we lost touch pretty soon after that."

"Well she's back now."

"Are you kidding me?" Ash says, punching my shoulder with a sudden burst of excitement. "And she didn't even tell me? I would've loved to hear from her again."

I hold up my hands in defense. "I only bumped into her by accident. She walked into the tattoo shop a month or two ago. Wanted a hand tattoo but we ended up talking about old times instead."

"Wow," Ash says, looking out over the city as she remembers. "Isabel... You know, I always thought she was kinda beautiful in this strange, subversive way."

"You should see her now. It ain't subversive anymore, she looks incredible. A trail of drooling guys wherever she goes. If the rock 'n roll chick type is your thing." I shrug, and Ash looks at me in open-mouthed awe. "Yeah. She's in a band—they just signed a deal with a major label after doing the indie thing for a few years. They're only in L.A. to record an album, I think."

"*Seriously?*" Ash says, looking almost proud. "God...she always talked about wanting to do that. I remember going to a couple shows with her, those fake IDs she got us, how she messed around with her old ukulele whenever I went to her house. This is incredible. I've *got* to see her before she goes."

"She wanted to see you too," I say, stopping short of admitting how much we had talked about Ash. I remember something and frown. "Actually, I think she said she was playing somewhere local in a couple of days. Put a flyer up in the shop."

"Wow," she says. "Living the dream, huh?"

I take a long moment to think about what I'm about to say. Then decide to take the risk.

"You wanna go?"

It takes a second for Ash to stutter over her response, and I imagine she's doing the same thing I am, trying to wrestle with a whole lot of complexity before she can give an answer so simple.

"Yeah...why not? Tell you what, call me when you figure out what night it's on and I'll see if I'm free. With the hours I work I don't get out much, but I can make an exception for an old friend."

"Let's exchange numbers," I say, pulling my phone out. "I could pick you up. Maybe we can get a drink afterward and catch up, or something." I don't clarify whether I'm talking about all three of us or just me and Ash, but she doesn't ask and I let it remain open-ended. No need to push things now—it seems smarter to just see how the night plays out.

We swap numbers and as she's putting her phone away Ash looks up at me through her side-swept bangs, with that mischievous look that always got me thinking unsayable things.

"You still ride a motorcycle?" she says.

I smile back.

"Nothing beats a bike for L.A. traffic. You still like riding in back?"

Ash lets out a furtive laugh, already turning away to leave.

"Give me a call. Let me know," she says, starting to run.

"Absolutely," I say, struggling to hide how good it feels knowing that I'll get to see her again.

3

ASH

I go through the morning at work like a coffee-fueled automaton. Executing the tasks on my to-do list with the detached determination of somebody who has bigger things on their mind. I buzz around the production office, handing out copies of scripts and shooting schedules, hashing out last-minute alterations to the night's program, and prepping a couple of guests, but mentally I'm still up there on Runyon Canyon, replaying the conversation with Teo, reading between the lines, searching for double meanings.

Even on the surface, it's crazy. An invitation to a concert? Casually delivered like we were just a couple of old high school buddies who did chess club together? No sense of the hurt and drama in our history. No acknowledgement of what he did to me, to us.

Then again, maybe it doesn't really matter to him, maybe it didn't mean anything. Maybe it was exactly what he seemed to treat it as: Bumping into some girl he used to know, and asking her out on some semi-date. Could he really have forgotten how badly things ended between us?

It was so easy—too easy—to be comfortable with him. Talking like we used to, laughing like we'd won. His eyes still fixed themselves on me like everything I said mattered, his presence so deep and strong I felt like I could fall into him. He still talked with that cool, guarded manner of holding something back. Still had the look of someone who didn't tell you everything, who kept himself a mystery, so that even when you were talking about one thing, you felt like he was thinking about something entirely different.

I used to love that, it used to make me want to unlock that enigmatic smile and find out what went on behind those narrowed eyes—but now that I know how much Teo can hurt me, I can't stop worrying about what could happen if I let myself get lost in him again.

For so many years I'd thought about what I'd say to him if I ever saw him again. I'd filled entire journals with the things I wanted to tell him. Angry, hurt, confused things. I'd imagined him turning up and begging for me to take him back. I imagined him turning up having completely forgotten about me. I'd envisioned passing him on the street, a battered, destitute criminal the way everyone in our town assumed he'd end up, or seeing him at a club partying it up, surrounded by sleazy hangers-on and pornstars.

And in all of those situations I knew what I would say. I'd had seven years to refine it, to practice. So that when I did get my shot it would really hit home. No room for him to mistake what I meant, no way he could ignore what he'd done to me.

Except the moment had come—twice in the last few days, in fact—and each time my mental script got thrown right out the window. What good was seven years' practice when the sight of that rugged jawline made me forget everything since then? What good was holding a grudge when that look made you feel so good?

Seeing him again made me realize what I really wanted, and it wasn't revenge. It wasn't to deliver the perfect 'fuck you,' or to gloat over some sense of high ground. All I really wanted was to go back to the past, seventeen and in our own secret world.

Except I can't. I can't forgive the unforgiveable. Not that it's even an option.

Now all I have are a bunch of questions, a half-promise we'll see each other again, and full confirmation that he's as beautiful and dangerous as I remember, maybe even more so.

"Crap!" I splutter, as my phone alarm goes off and I realize I've been staring at a blank sheet of paper on the desk in my new office for nearly an hour.

In five minutes I'm about to have the biggest meeting of my career. A pitch meeting with the higher-ups that I had to push, pull, and fight for like some lawyer on an unwinnable case. I may be new to the job title of producer, but I've been working my way up on this show for years and I know its internal workings like the back of my hand. I'm ready to push boundaries and forge my own path. I just need to get my head back in the game, and stat.

"Crap crap crap crap crap," I mutter to myself like some nihilistic mantra as I snatch and sweep up the papers I'd prepared for this.

This is my first real chance to drag some quality kicking and screaming into *Hollywood Night*. To take the televisual equivalent of a gossiping neighbor with a bad sense of humor and try to make something meaningful. Something people tune in for and remember, instead of just leaving on as background noise, or because they're too lazy to change the channel.

Clutching the stack of papers unevenly to my chest, I leave my new office (still only half-furnished) and blast through the corridor to the meeting room. At the door I see that two of the execs are already there. I knock lightly and force a bright, confident smile as I enter.

"Hey," I say, trying to hide the fact that I'm a little breathless with a swig from my coffee mug. "Hope I'm not late."

"Right on time," Sean says genially.

Sean's in his fifties, and has the gentle, detached presence of a man who doesn't seem to stress all that much about his work, but is so experienced in his field that he doesn't really need to. With his bald head and Lennon glasses he could pass for a New York Times columnist, though any one of them would probably swap places with him in a heartbeat. If you watch any primetime TV at all, chances are Sean is behind at least a third of them.

Love & Ink

"Just to let you know," he says, "Ted won't be able to make it today. He's got some other things to attend to."

"Oh, ok. I see," I say, pretending to be surprised. The truth is that I've only seen Ted once in all the years that I've been working here. If you could call Sean's engagement with the show 'hands off' then Ted's involvement is 'not even in the same hemisphere.'

The wiry woman with the red hair in a tight ponytail and permanently pouted lips looks at Sean, ignoring me. I grit my teeth and work hard to keep my smile firmly in place.

"How long are we giving this?" she says in a dry, bored voice.

"However long it takes, Candace," Sean shoots back, chuckling nonchalantly toward me, almost apologetically.

Candace McGill has a reputation for being rude, manipulative, and arrogant—and that's the nice version. As the executive producer and show runner, *Hollywood Night* is her baby—and by baby I mean the excuse she uses to party with celebrities and hit on young actors. She's as slim and dangerous as the cigarettes she chainsmokes, with a team of surgeons at her beck and call to keep her looking fantastic for her age—which I suspect is just a little younger than the Easter Island heads she looks uncannily like. My only hope for pushing through some of my ideas is that she doesn't care enough to bother shooting them down. Judging by the amount of work she does, that's not entirely impossible.

"I'll keep this quick, I promise," I say, sliding my papers around on the meeting desk. "I just wanted to go over a few ideas for some slightly longer features we could run. Interesting, more in-depth subjects that could give viewers a little more actual insight into Hollywood. You know, a more unique perspective that people might really respond to."

"Oh God," Candace sighs, looking out of the window in boredom. "This again. Honey: We're a late-night gossip show, not PBS. All you've got to do is put pretty faces on the screen, get actors to look like well-adjusted people for the interviews, tell rumors nobody cares about as if they're worth anything, collect a paycheck, and thank the Lord there are enough morons in the world to keep us in a job."

Sean laughs gently, though we both know Candace isn't really joking.

"I hear what you're saying," I reply, hoping to appear calmly diplomatic, "but even still, don't you think there's a little room for some more—"

"To be honest," Sean interrupts, "ratings are decent, but we're having to work pretty hard to keep them there. It's competitive now, what with TMZ and TrendBlend, no doubt about it. Sorry to say so, but it may not be the best time to take risks." He shrugs in apology.

"That's exactly my point," I say, leaning forward eagerly. "Most of our competition is coming from internet sites, right? And the whole 'celebrity scoop,' fast news cycle, short attention span thing is something we can't really compete with. They're always going to get there faster and more easily. Production value is our strongest suit. That's why—"

"Sweetie," Candace says, looking at me fully now, as if finally interested, "we don't *have to* compete, because they don't have the access, the power, or the money. And if the geeks posting online do want to come after us, they'll have a hell of a fight. If people want rumors, we'll have the sleaziest, dirtiest ones. If people want scoops, we'll make them ourselves."

Sean laughs again, this time a little more nervously.

"Right. I'm not saying we should change the show entirely," I say, backtracking a little to take the sting out of Candace's words. "But we could also do things that a lot of the internet blogs and video sites can't, such as really insightful features." I grab the printouts I'd made and slide them across the desk. "Remember last Christmas when we had to pull two segments at the last minute? I used the b-roll I had with some make-up artists just telling personal behind-the-scenes stories about actors and projects they'd worked on. It was a thirteen minute segment."

Candace rolls her eyes.

"How could I forget?" she says dismissively.

"Well, we didn't put the segment up on the site—but somebody took it and uploaded it anyway. It got thousands of views, and a ton of comments. People really seemed to like it. If we had put it up on our site it would have been in the top three videos for the year—and that's without people bouncing from our other videos."

Sean studies the sheet of figures and nods slightly, while Candace glances at it and pushes it back toward me.

"So what were you thinking?" Sean says.

"Ok," I say, leaning forward and taking a deep breath. This is it. "I've been talking with this really interesting woman who owns a yoga studio downtown. Just a couple of years ago the place was really struggling, but then these MMA fighters started going there, and in turn a lot of celebrities started going too. Apparently they really love this place. It's the new hot thing for actors here. We could take tons of angles on this. The feel-good story about a business turning things around. The idea of celebrities and regular joes going to the same classes, the way something like yoga can bring people together on equal ground—"

"Somebody pass me the remote," Candace sighs. "I'm already bored."

I let the comment slide. "Frankie—the woman who owns the studio—tells me there are some big actors who'd be willing to talk to us about how much they love the place."

"Sure," Candace says, "and there's a bum down the street who'll give you Clooney's number for the price of a forty. Honey, this is L.A. Everybody is somebody's cousin when they want something from you. We're not a charity organization set up to dole out free advertising. We run some infomercial crap like this and people will change the channel."

I clench my teeth, if only to stop me from saying something that would get me fired on the spot, and though the silence only lasts a few seconds, it's tense and hard.

Sean lets out another gentle chuckle to break it.

"It's a good idea, Ash," he says, though it sounds like a consolation. "Maybe we could revisit it at a later date, but for now I think we shouldn't rock the boat too much. Let's keep things running as smoothly as possible. You've only just started as a producer, so let's see how you do on the show as it currently is."

"Ok," I say.

"But great idea, and it's good to see you're thinking of ways to improve the show. Always good to see."

"Thanks," I say, already stacking my papers, grabbing my coffee, and standing up to leave.

I almost bolt out the door. Blood boiling so hot I want to scream like a kettle. I stride back to my office wondering if the door is sound-proofed, but halfway there I hear Jenny's voice.

"Ash! You having that meeting today?" she asks as she struggles to keep up beside me.

"Just had it." I refuse to make eye contact as I power walk down the hall, and I see her shoulders slump as she takes in my demeanor.

"Guessing it didn't go well then?"

"Your guess is correct."

I turn into my office and slam my papers down on my desk while Jenny closes the door behind her.

"You wanna talk about it?" she says, her voice gone low and soothing.

I turn around to face her, and at the site of her cute-as-a-button nose and thick, red, hand knit wool shawl, find it hard to maintain these levels of atomic frustration.

Jenny was one of the first people I met at this job, and now one of my closest friends. She's a writer, though nobody who saw her would have too much trouble deducing that. She looks like Virginia Woolf if Virginia Woolf smiled all the time, wore hoop earrings, and constantly dyed her hair whatever the most hipster shade of the month happened to be, in this case a glistening shade of greyish-blue.

"You were right," I say, throwing my hands up in the air and slumping onto the office couch, body limp with defeat. "Candace is never going to change. And neither is the show as long as she's in charge."

"She didn't like the yoga studio feature, huh?"

Love & Ink 21

"She didn't just dislike it, she spat all over it. You would think I was trying to allocate a segment to a Vietnam documentary the way she tells it. All I'm trying to do is add a little more substance to the show."

Jenny murmurs sympathetically.

"Was Sean there? Did he do anything? He loves you."

I shake my head. "Sean is Sean. He was into my ideas, but at the end of the day he's as scared of Candace as anyone. To be honest I don't blame him."

Jenny settles herself beside me on the couch and puts an arm around my shoulder, saying nothing, which I know comes hard to writers like her.

"Why am I even here? What's the point, Jenny?" I say, entering the 'despair' phase of this informal psychotherapy.

"The point is that you have a job that pays pretty well, you're great at what you do, and that you get to work alongside such cool and talented persons as myself."

"Such cool and talented persons that are allowed to do nothing better than write bad puns for segments about butt implants."

"You'd be surprised how challenging that can be."

I laugh a little, then stand up in a huff and start to pace, trying to shake off the bad energy that crackles through me. Jenny folds her arms and smiles.

"You gonna pretend that this is actually what's bothering you?" she asks.

I stop and look at her.

"What do you mean?"

"Come on. You don't expect me to believe you're this mad about a rejected segment, do you? You've worked here for two years—you know the drill." She pauses a moment, eyeballs me, and then nods slowly. "Alright. I see how it is. What's his name?"

I can't help but smile and shake my head a little, looking away in slight embarrassment.

"It's complicated."

"Great," Jenny says, leaning forward. "I love complicated. I read

Pynchon for the jokes."

I sigh a little, taking my time as I try to pick the right point to begin.

"It's not just any guy. I bumped into an ex yesterday."

Jenny rubs her hands together and grins. "Mm-hmm. I'm hooked already."

"He was, like, my first love. I mean real, deep, carve-your-name-in-my-skin love. Leave-your-shirt-behind-so-I-can-smell-you-after-you've-gone love. Kill-me-now-so-I'll-never-come-down-from-this-moment love, you know?"

"Whoa," Jenny coos on a heavy breath. "No. I don't know. My first love was more 'I'll-come-over-tonight-but-only-if-you-can-give-me-ten-bucks-for-gas' love."

I shake my head. "Anyway, we dated in high school and every-thing was magic and I thought it was forever until one night...he just skips town. Doesn't tell anybody anything. Just...gone. Nothing left behind, no clue where he went. Just gone. Never heard from him again. Until now."

Jenny sits back and frowns.

"You really don't know why? Did he act weird before he left or anything?"

"No. Nothing. His dad was always in and out of jail, involved with a lot of shady stuff, I don't even know what. Teo used to get picked up a lot by the cops too. But for nothing."

"Maybe that was it, though. Maybe this guy—Teo—committed a crime, like with his dad or something, and then left before he could get caught."

"No!" I say, sounding just like I did back then, always first to defend him. "Teo wasn't like that. Sure, he'd get into fights some-times, but he wasn't anything like his dad. Besides, he would have told me. We didn't hide anything from each other...or at least, I thought we didn't... I don't know. Maybe I'm wrong. Maybe he was just really good at pretending to love me, and I was really good at believing it."

Jenny lets the sadness linger in the air a moment before sympathetically sighing.

"How long since you saw him?"

"About seven years."

"Whoa!"

"I know. Long time, right? I tried to get over it. God, I dated some awesome guys. Smart, funny, talented, interested in *me*. But every time, I knew from the first date I wasn't going to fall for them. That it'd always feel...like an imitation."

"So you bumped into him again in L.A.? Just randomly?"

"Yeah. Just out of the blue. I went to a tattoo shop, and there he was."

"And you didn't say anything about your past? Or ask him why he left?"

"No. I mean, I wanted to, but...I don't know. It was confusing. A shock just seeing him. And I feel like I'm supposed to act like it's all water under the bridge. Like we've both moved on and it doesn't mean anything now. But..." I trail off, shaking my head.

Jenny sighs and nods sympathetically with the kind of expressive sadness only her big brown eyes could manage.

"Damn. And you'll never see him again. So now you'll never know."

"Actually, no—we're meeting again. He's supposed to call me."

"What?!" Jenny jumps up from the couch and paces toward me determinedly. "You'd better tell me you're gonna ask him what happened this time, because at this point I feel like I'm reading an Agatha Christie with some missing pages."

I laugh a little and move back to the desk, ready to take my seat and get back to work.

"That's not a bad way to describe how I felt the past seven years."

"Don't be afraid to talk to him, Ash. You can do this. You just gotta stand up and be your badass, take-no-shit, awesome self. You deserve some answers."

I nod and pick up my now-cold coffee, taking a big gulp and steeling myself for the day ahead. Jenny's right. I deserve answers. And I'm going to get them, no matter what.

4

TEO

It took me the bigger part of my life, but eventually I figured out that if you don't have much of a home, you can always make a new one yourself. That's what Mandala Ink feels like now. Home.

It wasn't easy. L.A.'s full of artists who can wield needles better than most surgeons, brilliant obsessives who could put a pore-perfect replica of the Sistine Chapel on your left butt cheek. I never saw the high standards of the city as a threat, though, more of a minimum requirement.

We don't do cute little dolphins for your ankle. We reject drunk bachelor party remnants and frat dudes for whom a tattoo is just a dumb story to tell to strangers. I make sure everyone who works for me reads up on the history of tattoos, on how they were used to distinguish warriors and women from Polynesia to Northern Europe, on how it became a mode of identification for Western militaries, and how tribes in India marked themselves to be recognized in the after-life. I tell them to treat every tattoo like it's going on their own skin. I take tattoos seriously—and how could I not? They pretty much saved my life.

Those kinds of high standards and strong principles are a hell of an overhead. For the first few years, Mandala was a couple dimes

Love & Ink 25

away from going under. But I figured that that kind of heavy investment was always gonna pay off. The thing about tattoos is that they're their own kind of advertising, especially with the internet and social media. We were putting stuff so beautiful and unique out into the world that eventually the world came to us.

Appointments started coming so thick and fast we considered hiring a full-time receptionist. People so famous we had to do their tattoos in private, or after-hours.

More than that, Mandala became as much of a community as it was a tattoo parlor. I left the brilliant art school grads with a penchant for pissing off their rich parents to the other shops, and instead the people that I hired as apprentices were dropouts, repentant ex-cons, drifters like myself. Young men and women who only needed to be given a chance, who would show you the kind of warlike loyalty only people like them can. Some of them weren't Picassos when I first started training them, but I believed that what you were born with only determined how much work you had to put in, that you could still win the pot with the worst hand at the table, and they were only too keen to prove me right. I've never had an employee that some other shop hasn't tried to poach, and I ain't never had an employee who took their offers. A few of my very first hires have even gone off to start their own businesses in other cities by now, and I've given my blessing to each one of them.

Though the front of the shop is all business, out back, behind a little door, we have a private lounge. Tatty sofas and stacks of beer that don't fit into the fridge. The smell of vinyl records and nickel-wound guitar strings. Just a chill place for the employees to hang out, I figured, except soon everyone was passing through. The back of my shop became a place for people to hang out until the bars ramped up later that night, a place to crash for kids who'd train-hopped all the way from the east coast, a secret club for people who knew what tattoos and music and good company could do for the soul. I can't tell you how many bands were formed there, how many bad-luck stories were drowned under booze and laughter there. Part halfway-house, part art collective, part underground club. I even got a legal permit to provide alcohol, just to keep the cops off my back. Shit—what else was I gonna do with all that money anyway?

That's where I am now, sitting back in the antique dentist's chair we used to use for tattoos, and which is now just a strange piece of furniture I got no reason to get rid of. I have the flyer for Isabel's gig in the one hand, my phone in the other, and I'm texting Ash to tell her where it is and what time I'll pick her up.

It's just me, until Ginger squeezes his big body into the doorway and slaps his stomach.

"Hoo-wee! I'm about ready for a beer, a girl, and the whole cow."

"Did you lock up?" I ask, still looking at my phone.

"Sure did."

Ginger's named after the red, braided beard that hangs from his chin all the way down his chest, which makes him look like some cartoon Viking. A four-hundred pound transplant from Alabama that I got into a fight with in a jail cell once, after we'd both been arrested for attending a house party that got a little out of control. The bastard used his Southern charm to wrangle a job out of me before the night was through. That was over two years ago now.

"We gon' start slipping if we don't get somebody else in here helping us out. You, me, Kayla—ain't enough. Whole damn city's fittin' for a tatt." Ginger comes close, casting a big shadow over the flyer. "Hey, I'm going to that. Want me to pick you up? Save yourself the DUI?"

I pocket the phone and put the flyer to the side.

"Nah, I'll be on my bike. I'm taking someone."

"Oh yeah?" Ginger says, perching his big body on a stool and popping open a beer. "Double-dipping on that brunette who keeps coming by wearing those booty shorts? Goddamn that girl, I oughta sue for public indecency—damn near put a needle right through a customer last time she brought that ass through here."

I laugh and shake my head.

"No. You remember the girl who came by yesterday morning?"

"The cute blonde with the Mona Lisa smile?"

Love & Ink 27

I almost wince as he says it—calling Ash a 'cute blonde' is like calling a Harley JDH 'two wheels and an engine.'

"Yeah," I say, biting my tongue.

"Wanted to ask you about that. Weren't she supposed to get a tattoo? Seemed like she ran outta here pretty quick."

I shift up in the chair, lean forward to look directly at Ginger.

"Remember that night we got blind drunk back here on the gin Kayla brought? Night I put the shop logo on your stomach?" Ginger lifts his shirt to reveal the mandala around his belly button with a sense of pride. "Kayla was talking about her kid, and I said I'd only ever loved one girl."

"That's about all I do remember from that night."

I shrug. "Well, that was the girl."

Ginger sips his beer quickly and widens his eyes, interested now.

"She just came by looking for you all of a sudden?"

"Not looking for me. Just a tattoo. It was a surprise for both of us."

Ginger laughs. "A good one—if you're taking her out now."

I try to sound nonchalant. "I doubt it's gonna happen."

"Ok," Ginger says with a sly smile. He gets up from the stool and reaches for the whiskey on the shelf. "I'm smelling a story here. A good one."

"Ain't no story. Definitely not a good one," I say, making it sound like the final word on the matter.

Ginger takes a swig and hands me the bottle, then looks at me like I'm performing a magic trick and he wants to figure out how.

Kayla steps into the back through the curtain. One side of her head shaved, the other side braided, long metal earrings that match the studs and buckles on her leather jacket and boots. She looks like she's stepped out of an eighties rock video, and is possibly the only girl I know who doesn't just make it work, but makes everyone else in the room feel underdressed because of it. Her tatt specialties are full color horror tattoos, which makes sense, and watercolor florals, which kinda doesn't. But she's amazing at both. Go figure.

"What's happening back here, boss?" she says, as she moves to the desk and starts packing some things. "Looks like a meeting of the sad bikers' club up in here."

With a big grin, Ginger says, "I've finally found a girl Teo's scared of."

"Fuck you," I say.

"Oh really?" Kayla says, turning away from her things to fold her arms and look at me with interest. "So the prolific Teo has finally met his match?"

"It's not like that. We've got history. Messy, complicated, dangerous history."

Ginger shares a look with Kayla.

"Can you hear that in his voice?" he tells her. "Sounds like fear."

"Fuck you," I repeat, but even I can hear the slight smile in my voice.

"What happened?" Kayla asks. "You gonna tell us? Or make us guess?"

"There ain't much to tell. We met in high school. She was in a lot of my classes—well, art class, that was the only one I really went to. Anyway, we fell pretty hard for each other. Except we had to keep it a secret from the whole town."

Kayla raises a pierced brow. "How come?"

"It was a small town. Everybody knew everything. I didn't have the best reputation. Well, my dad didn't have the best reputation, but it was the same thing to everyone else. Problem was, her family was pretty straight. Her dad was some big shot in the town. Sat on the local council, political bullshit, 'pillar of the community.' Mom was one of the teachers at the school until she passed from cancer our sophomore year. Last I heard, her sister was going to run for mayor."

"Man, some people are just born into it," Ginger says.

"Yeah," I say, taking the whiskey back from him for another swig.

I hand it over to Kayla and she takes a swig herself, then says, "Too good for you?"

"Pretty much. Ash and her sister were like the 'golden children.' Destined for great things. Whole town loved them. They lived in this big white house, clean as the sky. Big gate, driveway you could drag race on, maids—the whole thing. Her mom used to donate a truckload of toys to the children's hospital every year. They were seen as living saints."

"Shit," Ginger says, stretching the word out for three full seconds.

"And there I was sharing an illegal trailer with my dad on the other side of town. Dodging cops who had no one else to play authoritarian with and trying not to go out of my mind with boredom in that shitty hellhole."

Ginger whistles and then says, "Man, just like Romeo and Juliet."

Kayla and I laugh a little, looking at each other.

"Sure. Shitty ending and all." I look at Ginger and notice that he's frowning in confusion, too thoughtful to say anything. "You know how Romeo and Juliet ends, right?"

"Sure," he says. "Those damned chick flicks are all the same. They've always got happy endings."

I look at him to see if he's serious, then shake my head in disappointment.

"Christ, Ginger. You don't know how lucky you are that I hired you. Romeo and Juliet die in the end. They commit suicide."

"Well shit," Ginger says, taking a long draw of whiskey as if to dull this shocking revelation.

The moment lingers a while, the whiskey starting to hit all of us, slowing our thoughts and making us contemplate the situation.

Eventually Ginger turns to me with a confused look and says, "So what ever happened with you guys? How'd you lose her?"

I take another hit of whiskey, never drunk enough to deal with the pain of just remembering. I drop my head, stare at my leather boots, but all I see is the moon that night, the empty road, the exit sign.

"I left."

"You left?" Ginger says after a few seconds. "You mean you just disappeared?"

I nod my head, heavy with the years of regret.

"Shit," Ginger drawls again. "Well that's a hell of a disappointing ending, I gotta say."

My phone vibrates with an incoming text and I grab it from the counter beside me. It's Ash, telling me that she'll be ready and waiting for me to pick her up.

"Not an ending," I say, feeling a rush of powerful determination fill my veins. "Just the end of a chapter. It's not over yet."

5

ASH

Ordinarily, the meeting with Candace and Sean would linger in my mind for days like a bad meal repeating on me. Candace's poison-tipped words just now starting to get deep into my bloodstream, to work at paralyzing and angering me from the inside. It's her greatest skill—irritating me even when she's not around.

But nothing seems quite ordinary anymore, not since Teo turned up in my life again. Everybody has their own kind of ordinary, and a few days ago my ordinary was a job that paid bills and drained souls, my non-existent love life way down on the priority list—somewhere between de-icing the freezer and making sure I didn't run out of sugar. Ordinary was carrying around a half-filled heart, a future unlived, a missing limb—the knowledge of what I'd always dreamed could make me truly, profoundly happy, and the knowledge that it had disappeared the night he left.

Now there is no ordinary, now all the rules don't count. I don't know if this is going to be a second chance, an opportunity for the closure I've needed for years, or a final twist of the knife that was stuck into my gut seven years ago. The only thing I know is that I'll stop at nothing to finally get my answer, whether I have to pull it out like a tooth or seduce it out of him—I'll find out once and for all why he left. Maybe that's all I need to truly move on.

"Ugh, too fancy," I say to my reflection in the tight red dress. "It's a rock show, not a gallery opening."

My online search results were pretty short on 'what to wear to a maybe-a-date-but-not-really-a-date with a guy you were madly in love with but haven't seen in seven years' advice. Jenny had pushed for over-the-top sexy, and I didn't want to go that route either.

I end up settling on a pair of tight leather pants and a short black leather jacket, but I agonize over the red tank beneath it. Too much cleavage, I think, too easily interpreted as me wanting him to look— not that Teo ever needed much encouragement to undress me with his eyes. Maybe the leather pants are enough—Teo was always more of an ass guy. Then again, why am I even thinking about all of this, I'm not trying to jump him...not until I get to talk to him properly, anyway.

I'm half-squeezed into the leather pants when my phone rings. I pick it up with all the intention of letting it ring through, then see that it's Grace, my sister. Getting to speak with her is rare, through no fault of her own—that's just how it is when you're mayor of a town.

"Hey!" I say, as I put the call on speakerphone and continue pulling on the pants.

"Hey sis!" Grace says with genuine happiness. "God I'm so sorry I haven't been able to call in a while. I've just been so busy."

"Don't worry about it," I say. "I understand."

Grace sighs like she's more relaxed now that I'm on the phone.

"It's been so hectic over here," she says, slipping out of her 'mayor voice' and into the one I grew up with. "Jared's obsessed with closing this deal on a vacation property in Florida. Eliza's getting ready to start at a new school for gifted kids—she's so nervous, the poor thing, even though she's excited to be going. Tim just got his license and is trying to wrangle a *ridiculous* sports car out of us, which I told him I'd pay for *half* of if he gets a job to pay for the other half, and I'm still trying to negotiate a peace between a local fracking initiative and the protesters."

"Sounds like a nightmare," I say, tousling my hair in the mirror. "How's little Jane?"

"Oh, she's as sweet and adorable as ever. She's already onto three words now. She misses her Auntie Ash, though."

"Just tell me when and I'll come by."

"We're planning something soon, I'll let you know. Anyway, how are you? How's the job going? Father was asking about you."

I ignore the job question, already getting defensive at the mention of our supposedly well-meaning but perennially overbearing dad. "Asking? Or preaching?"

"Oh, come on, Ash. You know he just worries about you."

"Well, he *should* be glad to hear that I did just receive a promotion, and I've got a lovely new apartment as well. Tell him I'm not going to be begging for his help any time soon."

"You should tell him yourself," Grace says. "He misses you. And congrats on the promotion."

"Thanks." I sigh. "I guess we should all have dinner or something soon. Emphasis on *all* of us."

"I'll let you know," Grace repeats, that 'mayor voice' slipping in a little. I groan a little as I check myself out in the mirror, the tight pants maybe a little too sexy after all. "What are you up to tonight?" Grace asks, politely changing the subject.

"Just getting ready to go out."

"Ooh! Is my baby sister finally going to start dating again?" she teases.

"Hmm. Sort of. Not really."

"Oh! That's great! What is he? Someone from work?"

I roll my eyes.

"He's not from work, but he is about ten minutes away," I say, playfully. "So I might have to go at any moment."

"I won't keep you," Grace says. "I should run off and get my statement for tomorrow ready anyway. I'll talk to you soon. Good luck tonight. Love you, sis."

"Love you too, Grace."

She clicks off the phone and I continue to frown at my ass in the mirror. Eventually, I decide to scrap the sexy outfit and try a basic ripped jeans and t-shirt combo—something I assume most girls will be wearing, a default outfit that says nothing—better to play the opportunities of the night. Before I can get changed, however, the decision is made for me.

Teo arrives early. He doesn't text or call, though. Instead, he revs the bike engine outside my apartment. Loud and eager, like a lion's roar. I rush to the window, pull the curtains aside, already knowing that it's him, the kind of gesture he would have made all those years ago, the kind of gesture I'm not surprised he hasn't given up on.

He sees me come to the window, and a slight raise of the eyebrow is all the acknowledgement I get, and all I need. Grabbing the last of my things, I take one last glance at myself in the mirror, figure the low-cut top might not be such a bad idea after all, and go outside to meet him.

He looks good enough to lick, to bite, to eat. Black jeans packing the powerful muscles of his legs, astride the bike. Black boots on the ground. White t-shirt from which those tattooed arms extend toward the handlebars in a tense grip. Even the helmet looks good on him, drawing attention to that broad jaw and Roman nose. I almost feel like stopping to take a picture.

Instead I move toward him, feeling the heat prickle up my chest, across the back of my neck, skin suddenly ultra-sensitive to the chill in the air, the nervous, jittery energy of heading into the unknown.

"You look incredible," Teo says, his voice the same low growl of the bike engine. His eyes move down my body with the slow gentleness of firm hands, just like I expected, and I try to remember how to speak.

"You're early," I tell him with a smile.

"Impatient," he replies.

I take the extra helmet from him and put it on, then swing my leg over the seat. The broad muscles of his back are inches away from my face, the hardness of his ass between my thighs. I can smell the mixture of the hot engine and his rough skin, a dark musk that makes me think of danger. My nerves jangle with paralyzing excitement at his heavy, powerful presence, so close to me. A mixture of adrenaline and nostalgic lust racing through me.

Tentatively, I put my hands to his waist as he picks a foot up off the ground and revs the bike. Pressing gently, I feel the muscular twist of his body, fingers nesting in the line above his hip. It feels too much like the past, doing this. Too much like the dreams I had after he was gone, where he showed up like this and I clung tightly to him as he made everything ok again.

He turns his head to the side, showing me his profile, outlined in streetlamps.

"You're gonna have to hold on tighter than that."

At his command I push my hands across his front, fingers following the lines of his abdomen through the thin fabric of his shirt. I let my eyes close as I squeeze myself against him, press my chest tightly to his back, nipples so hard he can probably feel them through my jacket. Thighs against his, cheek to his shoulder. My whole being so sensitive, and his body so hard I feel every movement of his muscle, every thump of his heart, every shift of his balance.

He lifts his other foot, twists the accelerator, and takes me away.

By the time we get to the venue I feel like butter, hot and melted against him, so blissed out from the ride that it'd taken me a few seconds to remember where we were going, so comfortable holding him to me that I almost tell him to screw the gig and keep on riding.

But I don't. Instead we pull up to a stop outside the gigantic converted warehouse that's located downtown, right beside the L.A. River. A big brick structure that would probably look derelict if there weren't crowds of people milling around outside it. By the light of the setting sun I can make out the coolness of the crowd. Half of them so detached and aloof that they look almost bored, the other half so intense they look like they're ready to fight. It's an edgy, hip crowd. Metal t-shirts and tons of mascara, combat boots and studded bracelets, red and black plaid and patterned tights. Strobing lights filter through the man-sized windows, and the rumble of a rock song emerging from inside makes people raise their voices to talk.

I get off the bike and feel suddenly awkward, suddenly aware of how long it's been since I actually spent a night out. Then Teo takes my hand, and even though it makes the nerves disappear, I instinctively frown at him for the forward gesture.

He shoots me a humored half-smile, as if amused by my reaction.

"What?" he says. "Surprised that your hand still fits in mine?"

I laugh a little, some of the nerves escaping on it, and Teo starts to lead me through the crowd.

It doesn't surprise me to see that Teo seems to know a lot of these people, and a lot of these people seem to know Teo. Guys call his name, hold out hands to clasp, break away from conversations to show their happiness at seeing him. Girls cast flirtatious, hungry eyes at him until they see me behind him and their looks turn curious or disinterested.

Teo leads me through a crowd that seems to go on forever. A mass of dancing bodies, jumping and moving to the driving bass that reverberates through the darkness, arms in the air, coaxing powerful roars from a searing guitar.

Just as I'm about to wonder where, exactly, he's taking me, we're attacked by a giant figure, who leaps out of the crowd to wrap long arms around both our necks.

"Guys! *Oh my God!* You came!"

The figure stands back and I see that she's a tall, striking woman with haute couture cheekbones and Joni Mitchell bangs. She's wearing black jeans and a denim shirt over a sailor shirt—but it may as well be a Margiela dress for how good she makes it look.

"Ash!" the girl squeals, almost hopping on those long legs, and I realize that I'm staring.

Suddenly I notice those round, intelligent eyes, that little dimple in the chin, the small gap in her teeth.

"*Isabel?*"

She screams again, and grabs me against her for round two of the bear hug. When we break apart this time I've got no doubt at all.

"No fucking way!" I laugh, full of incredulous shock. "Look at you! You look amazing!"

"Look at *you!* I didn't think you could be any more gorgeous than you were in high school but you're blowing my mind!"

"No, seriously," I interrupt. "I didn't even recognize you. Shit, Isabel!"

"I love your hair," Isabel coos, shaking her head in disbelief.

"Have you been working out? You look like a dancer or something!"

"Girl, that's from all the guitar-wrangling and the adrenaline and the cross-continental tour schedule," Isabel laughs. "But I guess you could call that working out for sure. So how are you? What are you up to these days? I wanna know everything!"

"I'm gonna go get us some drinks," Teo interjects. "Let you girls finish telling each other how hot you both are."

"Ok, sure," Isabel says, ushering me away and pointing in a direction. "We'll be over here."

Once Isabel gets me to a quieter part of the warehouse she leans in and through a semi-conspiratorial smile and says, "Ok Ash, you've got to fill me in. I feel like I've been away for *far* too long. *What* is going on with you guys? I thought after everything that happened... you know? Game over. And now this?"

Isabel was the only one of our friends I actually told about me and Teo, after the fact. That summer, after prom, before we both left our town to go away to college, I poured my heart out and told her everything. About our secret relationship, about our pact to show ourselves together at prom, about Teo's sudden disappearance. Isabel even tried to help me figure it out. Where he'd gone, or what had happened on that last night. It makes a kind of sense that the first thing she'd ask me about when we saw each other again was what happened—especially considering I showed up here with him.

I shrug as I search for where to begin.

"Are you back together?" she prods.

"No."

Her brow crinkles. "Did he finally get into contact with you, then?"

"No."

"So..." She screws up her face in confusion. "How did all this come about? Did you find out what happened?"

"No."

"Does he..."

"I don't know," I say with a shrug, pre-empting the question and unable to even hear it right now. Isabel frowns and I let out a sigh. "Honestly, I know as much about what's going on between us as you do. I bumped into him by accident at the shop last week and this is the first time we're seeing each other since that day. There's still a lot we haven't talked about."

Isabel glances through the crowd to see if Teo's coming, then turns back to me.

"Well, I don't know anything either. About a month ago he commented on my band's Instagram and then I wrote back on his and then we met for coffee, but when I asked him about you he didn't say anything. Just clammed up...you know, *Teo*-style. I didn't even think he'd come to the show. Then all of a sudden he sends me a message telling me he's coming to the show with you. To be honest, I thought it was some autocorrect error when I read that."

"Really? He didn't say anything to you about—"

I stop myself when I see Teo emerge from the crowd carrying three beers. He hands us a couple and smiles as he takes a sip.

"You girls want me to leave so you can talk about me a bit more?"

"Oh please," Isabel groans playfully, then looks at me. "What an ego."

"Anyway," I say. "Tell me what all this is about. You're in a band? You're recording an album here?"

"Yep."

"What happened to studying fine art in Paris?"

Isabel shakes her head as she looks away, as if looking back at a memory.

"I dropped out in the second year. I mean, I loved art, but

everyone around me was struggling to find work, taking a long time to get their foot in the door. Nobody's really paying for art criticism, you know? Eventually I figured that if I was going to be unemployed and frustrated, I may as well be that way doing something I loved. And I love music—so I picked my guitar back up again and started jamming around with different people and finally met these guys and something just...clicked. We started playing shows, put out a demo, got some label attention. And now here I am."

"Good for you," Teo says. "Amazing things can happen when you decide to just go all-in and chase your dream."

"Yeah," I say. "That's so great."

"What about you?" Isabel says to me. "Are you tearing up the movie business?"

I laugh a little abashedly.

"I'm not actually in the movie business. Not yet, anyway."

Isabel shoots me a confused look.

"Wait," she says. "I thought your dad was going to hook you up with a job after college? Something in a big studio."

"He was," I say, feeling a little awkward noticing Teo staring at me with narrowed, focused eyes. The way he always does when he's keen to hear what someone's gonna say. "But I didn't take it."

"Seriously?" Isabel says.

"Yeah," I nod. "I just...I wanted to make my own path, you know? I work in television right now, as a producer, but I'm not exactly where I wanna be just yet."

Isabel squeezes my shoulder reassuringly. "You'll get there. I know you will."

I glance up at Teo, just enough to notice the upturn of his lip, a trace of a sad smile.

Suddenly there's a unanimous roar from the crowd that draws our attention toward the stage, now empty but for the host walking up to the mic.

"Shit, that's me," Isabel says, shoving her beer at Teo and running backwards into the crowd. "Love you guys! See you after the show!"

"Make it a good one!" I shout after her as she disappears into the crowd.

She reappears with her bandmates on the stage, and they get their instruments ready as the audience whistles and shouts. Isabel steps up to the mic, eyes closed, and puts one hand on it, the other on her guitar. The drums tap a gentle rhythm, bass throbbing like a melodic heartbeat. The warehouse is getting packed as more people come in from outside, closing up the space until we're all shoulder to shoulder. One solid mass, entranced by the hypnotizing figure of Isabel on stage. She starts to sing softly, like a half-whisper, and goosebumps run their way down my entire body.

"Pretty incredible, huh?" Teo says, leaning close so I can hear him.

"Yeah," I say, our faces close enough to almost touch. I lean toward his ear, smell his cologne, and say, "Do you remember the Jawbreaker gig we went to in San Diego?"

When I pull back to see his face I can see he's already grinning with the memory, already smiling just like he did back then when we were seventeen and shoved together in a moshpit, making out as the walls vibrated and people danced all around us.

"I love the way you dance," he says, and in that single phrase it feels like we're back there again. Not 'danced,' but present tense, as if I'm the same, he's the same, *this* is the same. I know that now, if I don't say something to stop this and pull us back into the present day, we may as well be back there all over again.

"You've got great taste in music," I say instead—the same words I said to him back then, as if we're reciting the old lines, an incantation that'll bring us back to the past.

I force myself to turn back toward the band on stage, feeling Teo's strong presence behind me. The song builds until it's too tender, too achingly beautiful to carry itself. Until the crowd is almost begging for some resolution. That's when Isabel clutches her guitar and the chords crash down like some satisfying explosion. The audience erupts into joyous shouts, arms in the air as they dance against each other in the cramped space. I lose myself in the darkness and its flashing lights, carried from moment to moment by the glorious shift of those chords, by Isabel's soaring, powerful voice and the roar of the crowd singing along with her.

I look up over my shoulder at Teo, still standing there behind me, his body barely touching mine. As the song builds I look at him and laugh in disbelief at how good this is, and he smiles as if he's enjoying my happiness.

Time seems to stop, catalyzed into one perfect moment of nothing but music and dancing. The drums possess me, the guitars send me into a trance of never-ending movement. Deeper and deeper I go, out of my mind and into my own body. The music shaking something deep in my core, rhythmically and primally.

It could be minutes, or it could be hours, until I feel his hands on my hips. Firm, tough hands that seem to know how to touch me. Fingers search under my tank top for skin, press inside the waistband of my pants against my abdomen as I gasp for air. I let Teo press me against him, against the big, hard front of his body. Both of our forms fitting together with a sensual satisfaction, moving against each other to the rhythm set by the bass.

I put my hand up behind my shoulder, where I know his face will be. I feel the grit of his stubble as I arch my shoulders backward into him, letting him take the weight of my body. He nuzzles my palm, bites at my finger, then tilts down to bury his face in my neck. His cool breath shivers against the sweat of my body, his lips brush against the soft spot behind my ear. A tease, he pulls away as I push into him. His hand still against my front, he pulls my swaying ass to his cock, straining against his pants. I smile as the music shifts, as I trace his bulge with the crease of my ass and make him growl, low and close, into my ear. The sound makes me wet.

"I love the way you move," he whispers again, so close to my ear that his lips brush against it, so close that I can hear him even over the raucous music. My body feels electric, more full of energy and joy than it has in years. I remember this feeling, and it's not just the music. It's him.

My hand in his hair, my ass on his cock, his fingers under my shirt. We grind against each other until I feel like my body is about to explode, until even this closeness isn't close enough. He must feel the same because he puts a hand on my throat, twists my jaw around to his waiting lips. In this moment, there's nothing I want more than his tongue in my mouth.

Teo tastes like lust and aggression, alcohol-hot tongue writhing in my mouth. His stubble grates satisfying against my skin as he holds me captive against him. My body fills with the taste of him, with the sensation of his rough hands, with music, with the atmosphere, with the smell of his cologne. I feel like I could stay here forever, and yet I'm desperate for more, desperate to get rid of even the small obstacles between us—this club, our clothes, my inhibitions. I want him inside me.

His lips break from mine, leaving me lost, disoriented. I bring a hand to my forehead.

"I'm a little dizzy," I laugh. He smiles back at me, then takes my hand and leads me back through the crowd. That tattooed arm leads me to the side of the warehouse. He pushes open a door and steers me outside, into a small alleyway. Out here, the air is cool and fresh. A single streetlamp out on the road and a half-filled moon reflect across puddles, just enough to exaggerate the darkness.

The door shuts behind us, turning the crashing guitars into a muffled monotone, suddenly distant. I turn to look at him, his narrowed eyes catching the light, the glint of his watch, his belt buckle.

He puts a hand on my cheek.

"You ok?" he says.

I take a deep breath and nod.

"I feel great," I say. "Just got a little overheated."

His eyes rove down my body and back up again. The heat between us is undeniable. For a split second the cool air stills us, until we crash into each other like animals, clawing at each other hungrily with hands and mouths. His hand reaches between my legs, rubbing me through my pants, and I grind into the delicious friction until I'm gasping for air. He pushes me back into the brickwork, and I'm ready to tear off his clothes, eager to put my mouth over every inch of his body.

His strong hands reach for my zipper, sliding it down as I grab fistfuls of his shirt, pulling him closer toward me. Every part of me thirsting for him, purposeful and untamed, so much I almost scare myself, almost forget who I am, forget who he is...

He traces a finger down my slit and pushes it into my aching pussy, sliding it so deep. Our eyes lock and all of a sudden I remember who he is, what he's done to me, and how close I am to letting it all happen again.

I shove him back onto the wall, push myself away from him, putting distance between us.

"Wait!" I say breathlessly, the word more instinct than thought. "I can't..."

"What?" Teo says. "What's wrong?"

He takes a step toward me and I take another step back, pulling my jacket tighter around me, closing it over my breasts, the air suddenly seeming cold and uncomfortable. My mouth goes dry, my head starting to spin without the music to orient me. I breathe long and deep, shuddering all the way.

"I can't do this, Teo. I can't just pretend like this is ok."

"Who's pretending?" Teo says, stepping toward me again, but I move away again and hold a palm up to stop him.

The air between us feels dry and brittle now, already crackling. I search for the right words, but all I can find are the simple ones, the self-evident truths. A wave of regret that I let myself get this far hits me, a sense of wrongness that I let it get to this point without even a second's thought for my mental and emotional well-being. The things I didn't say—at Mandala, at the Canyon, back in the club—bubble to the surface now, raw and powerful. I can't pretend anymore. I can't keep acting like it all doesn't matter.

"You left me, Teo," I say, almost choking on it. "Three years together, and we went through everything, my mom dying, you finding your way through your art, all the highs and lows. In love... and on the night you were supposed to prove it to everyone, you left."

In the dim light I see his face go hard, his eyes look away.

"You just disappeared," I say, shaking my head. The disbelief and despair I felt about it still fresh. "We were so happy. All the things we did, the things we said to each other...gone in a second. I still can't understand...you lied. Did you think I'd forgotten? What happened to 'us against the world,' Teo? I gave you everything. We had a future."

I hear him sigh heavily, angry and challenged. But he says nothing.

"Tell me," I urge, "what happened?"

Teo's boots shuffle on the ground, he folds his arms and looks around him. Like a cornered animal, prideful and trapped.

"Is that really how you remember it?" he says, finally directing an intense stare at me, lasering the words home on that stoic look.

"*Remember it?*" I reply quickly. Despair turning to indignation. "I've remembered it every day since, Teo. I remember living my life like a half-conscious zombie for years afterwards, until I went numb to cope with the pain, to cope with the heart you stole from me.

"I remember staying up late every night for years afterwards, *sure* that tonight would be the night you called me, explained yourself, begged me to forgive you. I remember each and every time you told me that you loved me, and I remember trying to come up with reasons for why each one might not have been a lie. I fucking remember it all, Teo. You know, seven years isn't a long time when you're stuck trying to get over the past."

"You know what I remember?" Teo says, voice firm and unfazed by my choking voice. "I remember asking you—over and over and over again—to leave with me. To leave that shitty town behind and build a life together. And I remember you laughing at the idea at first. Then changing the subject. Until eventually you just shut it down and said you didn't want to talk about it anymore."

"We were *seventeen!*" I say, loud enough for it to echo against the tight walls of the alley. "We had no money, Teo! No jobs! What were we going to do? Where were we going to go? You used to spend half the time complaining that you couldn't even afford to put gas in your bike. About how much of a hard time it was finding work."

"I couldn't find work because to everybody in that fucking place, me and my dad may as well have been the same person." Teo opens his arms wide with hopeless frustration. "Nobody wanted to hire my dad's son. I didn't stand a fucking chance there!"

"And you think skipping a state border or two would make things so much easier? For a couple of teens who hadn't even graduated yet?"

"It would have been a clean slate. A fresh start. We could have made a new life together."

I sigh heavily, feeling like he's not getting it.

"A clean slate might have sounded great to you, Teo, but what about me? I'd just gotten a scholarship to Berkeley, I was about to follow my dreams. I had ambitions and I wanted to do something meaningful. I wanted more than to get some shitty job to pay for a crappy apartment in a place I hardly knew. I had friends, family—was I supposed to cut them all off? Throw all of that away?"

Teo lets the words linger in the alley, as if waiting for them to settle before he speaks again, his tone lower, faded, resigned.

"Well there's your answer, Ash. That's what happened to 'us against the world'—you decided the rest of the world mattered more."

I look away, pace a little to shake off the chill of the night, the emptiness left by the kiss.

"That's unfair," I say slowly. "Even if you felt like that—even if you hated me for it—you could have told me. Could have said something before you left. You know I wouldn't have told anyone where you went. I deserved better, Teo."

"You did," Teo says, regret in his voice. "But I didn't plan it out like that. It was...complicated."

"Sure. Call it whatever makes you feel better. Complicated...difficult... You can't call it right, though, can you?" I walk up to him now, close enough to see the hard, blank expression, but those blue eyes pained and broken. "You had seven years to explain, Teo. A phone call, a letter—that's all it would have taken. But even now, even with me standing in front of you like this, you still can't tell me the *real* reason why you left, can you?"

He rubs at his temples, the muscle in his jaw tensing. Then he fixes that icy glare on me, gazing straight into my soul. "Listen to me, Ash—there are some things better left in the past. Please trust me on this. Whatever happened that night, it's nothing you need to know, and it would only hurt you—hurt us. It'll do the kind of damage neither of us can repair."

"Quit being cagey. Just tell me the fucking truth, Teo!"

I wait for him to speak, both of us aware that the only thing he can say now is the only thing he won't. I wait until I can see the pain he carries holding it back, until I know for sure that Teo won't ever tell me.

I look down, step away, and shake my head.

"Do you think that whole 'tough guy who doesn't care' act works on me? Withdrawing into yourself, shutting down everybody else... You haven't changed a bit. You're still the same scared little boy who can't take responsibility. Who runs away when things get tough. And now this...as if you can just step back into my life and hook up like none of it mattered."

"Hey," Teo says, "*you're* the one who walked into my shop."

I look at him and laugh in disbelief.

"You never give up, do you?" I say, holding palms up as I walk backwards, away from him. "Well, I do. I'm done trying to understand you. And you know what else? I deserve better. See you in another seven years, I guess."

I turn around to face the street and turn the corner, feeling some slight sense of half-victory, of bittersweet conclusion—nothing like what I wanted, but maybe enough to survive.

6

TEO

The morning after the gig I wake up feeling like hell, head spinning and a deep nausea in my gut. Except I barely had anything to drink. A psychological hangover. A twisting, engulfing, discomforting sense of something wrong that it'll take more than an Alka-Seltzer and some aspirin to get rid of.

Not that I ever really get rid of this shit—the bad memories of mistakes and struggles, the guilt and grief. I'm just good at burying it. I never claimed to anyone that I was a good person—least of all myself. I know what I am: The high school dropout son of an alcoholic criminal. The kid who lived in that shitty trailer by the woods, the kid you wouldn't trust to watch your jacket, to hire for your store, to be near your daughter. What good's a free country when you're given every chance you'll ever get at birth? When the world takes one look at you and decides who you are?

It's in my face. In my eyes. The way I stand, the way I talk. Bad boy. Unpredictable. Unemployable. Dangerous. You don't get to choose that. The world does. Assumptions become inevitabilities. And before you know it the only friends you have all seem to possess criminal records, job interviews only last five minutes, cops like to ask you where you're going, and girls wanna ride you to the wild side before they settle for the nice guy.

I don't mind, except it meant I had to leave the one girl I ever wanted.

You don't survive the kind of life I've had unless you get good at burying your feelings. The sensitive don't last with fathers like mine, the expressive get into a lot of fights in the crowds I run in, and there sure as hell ain't no time for self-pity when you've got to figure out how you'll make rent.

It took me years to get where I am. After I left that town—left Ash —I just about did a grand tour of every cockroach-infested hellhole in America. Hustling money wherever I could, both sides of the law. Working the kind of jobs where the only topic of conversation was what we'd do when we had enough money, until I finally got to Europe, found something to get passionate about, something to build a life around, only to realize the hurt was still there.

I thought about Ash every day, even though I didn't want to. As far as I knew that part of my life was over. I sealed the feelings up real tight and dragged them around like a weight, held them underwater until they stopped moving. I numbed so much of myself—just to avoid that pain—that it got hard to experience even joy. I had to drink more, fuck more, ride faster and fight harder just to feel the same as the next man.

Now she's back. And all those things I buried like the dead, all those feelings and memories I tried to leave behind, are back. Like ghosts here to haunt, a hurricane that's been brewing for a long time.

I call Kayla and tell her I won't be coming into work today. I haven't missed a day in over a year, but I can barely focus on myself right now, let alone somebody else's tattoo. I take Duke out for a long run but it only tires him out, so that when he comes home he eats half a bowl of his food and settles in the yard for a long nap. I'm still pacing around the house with a static I can't get rid of, however, so I grab my gym bag and leave.

The boxing gym's half-empty when I get there. I nod to the few faces I know, making it clear I'm not in the mood for small talk. Once

Love & Ink   49

I get my gloves on I skip the warm up and head straight for the bag—the old one, the one that never breaks.

For a half hour I play with it, moving and swinging, ducking and weaving, throwing combinations and staying on my toes like it's a real fighter. This is how I let off steam, how I burn myself out enough so I can relax—except this time it isn't working. The more I try to forget about her, the more I can't. I move and jab but my body only gets tighter, more tense, more frustrated. I stop moving and just start hitting. Big, thunderous punches that echo like a quake throughout the gym, drowning out the loud grunts of anger escaping my body. Slamming my fists into it like I'm trying to break down a wall.

"Teo!" I hear somebody shout in between punches, in a loud tone as if it's not the first time they tried to get my attention.

I stop the bag swinging against me and turn to look. It's Bobby, the co-owner of the gym, who's in here almost every day training young boxers. He's a good guy. Old school. Looks like an aging comedian but has a voice that sounds like a New York deli owner with severe tonsillitis.

"Hey Bobby."

"You're hitting pretty well these days," he says. "Wanna spar with my boy?"

I raise a glove and say, "No thanks. I'm good," before turning back to the bag.

"Come on! He's a tough one—little green, but real natural. He needs a moving target though. Be good for both of you."

Bobby's thumbing back over his shoulder and I lean to look at the ring. The kid looks like he's half-bull, about two weight-classes higher than me. I'm tempted for a second, but the only thing I want right now is to be alone while I try to get rid of this monkey on my back.

"Looks good," I say. "But like I said, I'm not in the mood."

"Hey, you owe me!" he says, smiling impishly. "You know how much business I've sent your way? Just this month?"

I can't help but smile at Bobby saying that—he knows I don't need the business.

"Ok," I say, stepping away from the bag and slapping my gloves together. "Let's see what he's got."

Bobby smiles gleefully and almost jogs back to the ring as I follow him.

"You're up, Alex!" Bobby says to the broad-shouldered beast in the ring, pointing at me as I get somebody to help me put the head guard on.

It isn't until I get in the ring that I truly see how big the kid is. He's got a couple of inches on me and looks like he's been drawn to life by an over-compensating comic book artist. We nod at each other, a quick exchange to show we're cool, and Bobby steps in between us, pulling us into the center of the ring.

"He ok?" the kid asks him.

"Teo?" says Bobby. "Don't worry about him—he can handle himself. Worry about you. Remember, *precision*. Don't be rash. You good to go, Teo?"

"Ready when you are."

"Let's do it," Bobby says, backing away.

I touch gloves with the kid and then we're away, guards up and circling for space.

I wait to see if the kid will make the first move, and sure enough he does, but I keep distance. I open myself a little, let him take a few shots, watching close for tells, to get a sense of his movements. Then I start throwing a few combinations myself—nothing too committed, just enough to see how he ducks, how he weaves, getting a sense for what kind of fighter he is.

Soon we start boxing proper, showing a little more aggression. He's good, jabs harder than most can hook, something of the Tyson about him. He tries cornering me, and I try to get past that jab good enough to counter. He gets close a couple of times, I land a few body shots but nothing he notices.

Then something happens. Some dark energy starts swirling at my core, winding itself around me. The ghosts back to haunt, the frustrations back to torture. Before I know it I'm thinking of Ash, of her leaving last night, of the uncertainty of whether I'll see her again.

Thoughts that anger and pummel me like the gloves striking at my head. Suddenly I'm not in a ring sparring with some rookie, I'm fighting demons, I'm trying to put the pain back in a bottle.

The kid's coming close now, like he senses a chance to really connect, and suddenly I'm weaving past his left to deliver an uppercut that lands on his chin like a homing missile. The kid goes down like a plank and I snap back to reality with a sense of guilt.

"Shit," I say, kneeling beside him. "You ok?"

The kid blinks himself back to sobriety and nods.

"I'm good, I'm good."

I hook my arms under his and lift him up.

Bobby runs into the ring smiling.

"Didn't mean to go that rough," I tell him. "Got a little carried away."

"You kidding?" Bobby says. "That's just what he needs. See how Teo lulled you in there? You thought he was dizzy there, didn't you? Let yourself get suckerpunched—that's the kinda thing you'll see *all* the time when you..."

I leave Bobby to lecture the kid as I exit the ring and pull off my gloves and head guard. I head back to the locker room, touching a sore spot in my side where the kid landed a few good ones. I make my way to my locker and open it to grab a towel, then run it over my face and arms. Then I start unwrapping the bandages around my hands.

"Hey."

I glance up in the direction of the voice, and find it hard to put my eyes back on my hands again.

I'm pretty sure I've never seen this girl before, pretty sure I'd remember a figure like that. Big hips and long legs in yoga pants so tight they leave nothing to the imagination, a sports bra that struggles to hold back giant, explosive tits. So many curves it looks like she's moving even when she's not. Her black hair in a ponytail so I get a clear look at those smoky eyes beneath seductively-arched eyebrows, lips big and pouted in a permanent expression of lust.

"Teo, right?" she says, stepping closer.

"Uh-huh," I reply, turning back to the task of unwrapping my hands.

"Riley," she says, offering a hand regally.

I shake it with my bandaged hand, noticing the way she trails her fingers against my palm when I pull away, and smile at her.

"Nice to meet you. You get lost on the way to the ladies' locker room?"

Riley laughs. "So you're hot as hell *and* funny."

She smiles now, those lips demure, and leans back against the locker beside mine. Back arched so only her shoulders and ass touch it, arms folded and pushing up those breasts, one foot stepping back, making those thick thighs impossible not to notice. The girl moves like she's acting in a porno, every gesture calculated and direct.

"I've heard *so* much about you," she purrs through those lips, her eyes studying my tattooed arms with the intensity of a starving man at a steakhouse menu. "You run a tattoo place, right?"

"Uh-huh."

"I was thinking of getting one."

"Oh yeah?" I say, grabbing a fresh shirt from my locker. "You had one before?"

"No. I'm a virgin," she says, swaying her shoulders playfully.

I let out a little chuckle without looking at her.

"Well, what were you thinking of getting?" I say.

I pull off my shirt, ready to put a new one on, but in the split-second it takes to pull it up over my head she moves closer, long fingers pressing against my abs, face so close to mine I can feel her breath on my chest, eyes looking up at me through long lashes, biting her lip.

In a slow drawl she says, "Maybe you can check out my body and tell me what you think would work."

Her fingers trace across my skin. Her eyes make promises that the breasts she's squeezing up against me are ready and willing to keep. Sucking breath through her teeth like a heated sigh. The testosterone should be flooding my body like poison now; I should be feeling a cold, hard lust just looking at this woman. I should be ready to slam her up against the locker, tear her clothes off with my teeth, to press my hard cock between those breasts, those lips, those thighs. About to do what I do best and enjoy most.

But I can't.

A wave of guilt passes over me so thoroughly I can taste it, can feel it on my skin, and I feel dirty because of it. Suddenly repulsed, by her, by the idea of doing this. I try to fight it. It's not like I'm married, I'm a free man, perfectly willing and capable of fucking anybody I like. Even as I try to tell myself that, though, I realize it's not true.

I remember Ash, remember how she looked last night, how she felt dancing against me, and suddenly Riley doesn't look so good. Those smoky eyes suddenly vacant and hollow when I remember how Ash's sparkle. Those forward lips, those giant tits, all seem so tacky and unreal, an imitation of beauty, a desperate attempt to manufacture the natural allure Ash doesn't even know she has.

I take her hand away from my chest and move her gently away from me, smiling almost apologetically.

"I'm flattered. Really. But no thanks," I say, pulling on my fresh shirt and slamming my locker shut.

Riley eyes me curiously, as if she's trying to understand if I'm just playing by different rules to her.

"Are you...taken?" she asks.

I heave my bag to my shoulder and shuffle aside past her, frowning as I think over the question myself.

"You know what? I think I might be."

When I get home I dump my stuff and pull out my phone to stare at Ash's number as I pace around the room, trying to shake these physical urges that course through my tired muscles.

I think about calling her, think about what I'd say. I wanna tell her how good she looked dancing like that last night, how she's been dancing like that in my head all day, my body aching and itching with unfinished business. How I still taste her lips, feel her body, see her face whenever I close my eyes. My heart still thumping with the rush of blood I got having her so close.

Only I know I wouldn't get to tell her all that. I know she'd only ask me once again why I left, wouldn't let it slide for long enough to see how much I want her. Have always wanted her.

I toss the phone onto the couch and pull my shirt off as I make for the shower. Still irritable, emotions still on edge. I step out of my shorts and turn the water up until it scalds, stepping under the stream and letting the heat force all the other emotions from my body.

I push water through my hair, close my eyes and try to let my mind go blank.

Her ass in those tight leather pants, the feeling of her wet pussy in my hand, her hands pulling my chest on the bike, the sun shining on her sweat-soaked skin in Runyon Canyon, her mesmerizing smile when she saw me in the tattoo shop... Soon the images and sensations run through my mind, flooding over me like the water. My lust manifesting big and hard in my hand.

I roll back my mind to last night, back before the argument, back to us grinding against each other, to that low-cut top, the pressure of her ass against my cock. I fix and focus upon the memory intensely, as if I can somehow bring it back to reality by force of will. Stroking my cock to the rhythm of her dance, feeling the softness of her belly under my fingers once more. In my mind I push them deeper than I did, in my imagination I tease those pants down around her ankles, spreading her thighs to lap at her pussy with my tongue. Then I spin her around against the wall, cock unleashed, and thrust into her from behind, her hands pressed to the bricks as she begs me to fuck her.

I picture how she would look laid out in front of me like an altar, tits shaking with the force of my strokes. I imagine her moaning, what her face would look like when she's losing control. Her mouth open to let the warm groans escape, eyes losing focus as I fuck all sense of reality from her. In my mind I kiss the glistening sweat from her body on the trail in Runyon Canyon, making her laugh that delicate laugh. I push her hand down into my pants as she rides behind me on the bike. Her cool, delicate fingers stroking as she whispers my name in my ear, tells me every single dirty thing she wants me to do to her, hard, fast, now.

It's too much, the idea of her, the memory of her—the tightness in me becomes unbearable to hold any longer and I release it into the hot water. A jackhammer thudding deep inside, pushing this energy out of me, leaving me panting and exhausted as the water massages away the tightness of my body. My muscles relaxed, my mind a little clearer, but something inside still rolling and twisting, unfulfilled.

7

ASH

Lunch with Jenny is more like a refueling of our bodies with caffeine —the wraps and sandwiches just help the triple-espresso shots wrapped in sugar flavoring go down. When things are really bad we'll head around the corner to the place with the cute waiters and replace caffeine with cosmos. Today's not that bad—but we considered it.

As we ingest caffeine/alcohol, and just enough calories to keep hunger from tipping our stress levels into breakdown territory, we bitch—about *Hollywood Night,* about Candace, about Carlos (the vain, sleazy host)—about the industry at large, about the pointless tasks we're given on a daily basis that stop us from doing our jobs. Like a couple of cynical aunts we tear into the lot of them, dismantling and exposing their idiocy like a couple of witches casting spells through insults, mean nicknames, and tutting eye-rolls. We say all the things we wouldn't even dare think inside the office, nothing that annoys us going unpunished. It's not pretty, and anyone overhearing us would think we're the worst people in the world, but we know it's just for us, just so that we can save ourselves the money and bother of the therapist's couch or the confessional booth.

Today, though, Jenny is more interested in listening than venting, and my issues aren't work-related. I give her the story of last night, dwelling longer than I probably should on how Teo looked when he picked me up, and getting a little embarrassed when I have to describe what we were doing in the crowd later on. It's the argument that I really want to talk about though, and Jenny leans forward, wide eyes almost filling her thick-rimmed glasses, when I tell her about the confrontation.

"...and then I just walked away. Left him there in the alleyway. Got an Uber, came home, and watched trashy television to distract me from thinking about it until I went to sleep."

Jenny says nothing for a second, her face frowning with thought.

"I don't get it," she says, as if I left something out. "He left town because you wouldn't run away with him?"

"No. I mean, *yes* he asked me to run away with him a ton of times, but he was supposed to meet me at prom that night—we'd talked about it for weeks. Either he was trying to play some cruel trick on me, or he isn't telling me something... I don't know. I just know I'm done trying to get through to him, trying to get him to explain it."

Jenny drains the last of her coffee and shakes her head empathetically.

"Well I can see why you're so confused. You think maybe he had someone else? Maybe he was just overwhelmed by everything? Or maybe he...you know, didn't actually love you like that?"

I look down at my half-eaten Mediterranean wrap and sigh—I've asked myself all those things and more way too many times to bother doing it with Jenny.

"Like I said: I don't care anymore."

"You sure about that?"

I look up at Jenny with a slightly shocked expression.

"I'm sure," I say.

Jenny holds her palms up and looks aside in a 'don't shoot the messenger' pose.

"I'm just saying, it sounded like you still cared when you were describing what a good kisser he was ten seconds ago."

I stare at her with full incredulity now, but Jenny's unfazed.

"You must have gone on a dozen first dates since I met you, and I never heard you talk about any of them with that kind of look."

"What look?"

"There was a look—when you talked about him."

"There was not a 'look.'"

Jenny nods.

"If you didn't even know you were doing it, then that says even more."

I fold my arms and sit back to glare at her.

"You're supposed to have my back on this, you know? Isn't that the third rule of Bitch Club? No devil's advocates?"

"I *am* on your side—that's why I think maybe you shouldn't cut him off so soon. You're clearly attracted to him, and he's clearly still into you. I know things didn't end well between you, but you're both different people now..."

"*Jenny!*" I almost shout. "Teo broke me so hard I almost swore off men for life. You think I can make myself forget all that just so I can... screw around with him?"

She shrugs apologetically. "Maybe screwing around with him will help you forget. At the very least it might put it all into perspective— he's just a guy, he doesn't define who you are or what you can do. Have wild, crazy sex with him, long enough to see his flaws and realize he's not the perfect boyfriend who exists in your head, then you can move on. Or maybe not. Maybe you're doing the right thing, running hard and fast from this and putting it all behind you for good. I just don't want you to have any regrets if you miss this chance."

I try to think of a comeback, something to dismiss the logic there, to avoid actually allowing Jenny's idea to breathe, but my phone vibrates on the table and distracts me. I pick it up and open the text message.

BRING CASUAL CLOTHES TO DOUBLETREE HOTEL. NAMES MR & MRS BORGES. ROOM 37. NOW!!!!

Jenny must notice how I slump miserably in my chair because she asks, "What is it?"

I hold the phone toward her so she can read the message. She frowns for a second until the penny drops.

"Oh," she says, looking up. "Candace still sneaking around with Carlos?"

I roll my eyes in disgust. "Did you think they'd stopped?"

Jenny frowns. "Isn't Carlos' wife pregnant?"

I nod my head gravely.

"Shit," Jenny whispers. "How can they not have been caught by now?"

"Caught? It's not like there's anybody in the office who doesn't know."

"Yeah, but his wife doesn't."

I look at Jenny with the look of someone sharing something secret.

"She does."

Jenny leans forward, knowing there's more.

"About three or four months ago—when I heard she was pregnant—I couldn't live with myself anymore, knowing that I was helping both of them cover it up. I sent her an anonymous email that told her everything."

"She didn't do anything?"

I shrug.

"I don't think so. Just last week she visited him in the studio, all happy smiles and cheek kisses."

"Wow. Makes you wonder how someone could just...not care."

I let out a sad sigh.

"Who knows? I'm sure she's got her reasons. Maybe she tolerates it to keep her family together. Maybe she's afraid of breaking away from him, and the paychecks. Maybe she still loves him enough to put up with it. Shit—maybe she just didn't get the email."

I look up and see Jenny smiling.

"What?" I say.

"Nothing," she says, still smiling. "I just think it's funny how much easier it is to give the benefit of the doubt when we're not involved.

Maybe you should cut Teo that kind of slack. At least for now. You can always run away again later."

"That's it," I say playfully, standing up and putting on my jacket. "You're paying."

Forty minutes later, after a quick stop at the studio to grab Carlos' clothes, I'm at the Doubletree hotel. After telling the concierge that Mr. and Mrs. Borges are expecting me, he directs me to room thirty-seven. I make my way up to the expensive suite and knock at the door with the 'do not disturb' sign hanging from the handle.

"Who is it?" I hear Candace's voice clearly, her sharp, abrasive tones slicing through the door, impossible to insulate against.

"It's me, Ash."

"You took your sweet fucking time! Get in here already!"

Bracing myself for the mental and emotional fatigue every interaction with Candace brings, I push open the door and enter the suite.

If I didn't know what they had done in this suite last night, I would have assumed a group of about twenty rock stars had spent the night partying here.

The place is a mess. There are sheets and clothes crumpled up across the entire floor, so that I have to pick my steps carefully as I also try to wince away the smell of day-old seafood, too-strong perfume, and the strongest sex smell I've ever encountered. There are plates on the bed carrying a smashed lobster shell and a series of sugary treats—all tasted, none finished. I accidentally kick over a bottle of wine and look down to find a dark stain on the hotel carpet.

"Careful!" Candace scolds from the corner of the room, where I see that she's applying make-up with the focus of a safecracker, pausing only to swig quickly from yet another wine bottle.

I shriek suddenly at the sight of the tall, half-naked man approaching me from the side in a hurry. I look, see that it's Carlos, shower water flinging off him like a shaking dog as he ruffles himself with his towel, knowing his cock is hanging there just a few feet away from me, then look away, suddenly fascinated by the pattern of the rug. Still, I see Candace glare at me with a sense of possessiveness you wouldn't really expect from a mistress.

"Those my clothes?" Carlos says.

"Uh...yeah," I say, holding them out to him while looking the other way still.

"Great," Carlos says, over the sound of him still vigorously scrubbing himself dry with the towel.

When he takes them from me, he says, "We've got a problem."

I look up, and finally feel comfortable enough to look at Carlos now that he's pulling underwear on. The host of *Hollywood Night* might look warm on camera, but in reality he looks too clean, too creepily perfect to be human. As if he were created by aliens to emulate humans—except these particular aliens only ever saw humans in toothpaste, fake tan, and hair gel commercials.

"What problem?" I ask.

"Did you see a guy down there, about five-nine, brownish hair, blue suit—looks a bit like Anderson Cooper?"

I pretend to really think about it.

"I don't know. There are quite a lot of people in the lobby."

Carlos groans with disappointment as he pulls on his shirt.

"That's my agent. He's here. Nearly bumped into him when I tried to leave this morning. He already suspects something. If he catches me here now, he's gonna find out about us for sure."

I nod as if I understand perfectly, though I still ask, "What's wrong if he knows? I mean, he's your agent. What does he care?"

Candace groans this time from the peanut gallery and I hear her mutter to herself in the mirror, still applying make-up.

"Just when you think one of them has a brain, they always prove you wrong."

"Anne," Carlos says, calling me by the wrong name as usual, leaning forward now and holding his palms together like he's explaining something to a child, "I'm Carlos King."

He says his name as if it's supposed to explain everything, and though I wait for more, there's nothing but an uncomfortable silence. Just as I open my mouth to say something, however, he continues.

"I guarantee you a certain demographic wherever you put me—a Broadway musical, a game show, a primetime sitcom, and you know why that is?"

Again the uncomfortably long silence that he only breaks when I open my mouth to say something.

"Because I'm clean. Straight. Pure as a priest. No skeletons in the closet, no blemishes on my record. I'm Teflon. My clothes don't crease; my shit don't smell. I'm a family man. I don't curse, I don't drink, I don't take drugs, I don't get angry. I always stop for fans, I reply to every letter with a signed photo. I'm primetime. Mainstream. I'm the guy your mother imagines when she thinks about you getting married. What I *don't* do," Carlos says, getting a little more aggressive now, "is fuck around on my pregnant wife. You getting the picture now, Anne?"

"Ash."

"Huh?"

"My name's Ash."

Carlos sighs heavily and continues pulling his pants on.

"Whatever," he says. "Point is, I need you to find out where my agent is and keep a lookout so I can get the hell out of this place without him noticing. Can you do that, *Ash*?"

I nod.

"You staying here, Candy?"

Candace turns around and smiles at him, and suddenly it feels like I'm not even in the room.

"I suppose I'll have to," she says slowly, as he approaches her. "Still need to recover."

"Planning next time, more like," Carlos says as he takes her around the waist and pulls her to him.

I try not to look as they kiss, in case I cringe so hard I develop a skin condition. But there's something almost horrific about seeing these two together—something that could make a person a very successful horror director if they could figure out what it was.

"I'm not gonna forget last night for a while," Candace gurgles in a creepy, babyish tone.

"Neither am I, considering those nails of yours left marks all over my body. If my wife sees them…"

Candace tries what I think is meant as a childish giggle, but comes out more as a throaty cackle.

"Better keep yourself away from her then."

I knew they were having sex, but now that they've got their hands on each other, and are puckering up to each other's lips noisily, the actual imagery of it forces itself into my mind. I'm gonna need the mental equivalent of bleach to feel clean again. Candace with the icy stiffness of a prototype waxwork, and Carlos with his hard vanity that ensures he's never less than three feet away from anything which could mess up his hair, and never more than three feet away from a reflective surface. I've seen shop mannequins placed too close together that had more natural chemistry between them than these two.

"So…should I go look for the agent?" I say, if only to halt the possibility of them fucking right there in front of me.

"Yeah, hold up and I'll show you a picture of him," Carlos says, breaking away to grab his phone and show me. Candace glares at me like I've just spoiled her party.

About a half hour later I've successfully led Carlos out to a waiting cab, away from the agent who I discovered having a business meeting in the hotel restaurant. Now I'm standing beside Candace as we wait for a car ourselves, feeling so uncomfortable around her I genuinely wonder if she emits toxic radiation.

"You know," I begin, feeling like if I can't make this work now, I never will, "I'm not supposed to be doing stuff like this."

Candace looks me up and down like I just emerged from a hole and asked her for a dollar.

"You're a producer—it's your job to make things run smoothly."

"Yeah, with *the show*."

"Honey, Carlos and I *are* the show."

"Still," I say, "I work really hard. I mean…all this. I don't complain about it. But it sometimes feel like I have so much responsibility without any of the freedom."

"Are you trying to blackmail me?" Candace says, her voice suddenly a directed hiss.

"What? No!"

"You're talking about your segment, right?"

"Yeah. I mean, sure... But I'm not trying to... I'm just saying I think I deserve at least a chance—just a chance. I've been working for you for years now, and—"

"Listen, sugar," Candace says, with fully patronizing dismissiveness. "You don't need a segment—you need a man, clear and simple. Look at you. Perky tits, tight little body. That annoyingly straight nose, ugh. You make me sick! You know how many divorces and lies and years of hard work it took to look this good? And there you are completely oblivious to how quickly you're gonna get old, and all you can fucking talk about is a ten-minute segment on a dumb gossip show. Don't you dare get all self-righteous on me. You're just sexually repressed."

"My personal life has nothing to do—"

"Oh Christ, you're annoying," Candace says, turning away to show she's not listening. "The only way I can tolerate you is thinking of what you'll be like a decade from now—God, that's funny!"

The car stops neatly in front of us, Candace moving toward it with perfect timing.

"Do us both a favor, Ash," she says, as she slides into the back seat, "get laid."

I move to follow her but Candace shuts the door before I can get close. I'm surprised for just long enough that she can tell the driver to go, leaving me standing there without a ride.

I hate Candace with the force of an entire social media mob, the kind of hatred most people reserve for politicians and rival football teams. But when both your enemy and your friends are telling you that you need to get a man, it gets pretty hard to keep on assuming that they're all wrong.

8

TEO

Mandala's already lively when I turn up at ten AM. I move past the curtain toward the blaring metal music, where Ginger and Hideo are working on a couple of customers. I grunt a hello—not wanting to distract them—and move on to the back room. A couple of girls, both dressed like goths, are lounging on a sofa, one of them flipping through a flash book while the other takes pictures of herself on her phone. Kayla's sitting at the work desk, drawing.

I move beside her, picking up the bundle of unopened mail and working through it.

"You done with those girl troubles then?" she says, without looking up.

I pause, mid letter opening.

"Girl troubles?"

Kayla stops this time, turning her head slowly toward me to reveal a knowing smile.

"That was the first day off you've had since I started. I doubt you even get sick."

I turn my eyes back to the letter, finish off opening it.

"Yeow," Kayla says. "That look tells me everything I need to know. Well, if you wanna talk about it—you know where to find me."

I pull out the bill, study it for a while, then realize I'm still in no state to focus. This thing's gonna bug me for days until I let it out. I sit down next to the drawing desk, watching Kayla sketch a bird in flight for a while. It's a departure from her usual repertoire but it looks incredible all the same, and I tell her so. Meanwhile I zone out to the sound of the buzzing coming from the tattooing chairs, the girls erupting into a conspiratorial laugh over something on their phones.

She's a good kid. Barely into her twenties, but far wiser than she ought to be. Having a kid young will force a person to do that. She's a survivor. Decided soon after her ex walked out on her and little Ellie that her bad neighborhood in Atlanta wasn't any place to raise her daughter by herself, and left it all behind. She was a mess when she first came here. An emotional wreck, full of crippling self-doubt, but I could see there was something in her eyes, something that said she'd give it her all if she had just half a chance. I was right. For the past three years she's worked harder, learned faster, and improved quicker than anyone I've ever known. She's already one of the best, and she's already thinking of starting up her own place. By the time she's thirty she'll have given Ellie everything she ever dreamed of.

"You know what's funny?" I say, after a while. Kayla stops and glances up at me. "My dad's getting out of prison soon. Five year stretch this time."

"Shit," Kayla says, putting her pen down to show she's giving me her full attention now. "Seriously?"

"Called me last month. Asked me to come pick him up."

"Are you going to?"

I shrug and look over at the girls. Suddenly they seem so young, so innocent, so oblivious. They laugh again, and it seems like it's in a different language somehow.

"Even if I don't, I'll probably be the first person he comes to see. No idea how he even got my number."

"You probably put tattoos on half the people he's in with."

I laugh heavily and let the joke linger in the air a while.

"Feels like my entire past is coming back this week."

Kayla looks at me keenly for what feels like a minute, as if reading my mind and trying to figure me out.

Eventually, she says, "Why don't you deal with it then?"

I snort a little.

"Ain't no dealing with a past like mine."

Both of us turn to look as a lanky teenager comes into the back, greets the girls, and sits down next to them. Kayla turns back to look at me forlornly.

"This girl..." she says. "She's really got a hold on something in you."

"Just an ex," I say, not believing it myself. "I've got a lot of them."

"And none of the other ones make you do those puppy dog eyes."

I shrug, trying to act casual. "I'll never understand why people go digging up the past, looking for answers to things already settled."

Kayla smirks. "Sounds like it hasn't settled for her, though. You either."

"She thinks knowing what went wrong between us will help. If anything, it'll only hurt more."

I smile at Kayla, but it fades quickly, and only makes the sadness a little heavier.

"Why don't you let her decide that? Just tell her what she wants to know if that's what she's really after. Lay those demons to rest, for both of you."

I shake my head.

"Because she wants to know why I left—and I swore I wouldn't tell. She wouldn't like it. In fact, it might ruin her. Maybe it's healthier for her to just hate me. God knows, I'm used to it."

The girls laugh again and Kayla waits for them to stop before speaking again.

"Maybe not. Maybe that's just a detail," Kayla says. "Maybe she needs to know if it was real, that what you had was genuine. That you really loved her. Maybe that's enough. You *did* love her, right?"

Of course I loved her. I never stopped.

I think it, but I don't say it. Still, Kayla sees it in my eyes, in my silence, her face going soft and sympathetic.

"Look, Teo, you're like a brother to me. I respect you so much. And I don't want to tell you what to do. All I know is, it ain't healthy to live with a bunch of loose ends. You either tie them up, or cut them off altogether. Otherwise they'll bug you forever."

It's amazing what words can do. Ever since Kayla said that, I keep picturing that nagging, unresolved feeling as a dangling thread in the back of my mind, something that's just gonna stay there until I figure out how to handle it.

The day's busy enough to pass quickly, even with four of us in the shop. I spend most of the afternoon working on someone's neck tatt; hard, exhausting work that needs a lot of concentration, and a lot of making the customer feel comfortable.

Ginger and Kayla playfully fight over the choice of music all day, more people drop by to hang out in the back room. By evening it's clear that this is going to be one of those nights where the back room gets so packed that people end up standing around like it's a house party. Folks start bringing crates of beers, and soon there's a perpetual, changing circle of people by the back exit smoking. It's a night where Ginger gets louder and friendlier because there are a lot of friendly faces around, and where even more people come around because Ginger's in a loud, friendly mood.

I like these kinds of nights, even when they get rowdy enough to destroy my stuff, even when they end with fights and people regretting that they drank so much. More intimate than a bar, more spontaneous and unpredictable than a party. It feels like a place where people can relax, say dumb things and not be judged for it. A place where it doesn't matter who you are, because if you're here now, you're cool. Even with the swearing and the boozing it feels compassionate, brotherly.

It feels like family—or what I presume most families feel like. A dysfunctional group of people that I didn't necessarily choose to be here, but who I know and care deeply about anyway. But tonight— family or not—I'm just not in the mood. That hanging thread keeps

Love & Ink   69

me from laughing as hard as I normally would, keeps me from truly experiencing the present moment.

A song comes on the stereo—one everybody knows the words to —and even those who hate it sing along, bonded together by the sound of their own voices. That's when I drain the rest of my beer and slip out the back.

I take a few steps away from the smokers' group and pull out my phone. Unconsciously I navigate to Ash's number, and just stare at it on the screen.

It's hard to face the past. It's hard to navigate the emotional confusion of hurting someone. It's hard to condense seven years of baggage into words. But I tell myself I'm not doing any of that. I'm just hitting a little green button on my phone, and seeing what happens.

The phone rings as I pace beneath the night sky. The sound of my boots on the concrete, the muffled noise from inside the shop, one voice—probably Ginger's—adlibbing a little over the chorus.

How many rings was that? I watch the shadows dance away from a passing car's headlights. Where am I at now? A *really excited to speak to you* amount of rings? Or a *this is an emergency and I desperately need you to pick up* amount of rings?

It feels like forever. So much so that when the rings stop I prepare myself for the machine, the long pauses and rambling I'm about to record into it.

"Hey," Ash says, sounding cautious and quiet.

"Hey," I say.

And then...silence. Maybe a whole minute's worth. No 'are you gonna say something's, no awkward 'are you there?'s. Just the silence of two people on the same line, listening. As if just knowing that the space there, for us to talk, is enough, that the connection of an open phone line is all we need for now.

The things I want to say tumble over themselves in my head. 'I'm sorry.' 'Are you ok?' 'About last night...' 'How are you?' until I get to the single thing I want to say most of all.

"I wanna see you again."

There's a silence again before Ash speaks, and I wonder if she's doing the same, sorting through all the things in her mind that she wants to say but can't.

Finally, she responds. "I don't know, Teo..."

"Could you really leave it like that? Like this?"

She's quiet for a moment. "No..."

"I wanna see you again," I repeat.

"Yeah," she sighs, and it sounds like resistance is leaving her voice. "I kinda wanna see you too."

I feel the smile stretching across my face. "You free Saturday?"

"Yeah."

"How about the pier?"

"Oh," Ash says, and I can hear the smile in her voice. "Sure."

"Outside Blue Plate? Midday?"

"Sure. I'll see you then."

There are another few seconds of silence, of things unsaid, of that open connection, and then we say goodbye. When I look up, I see Kayla standing a few feet away, a knowing grin on her face.

"You eavesdropping on me now?" I ask, but I'm not really angry. "How long you been standing there?"

"Long enough. You taking care of those loose ends?" she shoots back.

I grin back at her. "Maybe I am." At least, I sure hope so.

9

ASH

In front of me, beyond the street, a big, shimmering orange sun starts to sink into the Pacific. Behind me people laugh and talk with pre-food energy as they wait for their tacos and corn dogs and lemonade; couples and families walk slowly, as if they have all the time in the world, casting long, dark shadows in the waning light.

I almost didn't come. At home, as I was getting ready, all I could think about was how Teo didn't deserve this second chance, about how I deserved better, about how I'd spent long enough chasing my past and the last thing I needed right now was to chase even harder.

Now I'm here, though, and the soft breeze blowing through my hair is stilling my mind a little. The warm, friendly chatter of people walking past me is charging the air with a satisfying kind of electricity. The smell of the sea mixes with the smell of hot grilled food, the heat of the day calming like an exhalation, and it's suddenly hard to think about past problems, possible futures. I'm just here, now, and I'm going to try and live in the moment.

Somebody looks at me a little too long as they pass and I realize I'm smiling. I look down, a little embarrassed, but still smiling. Teo always said I should live in the moment more.

I scan the street again, unsure of where he's going to come from.

When I do see him, it's because he's pretty hard to miss. He stands almost a foot taller than most people on the street, and walks with a kind of shoulder-rolling, rock star swagger that cuts him apart from anyone else around him. He's also wearing the same kind of outfit he was wearing at the concert: Black jeans and boots, a tight white t-shirt. He wears it better than most guys in tailor-made suits, however, and those densely-tattooed arms and narrowed eyes are accessories enough.

Suddenly I wonder what the hell I'm doing, why the hell I'm back here, meeting with him. As if he hasn't hurt me enough, as if the argument at the gig wasn't proof enough that he's never going to change, that I'm never going to get the answers I want—that I need—out of him. I feel like a moth being drawn to that flickering blue flame of his eyes, burning myself, killing myself bit by bit. My own curiosity, his impossible beauty, compelling me to do the things I know aren't good for me.

I wave at him to draw his attention, even though he's looking right at me, and he salutes casually in response, a warm smile lighting up his already perfect face. I realize I'm smiling back twice as hard and try to stop myself by biting my lip, but it doesn't work. I could watch him walk toward me forever. A voice in my head tells me to turn around and run away, before Teo crushes my beaten heart even more. But my body weakens, and my blood starts to thump, urging me to get close to him, to touch him, to get him somewhere and take my time tracing out the muscles of his chest...

"Hey," I say, trying to hold back the quiver in my voice.

"Hey," he says, his voice slow and sexy. "I'm glad you came."

"Yeah. Well...I didn't want to leave things like..."

I trail off, unwilling to bring up the bad taste of what happened at the gig, unable to find the words to explain the complexity of what I'm feeling. That I still hate him for holding so much back, but that I still want to know him, who he is now, and what he's done for all these years.

"I get it," he says. "We got off on the wrong foot. No time to breathe. We'll take it slow this time."

Love & Ink 73

I nod, more at his calm, steady tone than the idea of just moving forward and forgetting everything that happened between us entirely. But he's right. We should take it slow.

"Ok. What do you wanna do then?"

He shrugs. "Are you hungry?"

"Actually I just ate. Drinks?"

Teo looks up and scans the beach, Ocean Avenue, Santa Monica, then gets a mischievous look in his eye that makes him look like a teenager again.

"I got it. Come on," he says, taking my hand, already leading me toward the pier.

A small part of me flares up at the familiar heat of his touch, wants to yank my hand back and kill his air of carefree easiness. To ask him once again why the hell he left, to tell him that it can't be this easy to just forget what he did, that I won't make it this easy. But so much more of me wants this.

"Oh no," I say, laughing as we move closer to the boardwalk. "Are you seriously taking me where I think you're taking me?"

Teo looks at me, still wearing that mischievous look.

"I just wanna know if you're still a crack shot."

I laugh, pushing up against him and hardly even noticing myself doing it.

"I told you, it's all about watching other people shoot first, seeing how the gun's misaligned and which one has the best air pressure or whatever."

I flash back to when we were seventeen. I ached every moment I couldn't see him, and though it made the brief, secretive meetings we had even sweeter, each one required the same amount of planning as an undercover military operation.

Sneaking off into the woods and following instructions like 'left at the mound of walnuts caused by the hill, at the fallen tree covered in moss.' Abandoned playground, the grim underpass, windows of time when our parents weren't around, when we knew we'd be the only people in some place or other. Sometimes wearing hoodies and baggy clothes so people wouldn't recognize me, joining so many after school clubs that tracing me to one was virtually impossible. I deleted so many messages from my phone that I wished I could keep (but remembered anyway) and our phone conversations were filled with so many code words they were almost a different language.

It was kind of romantic for a while. A secret that bonded us together, our love growing stronger for all it had to endure, for the difficulty we had to go through just to share it.

"Ooh," I say, pointing at a stand. "You gonna get me some cotton candy?"

Teo shoots me an amused look even as he changes direction to head toward the stand.

"Thought you said you weren't hungry?"

"I'm not. It's just been a while since I had it."

Teo's eyes narrow a little and his half-smile gets a little more directed.

"That's as good a reason as any."

It was hard work though, hiding something so big. Having to cram so much we wanted to express, so much we wanted to share, into just a few stolen moments. Always looking over our shoulders. Living in two worlds, never overlapping. Holding back and never talking about this part of our lives that felt so natural at the dinner table, in between classes, or at the hangout. But what begins as romance can start to feel like a heavy burden when you have to keep hiding it.

More than anything, I remember just wanting to walk down the street with him, holding his hand. I wanted to stop at some place to eat, sitting at the tables with people around us. To laugh as loud as I wanted to, to relax and do what normal couples did.

"Strange how this place doesn't ever seem to change that much," I say, sucking down the sticky sweet pink and blue spun sugar as we stroll away from the stand.

"Why would it?"

We planned it for ages. A weekend away, just the two of us. Isabel helped me construct some story about how we were both going to go camping up north, and how it was somehow related to a school science project. Teo scrapped together some wages from odd jobs around town, and I used some birthday money for us to afford a small motel room and gas, and we went to L.A.

That first time felt like a dream. Scary and alien at first, until it went warm and satisfying, wonderful and perfect. I almost skipped beside him, the freedom of just being out with him a weight off my shoulders, making me feel physically lighter. The vivid colors and entrancing sounds of the pier made me feel more alive than I had anywhere else. We sat at a restaurant side-by-side and ate slowly, talking between every bite, our hands going to each other's legs, leaning over to kiss tenderly when we couldn't find anything more to say. Then we sat on the beach and watched the sunset, my head against his chest, his arm around my waist. I felt as happy as I ever had, knowing this was all I wanted, and as sad as I ever had, knowing that it wouldn't last.

We went down to L.A. a couple of times after that, and each time was as good as the first, but coming home only got harder.

"Okay, killer," Teo says, snatching my cotton candy from me and pointing at the midway booth. "Time to show me if you've still got it."

I look at the shooting stand. It's one of those where you have to shoot out the red star on a sheet of paper. There are three BB guns—somebody's already using the left, and the booth employee is standing over the middle one, making eye contact to beckon us over.

I suck the stickiness off my fingers, slow enough to give him a little show, eyes locked on him, and nod. Playful, innocent, but I know how dirty his mind is.

"Just figure out which toy you want," I say with a wink, and move toward the rightmost gun.

Teo lays five bucks down and I peer at the stand worker as he loads the BBs, making sure he doesn't short me.

"Here you go, sir," the stand worker says, offering the gun to Teo.

He laughs gently. "The lady's gonna do my shooting for me," he says.

It takes the stand worker a second to understand—too long, so I take the gun from him, and while he's still looking befuddled, raise the gun and aim. I'm slow, patient—squeezing off only a few rounds at a time—not aiming for the red, but around the star, cutting it out point by point.

"God damn," Teo mutters with appreciative awe, as the last of the star falls out with ammo to spare.

"Well how about that..." the stand worker says.

I lower the gun and try not to look too smug.

"Your lady's pretty dangerous," the stand worker says, his smile a little forced now as he takes the gun from me. "You better treat her well."

I turn a satisfied smile back to Teo, who doesn't bother correcting him.

"So, what do you want?"

Teo's still looking at me with a sense of bemused pride, then turns to study the fluffy toys at the back of the stand.

"Hmm..." he says, scratching his stubble. "Well, I gotta go for the goofy-looking dragon. Duke's got a thing for dragons. You just made my dog very happy."

The stand owner plucks the toy, hands it to me, and I give it to Teo, who nods at me with a grin, not even looking at the toy.

"Ok. Now you've got to win me something," I challenge.

Teo laughs, then looks around at the other booths. His eyes fall on the game with the basketball hoops.

"Ok. Let's go."

A little while later we move away from the games, toward the end of the pier, feeling like Bonnie and Clyde. Teo holding his goofy dragon and me holding a stuffed lion.

Tempted by the baseball toss, Teo ends up winning a toddler-sized teddy bear.

"There you go," he says, handing it over to me.

I laugh.

"I'm good with the lion," I say, raising it. "What would I do with that? It's huge!"

"You sure?"

"Yeah," I say, still laughing a little. "I don't have the space for it."

Teo notices something behind me. I hear a wail, and I turn to look. There's a little girl crying as she holds an empty ice cream cone, standing in front of a pink and green splat. Her mother tries to console her.

"Hold up," Teo says, and I watch as he walks over to them.

He exchanges a few words with the mother, then lowers himself to the girl's level, her face frozen in an expression of despair as he stands the teddy bear up. He nods the bear's head, sticks the bear's hand out, as if the bear's talking, and a shy smile breaks out on the little girl's face. He says something else, glances up at the mother, who nods, then the little girl opens her arms wide and takes the bear from Teo.

He returns, the mother and daughter smiling in his wake.

"Problem solved," he says.

I look away, trying to hide how much I'm blushing.

We grab some hot dogs and walk slow as we eat. Teo wipes a smudge of ketchup from my lip with a paper napkin, and the fact that it doesn't make me feel awkward makes me realize that I haven't been protecting my heart today, not at all. But I can't bring myself to shut down, not yet anyway. Moving toward the sunset on slow, light steps, it's like we don't want to run out of pier. The sky dims to an ethereal shimmer, the Pacific breeze making me light-headed.

"You know, it's funny," I say, feeling the space between what I want to say and what I allow myself to say fade, "I keep thinking of what I wanted to say to you the last time we met, and now that I'm actually here, I can't think of anything."

Teo smiles as we near the pier's end, and he leans over it, dangling the dragon over the water.

"Treppenwitz."

"What?" I say, leaning back against the rail beside him.

"It's a German word, for the things you only think about saying after you've left someone. The Germans have a lot of words for little things like that."

"Huh," I say, looking at his face, half-lit by the sun. "When did you learn German?"

He shrugs, almost seeming embarrassed. "I lived there for a year."

"Seriously?"

Teo looks at me and laughs.

"Yeah... After I left...I spent a couple years skipping around the states, grabbing work wherever I could. Construction, fixing up cars and bikes, even a little ranch work. Wasn't any kind of life, just enough to get something to eat, and just enough beer to keep me from thinking too much about what a waste it was. Anyway, I was working security down in Miami for an illegal backroom card game —pretty dangerous, but the money was the best I ever had. Shit happened, though, and I had to leave fast. Figured the best thing to do was get out of the country and lay low for a while. A lot of the people involved went south, to Mexico and Brazil, but I decided to go to Europe. I don't know why...or maybe I did."

"Wow," I say, taken aback by the thought of Teo being in that kind of danger. The wind picks up and I pull my light jacket around me, Teo reaching out to tuck my hair gently behind my ear. His finger traces my jaw, leaving a tingling trail on my skin. When his thumb brushes my lips, I let out a gasp. I want him so bad I can taste it. I feel my cheeks flush under his intense gaze. But then he pulls away.

"Berlin," he continues, his voice a little wistful, his expression a little more contented as he says it, "I'd heard it was the place to be. Full of artists, musicians—a good scene. Good place to be forgotten, to make a new identity." He shifts to show me his left arm, pulling his shirt sleeve over his huge bicep to reveal a tattoo of a falcon, the wings tensed in mid-flight, feet extended. Poised and dynamic, as if it's just taking off. "Few days after I got there I decided to get a tattoo —mark the occasion. Managed to get some time with Esther—the best artist in the city. I drew the flash myself, and she was impressed. Asked me if I'd ever handled a needle before. Next thing you know I'm apprenticing under her. She was incredible, taught me everything I know."

"That's pretty amazing," I say, feeling a sudden sinking feeling even as I enjoy the obvious happiness he has in remembering all this.

If I wasn't sure how I felt about Teo before, hearing him talk in

Love & Ink

79

such glowing tones about another woman puts it into sharp focus. Even as he confides in me, I feel a distance between us. A realization that this isn't the Teo who left me, but another Teo. One who's lived a lot of life in between, met a lot of other people, done a lot of things I know nothing about. Suddenly I feel a little silly about being indignant, about feeling that sense of ownership, and I start to get the same danger signals that made me abandon him in the alley outside the gig—the feeling that even though I want him so bad, I need to keep my guard up.

"Yeah. She even let me crash with her for a while since I didn't have a place—until she moved in with her girlfriend, anyway."

"Girlfriend?" I say, too quickly to stop myself sounding overly interested.

"Yeah. They'd been together for four years, so I knew she'd be moving out soon. But it gave me the time I needed to get my shit together. Man," Teo says, laughing a little as he looks out to sea. "It was a hell of a culture shock—but a good one. One minute I'm working the crane at a junkyard making just enough for some canned beans and cheap whiskey, surrounded by country music and bitter old men; the next I'm being invited to punk rock roller derbies and fancy club nights. Bars full of craft beers and seventeen languages. Even had some of my art up in a gallery at one point." Teo turns back to me, eyes narrowed, turning me to stone under his gaze. "I never got the chance to say thanks. You were right. You had me figured out before I did. Who I was."

I look at him, struggling to understand.

"What do you mean?"

Teo laughs a little.

"You probably don't even remember..." he says, shaking his head.

"Remind me?"

After a pause, Teo says, "You remember that spot under the highway overpass, with all the trees? We went there a few times. I used to go there a lot to clear my head."

"Sure. Where you painted those animals?"

Teo smiles broadly now, looking at me tenderly when he sees I remember.

"Right. Just some graffiti, something to pass the time, take my mind off things."

"It wasn't just graffiti—it was beautiful."

Teo pauses again, as if to savor what I said.

"I didn't think much of it. Nothing important. Until one day I go there," Teo says, his face darkening, a flash of frustration, "and saw they'd cleaned the place up. Steam cleaned the whole damned thing. Columns, walls—not a dot of color left. Then that night I came to see you. Climbed in your window and sat on the edge of your bed. Told you about it, trying to figure out why it got me so cut up. It wasn't like anybody went there, or actually saw what I did. Half of it was fading anyway. I just couldn't understand why it made me so angry..."

He turns away from the ocean, directing his body at me now. He turns me to face him, his hands on my shoulders.

"And you put your hands on my shoulders, like this, and looked me right in the eye, and said: 'Teo, you're an artist. Of course you're angry. You've every right to be.'"

He holds me there for a second, our eyes locked, heat flickering in the small space between us.

"I remember," I whisper, my heart pounding.

I part my lips, but Teo pulls his hands away and continues.

"You don't know what that did to me," he says, looking out at the waves again now. "I thought you were just being nice, saying whatever to calm me down—maybe you meant it like that. But it stuck with me. I'd be halfway through a bottle of whiskey, or dragging feet across Michigan snow for a half chance at a job, thinking about what a fuck-up I was, remembering all the times my dad said I belonged in jail with him...then I'd feel your hands on my shoulders...see your face right *there*...and hear you say that to me again... It was the only thing that kept me going sometimes, knowing you believed in me. God knows where I'd've ended up without it."

As he says it, a flood of emotion holds me still, unsure of what to say, but certain of the need to say something meaningful. In an instant I feel like I understand, the way I understood before. The beautiful soul born to a deadbeat dad, who painted highway columns nobody would see, for whom a few words were enough to keep going.

Right now I feel closer to Teo than anyone else in the seven years since he left, more intimate and understanding. I try to think of how to tell him this, of how to express that he meant as much to me as I did to him, but there aren't words for it.

I put my hand on his arm, and he turns those eyes to me, a little soft, but never unfocused, never unaware. I move my hand up to his shoulder, turn his body to face me, move my hands to his neck, and pull him close to kiss with parted lips. Softly, tenderly, as if to slow down time. A kiss that makes my skin shiver in the breeze, my knees weaken until Teo holds me to him tightly and it feels like I'm weightless.

Then something shifts, our kiss gaining urgency, my insides going taut and white-hot. His hands pull at my ass, his cock hardening against me. As his tongue presses into my mouth I can feel his hunger for me too. A growl in his chest reverberates through my breasts, and I know he's on the verge of losing control, desire roused fully now.

I pull my lips away, our foreheads together, my hand on his cheek.
"Do you have your bike?"
"Yeah."
"Come home with me."

10

TEO

She grips me hard as I drive her home. Harder than she needs to. Fingers claw-like against my abdominals, as if she wants to tear me apart. Her nipples stiff enough that I feel them against my back, through her tank top, through my t-shirt, so all I can think about are those swelling breasts, so close and yet still out of reach. It sends me half crazy, so that I jump reds and push the bike hard, making it rev and roar, a voice for the almost angry lust that she's stirring inside of me.

By the time we get to her apartment I'm seven different kinds of twisted, cock pressing against my jeans like a wound-up spring, feeling like a loaded gun.

"This you?" I say, once we're off the bike and standing in front of the apartment complex. I want to fuck her so bad I can barely keep from picking her up in my arms and kicking down the door, but I force myself to stay in control.

"Yep. Just moved in about a month ago."

I follow her up a flight of stairs, the view of her ass torturing me all the way, even in those boyfriend jeans, still testing the limits of my self-control. She opens her door and I follow her inside.

"It's still a work-in-progress," she says, as she tosses her jean jacket and keys aside. "I need to get some more furniture. It's a lot bigger than my last place."

It's dark outside now, only the dim streetlights casting a yellowish glow through the night beyond the window. Ash turns on a lamp shaded in red, and it's like she's unveiling a masterpiece. I move through the hallway, soaking it all up. The art books stacked on the reclaimed wood coffee table and thick, knitted throws covering the low couch. The line of succulents on the window sill and the wood-framed paintings in small groupings across the walls. The antique cabinets painted in reds and yellows, topped with fading white flowers in mason jars, and the old, faded, country guitar in the corner by the French window.

It feels like her. Colorful, warm, interesting. Even smells like her, like wood and honey. It feels like a home. Somewhere a person can breathe and be themselves. I think about her room, back then, the one I would sneak into at night, and how that also felt like some expression of her.

I think of all the places I've called home. Weather-beaten trailers and old cabins not much more than barns. Even now, my place in L.A. Big and expensive, filled with slick electronics and black leather furniture and shit I don't actually need—a home only in name. I might be able to draw nice, but Ash always knew how to live beautifully.

"You want something to drink?" she calls from some other room.

"Sure. Something strong."

"Vodka ok?"

"Always."

I pace around the room a little, lust still pumping me full of adrenaline, taking in the details, stopping to study a Basquiat print above a bookcase. Flashbacks of conversations we had in her bed rushing through my mind, until she clinks some glasses behind me and I turn around.

"Here you go," she says, handing me the glass.

I take it from her, sip slowly, but my eyes stay on hers—a living work of art even more captivating than what's on the walls. The alcohol burns, hitting the spot, but I'm intoxicated enough by the room, by the smell, by her. She must sense it, because she breaks my gaze, eyelashes flickering away as she smiles down, but her coyness only ignites the fire building within me.

I put my drink down and throw her on the couch so I can gaze at those lush curves, trace my eyes down the length of that magnificent body.

I trace a finger around her ear, down her neck. She trembles like a leaf under my touch, skin cool with goosebumps. Her breath quickening, hot and heavy.

I climb on top of her and we devour each other's mouths as I tug her pants off and she pulls her shirt over her head. We roll around on the couch, her hands squeezing my cock, my mouth sucking each nipple until her breath shudders, her fingers clawing down my back. I need to taste her.

I pull away, enjoying how she hisses with unresolved desire.

"Why are you stopping?" she asks, her voice tinged with desperation.

I growl, low and firm, "I'm not. I'm going to eat you."

I pull her ass closer and rip her panties off, spreading her open and giving her one long, slow lick. She tastes delicious. I kiss and suck and tongue her pussy like I've been starving for her, for this, until she's panting and moaning, a dreamy smile on her face.

"You like that?" I say, and before she can answer I suck her clit between my lips, slipping a finger inside her to curl back and hit the spot I know drives her crazy.

She cries out, "Fuck me, Teo."

The lust in her voice drives me wild—it always did—and sets a fire through my body. I lick her again and again, lapping up her juices, pumping my finger inside her until I hear her moans grow in strength and her body begins to writhe and shake. I nip at her clit until she comes with an intensity I don't remember.

I pull back, looking down at her, oceans of desire swirling inside me. She bites her lip, puts her hands on her breasts and squeezes them.

Love & Ink

85

"You have no idea what you're doing to me," she says, the words coming out like a low, thudding drum.

"No. I do," I say. "But I'm not done with you yet."

My words make her smile. There's a twinkle in her eye. She brings a finger to her mouth, and something inside me triggers. I pounce on her like a predator. I bite at that divine flesh, run a rough tongue from nipple to neck and back again, take those perfect tits in my hands and mouth, pulling and grabbing. Ash tugs at my pants, undoing my button fly and wrapping her hands tight around my throbbing cock. We push and pull against each other until we fall to the floor, knocking the stack of books on the coffee table over, glasses clattering against the wood, a chaos of sounds that only sends us further into frenzy

I pull back from her to sit on the floor, so that I can pull and yank at my bootlaces, kicking them off. Ash tugs off my jeans just as quickly and then I stand up and let her peel my shirt off.

I smack her ass, making her moan deliciously, and then pick her up and carry her to the bedroom.

I toss her onto the bed but she laughs and climbs off, kneeling on the floor in front of me to pull down my boxer briefs. "I have a little favor to return," she grins.

"Do you?" I grab a handful of her hair and bring her mouth to my stiff cock. "You still love giving head, you dirty girl?"

She moans hungrily in response as her lips stretch across the head, soft and warm. Satisfying sensations making me slam back into her dresser, knocking into a lamp and upsetting a pile of folded laundry. But Ash doesn't miss a beat. Her tongue wraps and tosses my cock inside her mouth, soaking me in the hot cavern of her mouth, conjuring all sensation from my body to centralize there on the touch of her sensitive lips against my sensitive shaft.

"Fuck...Ash..." I snarl through gritted teeth. "Ash...that's good."

I can almost feel her satisfied smile, a shuddering laugh that shakes through my entire body. Her head twists around my cock, her hand working my balls with the tender care of somebody who knows they're in control, someone who remembers all the things that worked on me all those years ago.

I pull her away, her mouth open and gasping for more, my cock feeling powerful enough to smash a wall. Too close to wait now, burning too much to stay like this.

"Get a condom," I command.

She runs to the bathroom, already tearing the packet open as she walks back into the room. Without taking her eyes from mine, she puts it on me, enjoying how I wince a little as she makes sure it's on tight and good. Then she takes my hand and moves past me, leading me over to the bed.

I press up behind and bend her over the mattress, feeling the curve of her front, grabbing fistfuls of those tits to squeeze and pinch, leaning over her arched back to sink my teeth into her shoulder as I tease my cock against her ass.

"Getting impatient?" she teases.

"I've waited long enough," I whisper into her ear, taking her lobe between my teeth as she winds her ass up, the tip of my cock playing around her pussy.

I guide those swaying, dizzying hips with my hands, cock rolling against her wetness. I want to hold back but we fit too perfectly together, it feels too right, too good to press inside her again, to have her engulf my hard center. She moans, long and low, pushing herself against me, fisting the blankets and using the edge of the mattress for leverage. My hands on her tits, my teeth on the back of her neck, I pound hard into her, giving her a little more inside, her trembling gasps escalating a little more each time.

"Fuck me, Teo," she moans, her voice thick with sensation. So I do.

Both of us yearning for each other, but both of us holding back, teetering on the edge, trying to stop time to linger in this perfect moment a little longer, until the weight of our lust gets too heavy, too unbearable, and something snaps. No more foreplay. No more teasing anticipation. No more dancing along the edge. Just pure fucking, beasts unleashed, urges rampant.

"Get up on the bed," I tell her. "On all fours."

I climb up behind her and slam into her again, finding the rhythm again, stroking harder and deeper until she's panting my name.

"Fuck, you make me wild," I growl, and pull back to gaze through the mad haze at the perfection of the curve of her back, the shake and tremor of her ass against my hips. Pounding into her almost angrily, with seven years' worth of unfulfilled need. I grab a fistful of her sweat-damp hair and pull her head back, guiding her throaty screams upward. She pushes, straight-armed, against the bed frame, urging me deeper.

I smack her ass as she pushes, as I ram, until her muscles go limp, her moans pitching higher and higher. I can tell she's close, so I flip her over onto her back and gaze into her eyes as I pump into her, watching the ecstasy take her over. She closes her eyes and her moans reach even higher levels as her orgasm slams through her, the sound of her pleasure echoing through the apartment as her body gushes with the honey-thick glow of satisfaction.

"Teo," she says, reaching up to pull me toward her for one last kiss. "I love you."

Suddenly I lose all control. With a frenzy of final thrusts I let myself go, coming deep inside of her, the last tightenings of her pussy taking the last of my lust. My own body almost numb as I lean over, breath slowing, and plant a grateful kiss on her neck.

A quarter of an hour later, we're lying on our sides in her bed, gazing at each other as we recover some of our senses, come down from the high.

"That was nothing like high school," Ash says, still biting her lip a little from the shimmering afterglow.

"Well, we never had much time back then," I say, feeling the stirrings of another lust begin deep in my chest. Pushing a cool finger down her side.

"No," she says, a little sadly. "We didn't."

I narrow my eyes a little, my finger reaching her waist and pulling her closer, until the cool skin of her breasts is pressed against my chest. Close enough to see the swirls in her eyes again.

"I'm done thinking about the past," I say, hands already roving across the mountain of her ass again. "I wanna make the most of this right now."

"And what about later?" she asks with a mischievous smile.

I pull her on top of me. "We'll figure it out," I say, drawing her lips down toward mine.

11

ASH

I wake up slowly, drifting in and out of sleep, unsure of which is the dream or not. So many times I've dreamt of him, woken up and rolled over to a cold, empty part of the bed. I'd get a pang of loneliness that made me close my eyes and want to go back to sleep quickly, to catch that dream version of the world again before it disappeared forever. This time, I roll over onto the sculpted hardness of his body, giving off a soothing, gentle warmth. I open my eyes and see those tattoos dancing across the lines and twists of his body.

We're uncovered—enough heat generated last night to hold off an Alaskan winter. Teo's on his back, hand behind his head as he sleeps peacefully. I lean up on an elbow and watch his chest rise and fall for a while. I soak in the lickable, skin-tingling sight of his smooth skin. The perfect shape of his abs enough to jolt me to full alertness like a shot of caffeine. I think about waking him up with a blowjob, but he put his tight boxer briefs on before sleeping. Eventually I can't help myself, though, and I lean over to put my mouth on those abs. I kiss softly, running the tip of my tongue across the definition.

"Hey," he says, smiling groggily. His muscles flinch, tickled by my tongue, and he grabs me as if catching me in the act, pulling me onto him so I lie between his legs, chin on his chest. He sticks another pillow behind him to sit up, his hands lazily running down my back so he can play with my ass.

"Morning," I purr at him.

"Morning," he smiles down at me.

We don't say anything else for a few minutes, his hands running slowly up and down my ass, my fingers tracing the lines of his tattoos conversation enough.

"You've got so many more tattoos since the last time I saw you."

"Lot of stuff's happened since then."

I look up at him with curious eyes.

"You saying all these tattoos have stories behind them?"

Teo nods.

"Most of them."

I look down, scanning the array of images and symbols across his body, before settling on a roughly-drawn skull with a crow on top of it.

"This one? It looks pretty dark."

Teo sighs when he sees which one I pointed at.

"I keep meaning to get that one done over," he says, a note of dismay in his voice. "I was rolling with a bike gang in Tennessee for a while. Not exactly nice guys, but as long as I was with them I had a place to stay, could make some decent money, and keep drunk enough not to care about what we did for it. The tatt was just part of the induction."

"What was the other part?"

Teo looks at me with a half-grin, though I know it's only there to hide some pain.

"Unless you want to spoil this perfect morning, I'm gonna hold on to that story for now."

I turn my eyes again to his body, then turn over his other arm to better see a young deer on the inside of his bicep.

"Kinda cute for you, isn't it?"

"I drove trucks for a winter. Hit a deer one night in Montana. Didn't stop—those rigs take a long time to get going again in the cold. Next day after breakfast I just walked into a tattoo shop—didn't really think about it. Only knew that I wanted a tattoo and I had the money for it. When the guy asked me what I wanted, all I could think of was that deer."

I frown at him a little.

"Are all the stories of your tattoos sad?"

Teo laughs a little, the shudder of it passing through his body to mine. He quiets quickly though, thinking about it.

"I guess the good things I have are all there. I don't need to get a tattoo to remind me of my friends, my shop. I don't think of these as sad... Looking back at all these...it only makes me appreciate what I have more."

I purse my lips, acknowledging it, but still a little unconvinced.

"Look," he says, shifting me a little to show me a simplistic-looking plant shape on the side of his ribcage. "This is the lotus flower. It's an old symbol—means different things in different cultures. In Buddhism, Egyptian hieroglyphics, Greek mythology, Tibetan mysticism."

I look down at it, trace it slowly with an appreciative finger.

"I like it."

"Generally, though, it means new beginnings. A new day. The purity of a fresh start."

I raise my eyes from the tattoo to him and smile.

"That's something I can get behind," I say, lowering my lips to kiss it softly.

Teo laughs as if tickled again and grabs me, pulling me up for a slow, soft kiss. His hands trace once again down the curve of my back, ride the hump of my ass where they settle. I feel the bulge in his briefs harden and grow.

We pull our lips apart and he looks at me with narrowed eyes, searching mine as if he's looking for something.

"How about you?" he asks. "You still thinking about getting your tattoo?"

I don't hesitate. "Yes. When I'm ready."

He nods. "I'll be here, then. When you're ready."

Teo traces the line of my jaw with gentle fingers and then pulls me into another dreamy kiss. When we finally pull away, his eyes have a mischievous sparkle to them.

"We keep talking about me," he says. "What I've been doing, where I've been. But you've told me hardly anything about what you've been doing these past seven years. I think it's your turn to spill."

"Ugh," I say, hanging my head so my hair drops to his chest, then raising it again. "Nothing as exciting as biker gangs and jaunts to Europe—trust me."

"Still. I wanna know."

I take a deep breath, and look away.

"Not much to tell, really. I finished college... Got a job assisting and then producing at *Hollywood Night*... And since then it's been a steady grind, a lot of hard work to get barely anywhere from there."

Teo looks at me keenly, pulling his head back a little, as if hesitant to say what's on his mind.

"That stuff you talked about with Isabel...something about your dad hooking you up?"

I sigh and move away to sit up beside him, cross-legged on the bed—not really in the mood to get intimate now that we're talking about my dad, and my work history. I shake my head and look up.

"I was supposed to go work at some big studio after college. My dad had this whole path laid out—pulled in his connections and influence to 'pave the way' for me. Associate producer on some big projects for a couple of years, which is actually just a title and means you hardly worked on the show at all, then move on to producing a few of my own projects, with the help of some 'real' professionals, a.k.a. hardly working on them yet again, and plenty of networking and schmoozing all the while, and then—if I followed the plan—I'd be earning seven figures and calling shots in Hollywood as a real producer by the time I was thirty. All without hardly lifting a finger. He was going to pay my rent and everything."

"Shit," Teo gasps in genuine awe. "What happened?"

I look at him, wondering if he really doesn't understand me after all this time.

Love & Ink

"Nothing 'happened.' I turned it down. Looked for a job on my own. I didn't just want the title and the glory, I wanted to learn on the job, get my hands dirty doing the work."

Teo's staring at me now as if I told him I killed someone.

"Seriously?"

"What? Would you have taken that deal?"

"Hell yeah! Seven figures and being able to call your own shots in Hollywood? Isn't that what you wanted?"

I shake my head at him, wondering if he's joking.

"Yeah, it's what I wanted. But getting what you want means nothing if you don't *earn* it. And it isn't a money thing, either. Forget the big paychecks. I want to work on projects that *move* people. That make a difference. The kinds of projects that really matter."

Teo pushes a hand into his hair and scratches it roughly.

"You're a stronger person than me, Ash."

"Come on. You wouldn't have taken that deal either," I say. "Imagine never knowing whether your success was yours or if it was just handed to you. My whole career I'd have been 'my father's daughter.' It would have hung over me until I retired—*fuck that*."

Teo laughs and looks at me with admiring eyes.

"What about now? How is 'going it alone' working out? Any closer to those big dreams?"

I roll my eyes and look away, realizing that I might defeat my own argument by answering that.

"Well...it's going ok. Not 'ok' enough that I don't wonder about whether I made the right choice sometimes, though."

"What's up? You having problems moving up?"

I throw my head back onto the pillow beside Teo and look up at the ceiling.

"Not 'problems,' per se. I mean, I just got a promotion, hence the new apartment. I'm getting tons of experience and making contacts and all that. But it's...just...it's... I'm working on this crap show that could be so much *better* than it is, and all I want is the chance to show that—to show what I could do with just a little more faith—but I keep getting stonewalled every time I try to spread my wings a little.

They're convinced our audience can't handle the kind of stuff I want to do."

"What do you wanna do that's so controversial?"

I lean forward, full hand gestures now as I get enthusiastic.

"Ok, so it's just a gossip show—real formulaic. Who's fucking who, somebody's got a new movie out, that kind of thing. And sure, I get that, it's the format. But what I wanna do, really, is produce some segments with a little twist, you know? Some depth. Something a little out of the ordinary, that doesn't assume the audience is half-asleep and only kinda listening. I've got ideas—*man* I've got so many ideas. And I know they would work. But the higher-ups won't let me do any of them."

Teo looks at me with a mixture of admiration and confusion.

"So why not just film them anyway?"

"What?"

"Just tape the segments you want to film. On your own."

I laugh and wave the idea away.

"It doesn't work like that, Teo."

He opens his palm wide in a gesture of bemusement.

"You're a producer, right? You're not some intern coffee-maker. This is your job. Making shows happen. You have the know-how and the contacts, you can rent equipment—"

"True..." I admit belatedly. "But I can't just decide to put something on the air myself. *Hollywood Night* doesn't work like that. There's this tight-ass, corporate hierarchy structure that dictates exactly what we—"

"Bullshit," Teo interrupts. "You didn't turn down seven figures just to take orders from someone else, right?"

I bite my cheek.

"No."

"So...could you do it? Rent some cameras, get a crew together and film your pieces? Is that feasible?"

"I mean...sure, I *could*... But—"

"So just do it."

"And then what? Say 'Hey, I filmed this segment that you told me you didn't want a dozen times already. What do you say?'"

Now Teo waves my idea away.

"Sometimes people don't know what works until you show it to them," he says, with a belief that's bordering on wisdom. "You know how many times people have come into my shop with some picture that would never work as a tattoo? You can explain and argue with them for a whole day and they still don't get why it'll look like shit. But if you draw them something similar that would actually work," Teo stops to click his fingers loudly, "they get it. People don't know what they want until they see it. So show them."

I let the words linger in my mind, turning them over like a puzzle.

"Maybe," I say softly, lost in my own thoughts now.

In the silence I hear my phone buzz in the hallway, and get up to go check it. It's a message from Jenny:

STEPHEN PEACE JUST DIED. WE THINK. GET HERE NOW!

I rush back into the bedroom, waving my phone at Teo.

"Hollywood emergency," I say, grabbing clothes from my closet. "I gotta run."

"No time for breakfast?" Teo says, surprising me as he comes up behind me, roving hands around my front, his beard grazing my neck.

I groan slightly, then give in to responsibility.

"I'm still full from last night," I say, turning to kiss him quickly before pulling away to get dressed.

After a few minutes in which he gets on his jeans and boots, he comes back into the bedroom carrying a coffee for me in one hand and his shirt in the other.

"You got a safety pin?" he says as I gulp down the liquid caffeine, showing me the torn fabric.

"Sorry," I shrug, grabbing my bag and stuffing my keys and phone into it. "I could lend you a shirt, but I doubt anything would fit." I move toward him, put a hand on his cheek and kiss him softly. "I'll try to be more gentle next time."

Teo pulls on his torn shirt and follows me to the door.

"Don't. I've got plenty of shirts."

People are bustling and moving when I arrive at work. They buzz around with a sense of urgency, holding phones to their ears even as they shout at each other across the workspace. An Oscar-winning icon of modern cinema dying is the celebrity show equivalent of a major tragedy, especially when that actor is relatively young, and currently experiencing a career resurgence. This is news that the major news networks are going to dedicate hours to—so for a show like *Hollywood Night,* dedicated to exactly this kind of news, it's critical to get it right.

I decide to find Jenny first, and head upstairs to the offices, but she calls to me as I approach the writer's room.

"Ash! Christ, thank God you're finally here."

"Jenny," I say, as she walks hurriedly toward me, balancing a phone on her clipboard as she writes something on it, "is Stephen Peace really dead? I checked online in the cab over here but nobody seems sure."

Jenny buzzes past me so quickly I can almost feel the slipstream. She waves a hand for me to follow and I try to keep up.

"We're not sure either," she says, voice jumping along with her bouncing steps. "Rumors are flying around online, but there's nothing I would risk a limb on. The thing is, we need a segment up on this *fast*—it's what we're here for, and if we get this story first we might just hit our numbers this month. The problem is that we can't call it without knowing. If the show gets it wrong it would be suicide."

"Of course."

"And *you're* going to have to make the call on this. I just got off the phone with Sean, and all I got from him was what I dreaded—the most polite, humble, and nicely-worded 'I don't give a shit' in the business."

"What about Candace?"

Jenny glances back at me just long enough for me to see her eye roll.

Love & Ink 97

"She's getting her nails done today."

Jenny slams through the exit to the stairs and I jump through before the door slams back.

"Well why don't we actually try to find out if he's dead or not?" I say, over the sound of our shoes quickly tapping down the stairs. "It shouldn't be hard."

"Everybody's been trying. Half the writer's room is on detective duty right now. His agent says he's alive and kicking, but a publicist for the movie he may or may not be filming in Croatia right now gave us some vague answer that sounded like something was up. Then we've got one source saying he was transported to a hospital in L.A. an hour ago, is hanging by a thread, and the reason there's no statement is that the death is pretty incriminating regarding his drug habits. One of our writers is convinced this is all just a case of mistaken identity started by some blurry photo of a guy on a stretcher, and we've also got a source telling us this is all some elaborate publicity stunt to promote the release of his new movie."

"So in a word, it's a mess."

"Precisely."

"What about producing a segment that just talks about all those rumors then? Go through all the rumors and make a funny little bit on it. 'Schrodinger's Steve' or something."

Jenny stops on the landing and turns backward, pointing her pen at me.

"That's good," she says, smiling. "But a little too high brow. And a little too tasteless. What if he *is* dead, and our primary segment on it is a jokey one?"

"Yeah, you're right," I admit.

She spins through the doors and into the hallway.

"What about this," I say, my mind still going a mile a minute. "We film all the segments. All possibilities. He's dead, he's not, it's a publicity stunt, he's hanging by a thread—all of it. Then, the second we *do* find out what's going on, we push the button and we're live. We might not be the very first, but we'll be one of. And we'll be accurate."

Jenny turns to me as we reach the studio doors. She nods, but she's not smiling.

"That's a good idea. We'd have to cut them together really fast and loose, but it could work. Except we also have another problem."

"What?" I frown.

Jenny answers by pushing open the door and gesturing for me to enter.

Inside, the studio is all set up. The cameras pointed and manned, the lighting on the set, and Carlos in his spot, ready for show time. Sandra, the director, is standing by one of the cameras, but she's got a hand over her face like she's experiencing a pounding headache. It looks like they're ready to film. Except Carlos isn't wearing the 'happy to see you' smile he usually wears when he's working—instead, he's flailing his arms and ranting at anybody who might be listening.

"...bonafide asshole! One of the biggest you'll ever meet! The world's a better place without him—"

"What's the problem here?" I shout at Carlos, marching into the light between the cameras.

Carlos shifts his attention from a cowering runner toward me instead.

"Problem? If Stephen Peace is dead that's a blessing, not a problem. The only 'problem' here is that you expect me to do a whole segment on some nobody asshole like him. We're scrapping this."

I sturdy myself for a drama queen tantrum and focus on keeping my tone all business.

"We are scrapping nothing. Stephen Peace has won two Oscars and a Golden Globe and been nominated for a ton of other awards, and on top of that he was in one of the highest-grossing movies worldwide last year," I say, as calmly as possible. "He's also a UN ambassador and a spokesperson for Autism Speaks. So no, this isn't 'some nobody.' He's our top story, and all the other networks' as well."

"Pfft!" Carlos flinches backward and makes a face as if someone just tried to force-feed him rotten meat. "Let me tell you about Stephen 'Peace of Shit' as I like to call him. He's a hack who doesn't deserve a single dollar he's made in Hollywood. I know the guy better than anyone—we went through the same acting program, and I spent three years carrying him on a sitcom called *Scoop*. The guy needed more takes to get his lines right than any actor I've ever seen. Always trying to steal scenes from me, always getting in my light—that wannabe knew *I* was ten times more talented. You know the role that made him big, playing the rookie detective in that serial killer movie?" Carlos jabs a finger at the fine silk of his purple shirt. "That was mine—it was *written for me*. I knew the writer and everything. Then, at the last minute, they toss me out for Stephen Peace of Shit. Said I didn't come across 'hungry' enough, that I was too 'polished' for the part—can you believe it?"

"No, actually."

"Yeah!" Carlos says, feeling vindicated and angry at the same time. "See, I know what really happened. Shit! The things I could tell you about that prick! If you wanna roll that camera I could tell you stories about him that would—"

"Let's just try to keep it calm and detached, shall we?" I interrupt, firmly. "Professional. Right, Carlos? You don't wanna look bitter or anything, do you?"

Carlos straightens his shoulders a bit and adjusts his shirt.

"I'm not bitter."

"Of course you're not. But people talk. So let's just get this short little bit done and we can all take a break until tonight."

Carlos nods. "That's what I'm talkin' about."

"Great. You good to go, Sandra?" I ask the director.

She sighs and nods. "We just need a take," she says.

Jenny comes up beside me, carrying large prompt cards.

"I've done some basic lines," she says. "One for if he's dead, one for if he's not, one for if he's hanging by a thread in the hospital."

"Ok, great," I say, turning back to give Sandra a thumbs-up.

"Let's shoot the dead one first. Ready, everyone? Roll sound!" Sandra says.

Carlos takes his spot as the cameras make a final adjustment. He turns on his primetime smile as easily as a flashlight, and beams into the lens. Sandra checks the studio, the PA holding Jenny's prompts, then calls action.

Carlos' voice sounds like a completely different person as he begins.

"Stephen Peace, the thirty-five year old actor best known for his role in—" Carlos stops himself and laughs. "*Thirty-five*? Come on, if the guy's dead we can at least be honest. Guy's knocking on mid-forties *at best*! You ever met him in person? You can smell the Botox from ten feet away. His face looks like it's been pounded by meteors—"

"Carlos!" I say, trying not to show too much exasperation. Beside me, the director puts her face in her hands again with a deep sigh.

"I can't," she says.

"Can we please stick to the script?" I call out to Carlos.

The host holds his palms up innocently.

"My bad, my bad... Let's go again."

Sandra takes a deep breath, looks at the camera monitor, and gives the signal. Carlos starts again and Jenny comes close to whisper in my ear.

"Maybe we should get somebody else to do this segment. You want me to call Kelly Greene?"

I lean over to whisper back.

"Kelly Greene's not doing stuff for us anymore. She got that role in a TV show, remember?"

Jenny frowns, seeming a little more interested than I would have expected.

"So who's our back-up now?"

I shoot her a stoic expression.

"We don't have one."

"*Seriously?*"

"Nope. We should have found one last month—except Carlos doesn't want the competition, and Candace has to sign off on it anyway. You do the math... I must have suggested about a dozen names so far, but it goes nowhere."

Jenny gets a look like she's holding something back, like she's prepping herself to suggest something, but before she can speak I'm distracted by the raised tones of Carlos going on another rant.

"Unknown?! Give me a break—it's drugs! Ask anyone in town they'll tell you what a cokehead that s.o.b. was! Guy couldn't hardly remember his name at an after party! Either that killed him, or the money he owed all over town. I ever tell you about the last time I was shooting hoops with that asshole, back in nineteen ninety-six—"

"Ok, Carlos," I sigh, dismissing Sandra for good and finding it hard to be firm anymore. "Let's go again."

About an hour after we call it quits in the studio, I'm still in the editing room with the operator trying to stitch together the usable pieces of Carlos' bit. I play the trickier edits over stock footage of the actor, and try out various soundbeds so that nobody can see where I've edited out the 'Peace of Shit's and 'asshole's Carlos kept interspersing.

It's hard work—made harder by the fact that the only news we get just seems to confuse the situation more than clarify it.

I've barely had a chance to consider what happened last night between me and Teo, but it lingers in my mind like a treat I'm saving myself for later. Occasionally, zoning out as I watch Carlos flail his arms on the tape, I'll remember tracing Teo's tattoos in bed, but I snap myself out of it quickly to return to this impossible task before me.

The whole thing starts to feel like a gigantic waste of time, an absurd comedy where I'm the punchline. I struggle to stop myself from wondering 'what's the point?' and 'is this really my job?' pushing those thoughts to the back of my mind as I try to focus, absently shoveling a carton of Chinese takeout into my mouth. Listening to Carlos' voice so much now that I can feel myself going mad, and start to imagine being committed to an insane asylum screaming the words 'Stephen Peace of Shit' over and over.

Then, just as I'm about to really flip, one of our writers bursts into the editing room carrying his phone.

"He's dead," the writer says.

"You sure?" I ask.

"A hundred per cent. Had a heart attack on set in Croatia—I'm half-Croatian, so I spoke directly to the hospital staff. No doubt about it."

My stomach tightens. "Has anyone else reported it yet?"

The writer shakes his head.

"Not yet. But I doubt it'll be long. Apparently the hospital's full of the actors and crew he was working with."

"Ok," I say, turning to the editing desk with a newfound burst of determination.

After a few more last-minute alterations, the piece goes live, views rack up almost as soon as it's up, and the three of us share some belated, relieved high-fives. The editor and writer leave me in front of the monitors in the editing room, where I slump into my chair, only just realizing how tired I am, how many hours have passed, and how little I've thought about anything else but this segment all day.

Other than that, the one thing that could lift my mood right now is seeing Teo, and when I check my phone to find a message from him, it's almost as good.

It's a photo, kind of dark, but I can make out the goofy dragon I won him at the fair last night, sitting on a cabinet behind the tattoo chairs. Something else catches my eye though, next to it, and I zoom in, peering at my phone as I try to make out the shape.

It's another fluffy toy, battered and torn, as if it's been dragged across deserts and roads. A small gorilla—the same one I won for him all those years ago. My lips start to tremble a little, the image goes blurry with the wetness in my eyes, and I look at what he wrote beneath it.

ONLY MEANS SOMETHING WHEN YOU HAVE TO EARN IT.

I feel some immense shift in my body, as if all my muscles are relaxing at once. Through the open door I hear the shouts of celebration from the corridor outside, but I've almost forgotten the trials of the night. I brush a few stray tears from my eye, and read the text again. My heart soars.

Teo always had a knack for saying exactly the right thing, just when I needed to hear it. I guess some things never change.

12

TEO

I see Ash a few more times before the week is out. Each meeting feels like slipping further and further into the past, an old, comfortable rhythm, a rediscovery of why we fell in love in the first place, and at the same time, something new and fresh. As if the fact that we've been through so much in between, built careers and lives for ourselves, yet still feel like this about each other, makes it mean so much more. No longer naïve kids with their whole lives ahead of them, for whom it was a self-contained fantasy, but adults who know too much now to be taken in by hazy summers and hormones.

This is for real. Each minute we spend together makes the seven year gap between us feel even shorter, even more like nothing but a bad dream. Affirming that we were meant to be, that *this* is normal, and all those difficult years apart was just some irregularity. Picking up where we left off.

But as much as we talk and laugh and fuck, that unanswered question still hangs in the background of everything like a trouble-maker biding his time. We talk around it, heading off any talk of that night as early as we can. When one of us accidentally stumbles on the words 'when you left' or 'prom' they drop like stones in the smooth flow of conversation.

I know she wants to ask me still. I can see the question twisting inside of her when we get close to it. Holding her against me a morning after, I see it almost come to the surface, dark eyes getting darker, holding something back.

So I change the subject, talk about something that makes her smile, or pull her in to kiss her lips and make the question go away. It never really goes away though, I know that. But I'll keep that secret as long as I can—knowing that if I tell her the truth, everything we have right now will come crashing down.

I'm sitting in the back of Mandala, finally getting that skull and crow changed into something else by Esther—my mentor from Germany who's in L.A. for a few days doing a guest spot at my shop— the conversation with Ash putting a sense of urgency in me about it. Kayla's out front, while Ginger and Hideo are working on a couple of customers in the tattoo chairs.

"Hey Teo," Kayla says, poking her head through the door. I look up at her and notice a sly twinkling in her eye. "Your lady's here."

Kayla seems to relish saying it, but I don't mind the teasing, because a second later Ash steps into the back room and it's hard to mind anything when she looks that good.

"Teo? Oh," she says, stepping tentatively back, looking shyly away from the needle that's rapidly buzzing against my skin. "I didn't know you were busy—should I come back later?"

"No—I was just finishing up anyway." I nod at the short but fierce, tattooed, purple-ponytailed woman working on my bicep. "This is Esther. Esther—Ash."

"Nice to meet you," Ash says warmly, coming over and offering her hand with genuine enthusiasm. "Teo's told me so much about you."

Esther takes Ash's hand briefly and laughs, hard and mechanical —she doesn't have much of an accent, but her laugh is unmistakably German.

"I hope it was as nice as the things he told me about you," she says, smiling back.

Ash glances at me, a little coyness about her lips as it soaks in.

Love & Ink 105

"Esther's just in town for a few days," I say. "She's doing a guest spot for us and she's fully booked up already, but she made time to squeeze me in for a little ink on her lunch. Thought you'd want to meet."

"Done," Esther says, setting the needle aside. "For now. Maybe a little touch up when it heals."

I get up and move to a nearby mirror, checking out the conversion of a battered skull into a colorful Day of the Dead figure.

"That looks incredible," Ash says, leaning in to see.

I turn to look at her as Esther brings some saran wrap to tape over the tatt.

"Do you want to get one done?" I ask Ash. "No one better for your first tattoo than Esther."

Ash hesitates, and I get a slight sense she still feels overwhelmed at the idea. Esther must sense it, too, because she waves the idea away nonchalantly.

"I'm sure she'd prefer for you to do her first, Teo."

Ash laughs gently, a little nervous relief.

"In that case, let's all go get a bite to eat. My treat," I offer.

"*My* treat," Esther insists, winking at Ash as she pulls her jacket on. "I don't want to eat in the cheapest place in the city."

A short cab ride later and we're sitting on a restaurant terrace shaded by overhanging bougainvillea, around a table filled with lime mojitos and Mexican food. I never had any worries that Ash and Esther wouldn't hit it off, but by the time we're through our meals, I'm almost worried they're hitting it off *too* much.

"So tell me what Teo was like in Germany?" Ash asks Esther, who grins.

"Ah," I say, leaning back and shrugging. "You don't want to hear about me."

"Yes I do!" Ash says, only gaining in enthusiasm. She turns back to Esther. "I just can't imagine him over there...speaking a foreign language..."

"Oh, well it took him long enough to learn—though he had

plenty of girls willing to teach him," Esther says, in a drily humorous tone.

"Did he now?" Ash says, smiling curiously at me.

"Gott, ja! Why do you think we nicknamed him the 'rogue wolf?' He was always on the prowl. Girls girls girls—all day long. That was Teo in Berlin. I took him to a lesbian club once, so that he would actually, you know, have fun and dance a little."

"What happened?"

"In half an hour he left with a couple."

Ash laughs and shakes her head at me. I shrug and hope somebody changes the subject soon. Those wild days make for good stories, but the stories never go deep enough. They never address how I was just burying the pain, just reeling from losing Ash.

"And I've never seen an apprentice do as many ass tattoos as Teo, either. It's like every girl in the city wanted him to get his hands on them."

"I was just the 'foreign guy,'" I explain, shrugging. "It's not my fault the German girls had a thing for it."

"You knew exactly what you were doing!" Esther laughs, then pats me on the shoulder affectionately. "I didn't mind. He was a great tattoo artist, and he learned fast—that's all I cared about. One of the best I've ever known. If he ever wanted to come back, I would take him on in a second," Esther pauses, directing a knowing look at Ash, "though I doubt he'd want to leave here."

I look at her warmly.

"Everyone who works with you ends up being one of the best," I say. "I'm just lucky you gave me a chance."

Esther sighs a little sadly.

"Ah, Teo. You still underrate yourself. You were destined to be a great artist of some kind or another."

"I agree," Ash says, happily.

"See," Esther says, gesturing at Ash. "Everyone could see it but you. Maybe someday the two of you can come to Berlin for a visit and I can get Teo to guest for me. My shop is always open to visiting artists."

Love & Ink

"Maybe," I say, noticing the way Ash looks suddenly bashful.

Esther and Ash return to their mojitos, and I look out to the busy street, the passing cars and strolling couples.

"Excuse me," Ash says, pushing her chair back and fumbling in her bag as her phone vibrates. "I'm so sorry to be rude but I need to take a quick call for work. Be right back, I promise."

"Sure," I say, winking at her and watching her all the way.

"Smitten," Esther mumbles.

I turn to see her grinning widely.

"What?"

"Nothing," she shrugs, smiling even harder. "It's just nice to see you happy. I always knew you were a true romantic underneath that bad boy exterior."

I look back to see if Ash is nearby, but she's out of sight.

"So what do you think about her?" I ask.

Esther gulps down her drink and raises a curious eyebrow.

"Since when do you need to ask me for my opinion on girls?"

I laugh and drain the last of my mojito.

"You were always keen on giving me an opinion in Germany."

"This isn't Germany, Teo. This is your home, not mine," she says. "But honestly? I think you two are perfect together. She's smart. Gorgeous. Seems grounded, obviously hardworking...the humble, steady type. I think she's just what you need."

I nod, twisting a coaster in my hand as I ponder over the words. It feels somewhat satisfying hearing somebody else say it, a confirmation I'm not just blindly hoping our future looks good.

"Thanks for telling her I was a hound in Berlin, by the way," I joke.

Esther laughs deeply, throwing her head back.

"Please—she's so besotted with you I could tell her you were an axe murderer and she'd ask to help hide the bodies. She understands... More to the point, she seems to *want* to understand you. How many of the other girls you dated could you say that about?"

I nod again, feeling comforted by the way Esther never shies from delivering home the hard truths.

"Still..." I say, looking at the coaster.

"What?"

I shake my head, searching for the words—or maybe the courage to use them.

"Sometimes I think I'm just setting myself up for a fall again. Maybe she's still too good for me. Maybe I'm not as put together as I've been pretending these past couple of years. Still a whole lot of room for things to go wrong—do you know what I mean?"

Esther shifts in her chair to direct herself at me.

"Listen, Teo: I hate to play armchair psychiatrist, but this just looks so clear to me. The whole time you were working your way through every heterosexual woman in Berlin, it was obvious that you were trying to compensate for something—trying to fill some empty space inside of you. Whatever happened between you and Ash before is in the past—and it would serve you well to remember that.

"Can't you see? I *watched* you change, Teo. You came to me as a guy running away from things, a guy with plenty of demons. And you left Berlin as a guy coming home, a guy with goals. Your work, your shop, Ash—you don't have to keep searching anymore, Teo. Just let yourself be open to everything that's going right."

I twist the coaster a little more quickly now, struggling to order my thoughts.

"I had a future with Ash before," I say, looking up at Esther, "and I lost it. How do I know I won't lose it again?"

"Because this time you won't make the same mistakes, Teo. This time it's up to you."

I meet her eyes, as if allowing her a glimpse inside my soul. Then smile it off and look away.

Yeah. That's exactly what I'm afraid of.

13

ASH

As the only producer on *Hollywood Night* who actually seems to do anything, it doesn't take me long to put Teo's advice into practice. Within a week I've already shot some b-roll of Frankie's yoga classes and studio, as well as a basic interview. It's still not enough to form the segment I want it to be, but it's getting there.

It helps that almost everyone at *Hollywood Night* seems to hold a grudge against Candace for something or other, so I can call in favors with all the editors and crew I want, knowing that they're not going to tell her I'm working on something of my own.

It's strange, thinking back to how Teo and I kept our relationship a secret because my parents would think he was a bad influence on me. He's been back in my life for all of ten minutes and here I am bribing people with boxes of donuts to let me smuggle some older, unused camera equipment out of the studio for a few hours, sneaking extra time in the editing room, and pretending that I'm location-scouting when I'm really at Frankie's yoga studio filming interviews with her students.

Sometimes it feels like I'm running an undercover operation, stirring up a revolution in the ranks—but I've spent way too long playing by the rules, and breaking them can be a hell of a turn-on. It also makes the rest of the celebrity non-news and pregnancy gossip I have to produce a lot easier to stomach. Maybe I've always needed a little influencing to follow my passions—bad or not.

Now that I'm doing this, I'm really thinking back to all the ideas I've had shot down by Candace over the years, all the quirky people I wanted to interview, all the serious topics I wanted to cover. The peculiar stories of actors who reached the very top only to fall completely off the map overnight, exposés of sexism and prejudice in film-making, the great Hollywood scripts that were never filmed because they got caught in legal or political limbos.

Of course, filming all this stuff might all mean nothing in the end, if I never actually get to put it on air—but you can't force everything in life. Sometimes you just have to be ready for when an opportunity presents itself. Besides, with a decent portfolio of actually-interesting segments, my own ideas, I might just finally be able to take the plunge and find a better gig than running condom-fetching errands for Candace and Carlos.

It's as I'm working through some of these ideas, at the end of a long workday of dealing with Carlos' hissyfits over his hair, that Jenny knocks on my office door. She pushes it open slowly, poking a strand of blue hair and half a yellow hoop earring inside.

"You busy?"

"No," I say, dropping my pen. "Come in."

Jenny steps inside.

"Just wanted to remind you that we're meeting at Hooper's for drinks in about an hour."

I purse my lips apologetically.

"Oh, I can't. Not tonight."

Jenny's face falls. "You have to," she says. "Sean insisted that you come, so he'll notice if you're not there. I think he wants to thank you for nailing that Stephen Peace segment...under all those 'difficult' circumstances."

"Can't. I've already made plans," I sigh, knowing that Jenny isn't the person I should be excusing myself to.

Jenny winces, then quickly turns around to close the door and approaches my desk.

"Honestly," she says, "I think you should really come. If only to keep *certain persons* from bitching about you too much. With all your secret projects on the side now...might be smart to keep up friendly appearances."

My pulse kicks up a notch. "You think she suspects something?"

"No...Candace is so self-absorbed you could probably come into work naked and she wouldn't notice. She won't find out anything unless she decides to start going over the schedules with a fine-tooth comb—which is about as likely me being offered a part in a remake of Casablanca."

I laugh gently as Jenny half-sits on my desk.

"But since you're filming all this stuff," Jenny continues, "you may as well kiss a little ass. Could help when it comes time to show them what you've got."

"I hear you," I nod. "The thing is, I made plans with Teo tonight."

"So bring him!" Jenny asserts eagerly. "It's about time I meet the guy who's got you walking in here in the mornings with a Miss America smile! God—" Jenny stops herself to look away flippantly, "you should ask him to bring a friend, if you really care."

I consider it for a second, then shake my head.

"It's not really his scene."

Jenny scoffs. "He doesn't like free bar tabs? Come on, half the crew always bring their girlfriends and boyfriends. You can swing a plus one."

"I don't know..."

Jenny frowns suddenly, putting a hand on her hip.

"How many times have you been to his tattoo shop? Spoken to his friends there? You even met his mentor from Germany last week. Don't you think it's only right you show him your world the way he's shown you his?"

"I suppose...although my 'world' basically consists of an unbearably vain prima donna and a boss who looks at me as if she wants to wear my skin."

Jenny leans forward.

"You forgot to mention the incredibly smart, funny, and talented writer who does regular unpaid stints as your psychotherapist, motivational speaker, and top secret project collaborator."

I laugh again.

"I can't argue with that."

"Good," Jenny says, leaping off the desk and heading for the door with an air of triumph. "And don't forget to ask about the friend—it's been years since I could smile like that before midday."

Hooper's is a large bar. Sleek, with its black couches and metal tables, but not too modern with its warm chandelier lighting and carpeted pool table area. More to the point, they have a great cocktail and whiskey menu which—even with my producer-promotion raise—I wouldn't want to afford unless it was on the company's tab.

Work drinks happen about once a month. Part morale-booster, part opportunity for a lot of the unappreciated employees to drink their fair share of compensation, and part opportunity for Sean to feel involved with the production—the whole thing is usually his idea. Even as a producer on the show, it's only when the whole crew bundles into the bar that I realize how many people work on *Hollywood Night*—wardrobe, make-up, writers, editors, set crew, assistants —and it's nice to connect with everyone. It'll be nice to introduce Teo to them, too. As soon as I arrive I'm checking the door every few seconds, waiting for him to show up like he told me he would.

Tonight follows the same tried and tested pattern. Sean begins by giving a little speech about how proud he is of everyone, special mentions for some of us, and how much he hopes we'll 'kick-on' and 'keep up the great work,' before we all turn off to concentrate on our orders. Sean then jumps from conversation to conversation, making smiley small talk and handing out pats on the back while Candace inevitably separates herself from the crew members she can barely name, and spends her time with Carlos and the showbiz friends they always invite to these things.

Love & Ink 113

Once the vibe settles a little, and I've taken my turn exchanging niceties with Sean, I take a seat at the bar and order another blue lagoon. As I half-listen to a conversation between a couple of the crew beside me, I feel a pat on the back and Jenny squeezes beside me carrying an empty glass.

"Another Manhattan, please," she says to the busy bartender, before turning eager eyes to me. "So? Where is he?"

"Ugh, must you keep nagging?" I tease, pulling my phone out to check if he's messaged. "I sent him a text—but like I said, don't be surprised if he doesn't come. This is really not his bag."

Jenny smiles and leans in to be heard over the vibrant chatter, pointing along the bar to the corner.

"Take a look," she says, as I follow the point of her finger. Carlos is flirting with a couple of tall women in tight dresses— and a few feet away, Candace glares at him like she's trying to see a magic eye picture. "You'd think with all that plastic surgery she'd be better at hiding her emotions."

I turn my attention back to my drink and suck a long gulp.

"They're both a time bomb waiting to happen," I say.

"It's so ironic..." Jenny says.

"What is?"

"Well, Candace loves nothing more than pieces about 'cheating celebrities' and 'who's the father?' pregnancies—all the while she's sleeping with a married man who puts himself across as some latter-day saint."

I look at Jenny for a second.

"Don't start pointing out contradictions in Hollywood—we'll be here all night."

Jenny laughs loudly and sips half her drink. She sways and bounces a little to the hip-hop tune barely audible over the noise of the bar.

I watch her for a while, smiling.

"What's got you in such a good mood?" I ask, eventually.

"What good mood?"

"Don't play coy," I say, turning to face her. "Spill it."

Jenny laughs and stops bouncing for a second.

"Well, since I'm keeping your secret, I suppose you can keep mine."

"What secret?"

With a dramatic pause, a look in her eye like she's giddy, she says, "I just got my first audition."

"*Audition?*"

"Shh! Keep it down! I don't want anyone to know."

I lean in so I can whisper forcefully.

"Since when do you act?"

"It's not really an acting role...more of a presenting sort of thing."

"Ok...since when do you present—sort of thing?"

"I don't...I mean, I didn't. It's just something I want to try, you know? I've been writing for crappy primetime TV and trying to have my scripts read for so long now...I'd just like to try something a little more...*expressive.* Something a bit more thrilling than staring at a blank Pages document all day."

"That's fantastic, Jenny! *God!* I'm so excited for you!" I say, grabbing her instinctively for a hug.

"You don't think it's stupid?" she says, her lips curled nervously. "A woman in her thirties trying to for a dramatic pivot in her career? Trying to get in front of the camera? I mean, I'm probably not even what they're looking for."

"Are you kidding? You're one of a kind. I think it's fucking incredible," I say, picking up my glass and clinking it against Jenny's. "And I think you're going to kick seven shades of ass as a presenter."

"Thanks," Jenny says, blushing like it's the first compliment she's ever received in her life. "It's not like I want to present for TV or anything, but something small...online, maybe. Or the kind of things you see writers do on sites like *TrendBlend.*"

I nod encouragingly. "I could absolutely see you doing that. You've got the look, the charisma, the attitude—totally."

Jenny smiles bashfully and waves her empty glass at the bartender again.

"Yeah, well, you have enough of your lines cut by some higher-up, or butchered by some half-wit, and you can't help wondering why you don't just deliver them yourself. Speaking of which," Jenny says, lowering herself on the bar to point again, "it looks like Candace is trying to get her groove back."

Once again I follow Jenny's finger to the end of the bar.

"I can't see," I say, after tilting my head side-to-side. "What am I supposed to be looking at?"

"Candace is flirting with some guy, trying to make Carlos jealous," Jenny says. "Although seeing the guy, I don't blame her...just, *wow*."

It's only after seeing the half-lidded eyes and open-mouthed awe on Jenny's face that I figure I better see for myself who she's talking about, and decide to stand on the bar rail to get a better look. My look is less of awe, and more one of horror.

"Oh shit," I say, almost cringing at the sight of Candace tightly holding onto him, hand pressed against his chest, the other I don't even want to think about. "That's Teo!"

Jenny lets out a low whistle. "Now I see why you want to keep him locked up."

"Damnit," I say, jumping back off the bar rail and pushing my way through the crowd toward him, Jenny holding her drink high as she follows in my slipstream.

When I'm close enough for him to see me, Teo breaks out of Candace's death-grip and darts toward me to land a kiss that's a little more intimate than it should be considering we're in a public place surrounded by people.

"Hey babe," he says as we break apart, looking at me like we're in private.

"Hey," I say, turning to Jenny and Candace, who is now glaring daggers at me.

I feel myself blushing as I introduce him to my BFF first. "This is Teo. Teo, this is Jenny—she writes for the show, when she's not being an awesome friend and supportive comrade for my ideas."

"Nice to meet you," Teo says, holding his hand out for the few seconds it takes Jenny to stop gawking and process the words.

"Oh," she says, finally, practically drooling as she shakes his hand. "You too."

Candace scowls so hard it's difficult to ignore, and we all end up looking at her.

"And this is Candace," I say, trying to break the awkwardness. "My boss."

"Yeah," Teo says, half-smiling away the unease. "She already introduced herself."

"*This* is your girlfriend?" Candace says, ignoring me to focus on Teo.

Teo squeezes his arm around my shoulder a little tighter, plants a kiss on my forehead.

"Sure is. Lucky me."

"Pfft," Candace snorts dismissively, rolling her eyes and then looking back at me like I'm a stain on her expensive rug. "I thought you were a lesbian—the way you dress."

"*Candace!*" Jenny hisses.

"It's ok, Jenny," I say, my boss's catty words bouncing right off me as Teo squeezes me even tighter. "I'm sure she's just had a little too much to drink."

Candace laughs at this, reveling in the discomfort she thinks she's causing, enjoying the tension.

"What? Am I wrong?" she goes on, cheerily, as if we're talking about sports. "I mean...look at you, Ash, and *look at him...* I'm sure I'm not being controversial when I say he's a little out of your league."

"You're right—Ash could do way better," Teo says, looking at me like I'm the only girl in the room. "I'm a lucky guy."

Candace laughs like Teo's flirting.

"Excuse me? Are we talking about the same person?" She looks at me and laughs again. "What's the deal? Are you paying his rent or something?"

"What's *your* deal?" he says, glaring at her in confusion.

"Teo..." I interrupt, pressing a hand on his chest to try and stop him. I'm used to Candace's insults, used to shrugging them off and keeping my nose to the grindstone. But Teo's having none of it.

"Ash is an awesome, talented, brilliant young woman—and if you don't see that, I've got to think there's something wrong with you. I don't know you enough to call it jealousy—but from where I'm standing, it looks pretty obvious."

"Teo..." I say again, a note of warning in my voice. Meanwhile, Candace just splutters, temporarily incapacitated by Teo's aggressive defense of my character. And despite my reservations about him getting involved, the larger part of me feels like I'm on a cloud.

"Yeah, yeah," he says, looking back at me and taking my hand. "I'm done." He turns quickly to Jenny. "Nice meeting you. Have a good night." Then he leads me through the crowd and toward the door.

We make for the exit, stepping out onto the cooler, quieter calm of the sidewalk. Teo turns to me and grimaces like he just fucked up.

"Ash...I'm sorry," he says, as if the slight breeze is cooling off his temper. "I shouldn't have done that. I don't know what came over me... Hearing her talk like that to you just made me lose it...I'm sorry. I hope that isn't going to cause problems when you get back into work on—"

I don't let him finish, a sudden urge pushing me to him, pulling his face to mine, pressing my lips to his, shutting him up with a kiss.

When we pull apart he gazes at me, looking a little confused, a little surprised. Our faces tilt close, so I can gaze into his eyes, lose myself in them a little, remind myself of his essence. He half-smiles, reading my intentions immediately.

"Why don't we take this back to my place."

14

TEO

Ash can barely keep her hands off me in the back of the cab, grabbing at my crotch like she's relieving stress, body pressing me into the corner of the seat. Somehow, we manage to keep from giving the cab driver too much of a show, but by the time we reach my house I'm burning up as much as she is.

My place is big, but nothing too fancy. A three-story condo in Wilshire Montana that I picked because of its proximity to the beach and the good view of the ocean. I don't sleep much, and I've never liked sitting at home, so the place is pretty much just a glorified wardrobe and a safe place to keep my bikes.

I push the door open for Ash and follow her into the front room, watching her twirl a little as she takes in the empty walls, the unplugged TV in front of the pristine couch. Duke runs inside from his doggie door in the back and almost jumps at us. Ash coos at him and ruffles his fur before moving further inside as I load up his food bowl.

"Is this really your place?" she says, standing in the middle of all that empty space. "Or one of those abandoned apartments like the ones you used to take me to?"

I laugh it off.

"I'm not much of a homemaker."

"You don't say. I feel like I'm in uncharted territory."

"Beer?" I say, moving through to the kitchen.

"No," she says, smiling woozily. "I'm high enough."

I crack one open for myself and go back into the main room to find her gazing at the empty walls like there's a secret message in them.

"It's so weird," she says, her tone lowering, a little of the fun leaving her voice, "you're so creative...so imaginative. Your tattoos are so rich and vibrant and detailed...and then here's your home and it's so...vacant."

I suck down some beer and look at the wall as if I might see what she sees there.

"Tattoos are permanent. Homes aren't."

Ash turns to me, scrutinizing me as if reading between the lines of my lips.

"That's such a strange thing to say."

"It's true—in my experience," I say, punctuating it with another slug. "I've slept in too many beds to ever think of one as mine, heard too many stories with bad twists in them to think of anything as my own. Anything can go, in a second. Your house, your job, friends, money—hell, I even try not to get too attached to my bikes. All I know for sure is that, in the end, the only thing you can count on having is your body. And maybe—*maybe*—the shirt on your back."

Ash thinks about it for a second, then gives me a look like she's thinking dirty thoughts. She moves near and winds her hands around my waist, pulling herself up against me.

"Good thing you've got such a nice body then," she says, tongue flickering between her teeth. "Though I'm gonna make sure you lose the shirt real soon."

I half smile as I lean in to press my tongue against hers but she dances away from me, snatching the beer from my hand and swaying a little to the music in her head as she moves back. She takes a sip and I nod for her to follow me.

"At least let me show you the bedroom first."

I lead her upstairs to the large master bedroom, French doors along one wall leading out to a balcony.

"Wow," Ash says, sipping my beer as she casts her eyes over the messy bed, guitar leaning up against the wall, record player on the floor beside the armchair, LPs scattered around it. "It's like a fourteen-year-old boy's dream home."

She circles the room slowly, and I find myself hypnotized by her hips. She walks like most women dance, captivating and thrilling. Her body so incredible that even the slightest movement seems charged with erotic energy.

I move to the French doors and open them, stepping out onto the balcony, leaning on the rail. Ash follows and leans beside me, breathing deep the smell of the ocean, the cool air of night.

We stay like that for a while, lazily watching the reflection of the moonlight on the shifting waves. A police siren sounds in the distance, a few car horns and shouts, faint and fading, carried only by the emptiness of the night. Somehow it makes standing out here on the balcony feel even more intimate.

I grab the beer back from Ash, finish it and put it down as she smiles at me. She turns around to lean back against the railing, arching her body back as she looks up at the sky, then turns to me, eyes lost in thought.

"You know...I guess that cliché is true. About opposites attracting," she says, dreamily.

"Who says we're opposites?"

She thinks for a while, then says, "Well, it's like, you've spent most of your life going from place to place, trying to find a home, some stability. And here I am trying to break free of the path that would be so easy to follow. Trying to make my own way instead of the one my dad wanted to hand to me, trying to take some risks at work, instead of just doing what people ask and taking home a check for it."

I don't say anything for a while, the conversation a little too close to the bone, a little too close to that question I still can't answer for her. *Why did you leave?* I try to think of how to change the subject, try to think of something I can say or do that'll stop us from thinking

Love & Ink   121

about the past, about all those years without each other—but I can't. Everything, from the way the moon hangs above us, to the distant sound of the water pushing and receding, seems determined to push us into thinking about the past.

"Maybe..." Ash says, a quiver in her voice now, trailing off as if retreating into herself. "Maybe I should have gone with you, Teo. Back then...when you asked me to run off with you. Maybe I should have just—"

I don't let her finish—I can't. I pull her toward me and kiss her, soft and deep. I squeeze her body to mine like I'm afraid it might disappear into the night, kiss her to show how much I don't care about the past, to stop her from thinking about it, to show her that all I care about is right now, right here, together. A kiss to show I'm not lying. A kiss that says I love her.

Our bodies melt together, our lips locked tight. I hold her close enough to feel the tremulous shivers run down her back, the swelling breaths pushing her breasts against me, the weakness of her knees. Her back against the railing, our torsos leaning over the edge of the balcony, it almost feels like we're floating in the ether, out of time and out of space. Her jacket slips from her shoulders, my shirt comes off, then hers, then her bra—both of us acting in perfect unison to remove all the barriers between us, until it's skin against skin. Softening breasts against my hard chest, her delicate neck against my taut jaw, her pure, shivering, moonlit skin against my tattooed, rough, flexed muscles.

She bites my neck, pulling away to gasp slowly in my ear.

"Don't leave me again, Teo."

My tongue traces the outside of her ear and I whisper inside it, "I promise.

The whispers and inhalations of the ocean match our own, half-breaths and groans over the soft rustle of our jeans, the swish of cool night air on warming skin. She throws her head back, arching over the railing again, and I run my tongue up the softness of her neck, fingers dancing down her spine. I stop under her jaw, where the scent of her hair mixes with the smell of her skin, where I can feel the stuttered breaths rise and fall in her throat, moans vibrating against my lips and setting my own pulse racing. At the nape of her neck I suck softly, running my tongue gently across her skin, making her fingers turn to nails on my back, scratching and digging in as if clinging on to reality.

"*Teo...*" she whispers up at the moon, as I kiss and blow my way across her chest, tasting my way across that perfect terrain, leaving a hot trail that's now sensitive to the soft sea breezes that unfurl over us. My hand under her jeans, finger between her ass cheeks, teeth grazing across her breasts, as if leaving her no room to pull away now, fixing her in my reach, my desire. I curl my tongue around her hard nipples, blow softly and feel her convulse in my grip, breasts shaking under my mouth. First one, then the other, where I bite softly and tug with gentle teeth until she can take it no more. Her hands in my hair, pulling me away—then realizing it's even more unbearable without, and pulling me onto her chest again.

Her legs wind themselves around my waist, arms around my neck, clinging to me. I turn and carry her back inside, lay her down on the bed and pull away, pausing a moment to drink her in. Soft and pliable, she slips out of her jeans easily, as I undo mine and pull a condom from them, rolling it on as she watches, writhing a little in anticipation, her finger in her mouth.

"I could look at you forever..." I say, solemn as a prayer, as I kneel on the edge of the bed and pick up her foot. I run my tongue slowly down the side of her calf, enjoying the way she squirms and twists, kissing softly at the back of her knee. "Every inch of you as perfect as I remember..." I say, parting her knees as I move my tongue up the inside of her thigh, sucking softly, darting kisses, cool breaths mixing with the gusts of ocean air that make the drapes dance. "The smell of you..." I say, brushing my nose across her thigh. "The feel of you..." I say, reaching up across her taut stomach to take her breast in my palm. "The taste of you..." I say, holding back until she shivers in anticipation. A moment of glorious expectation, where the feel of my breath against her pussy makes her moan through closed lips, makes her squeeze her thighs around my head, fistfuls of pillow, urging me to her.

My tongue is light, a brush stroke working its way up her pussy, agonizingly slow. I watch her in the dimness of the night all the way, her face contorting, losing control, gaze tipping backward. When I'm almost there, at the clit, she looks down and meets my eyes, suddenly throwing her head back again in a spasm of joy, an outburst of heat that I feel rush over me. I take it into my mouth, soft and full, curl my tongue around it and flick it to the rhythm of her convulsing back, always a little slower than she wants, making her ache for me, making her beg on unresolved sighs and desperate moans.

"Don't stop," she pants.

I kiss and suck, tongue and lips and teeth working her clit until she's senseless, until her toes curl and her grip is almost tearing my pillows apart, almost pulling my hair out, until her body is surging with bliss, hammering intensely with every movement of my tongue, my lips, my teeth. Until I can ignore my own lust no longer, condensed and hard enough to explode, until waiting a second longer would send me permanently insane.

I kneel in front of her spread legs, finally feeling the blood thumping through my muscles like tribal drums, the jaw-clenching rush of testosterone, the cock-aching sight of her wet and writhing in front of me.

"God damn you're incredible," I growl, taking her leg on my shoulder, opening her up to push myself between those wet lips, to press myself into her warm tightness. I savor it, go as slowly as I can, to relish every squeeze of her pussy walls, the music of each drawn-out moan, the magnificent sight of her breasts shaking in front of me as I pound into her deeper and harder with every thrust. I savor it, until my body won't let me anymore, until every fiber of my being wants to be inside her, wants to be one with her, wants to fuck her so good it'll leave a mark on her essence, to push her so far into ecstasy she'll know she's forever mine.

"Yes...*yes*...fuck me," she whimpers over her own wails and groans.

Clinging to the bed as if afraid to let go, we find the rhythm of our bodies together, slowly building up the synchronicity of our desires. The slow and steady push inside of her gathering like waves before a storm, turning into a hard, forceful rumble, a quake that shakes her bones, that makes the sweat pour. I lean over her, her leg still on my shoulder, never deep enough, never hard enough. Fucking her until her entire body is almost vibrating, and the screams sound like a whole crowd is making them. Each thrust lighting the fire in our bodies, pushing us closer to burning up, to flaring one final time.

"Ash..."

Her name comes out like a low roar, as I look down at her one last time, the sight of her raptured face, of her shaking body, finally too much for me to handle. Explosions going off in my body, the hardness of my lust breaking down into the tender form of her juddering body.

I fall beside her on the bed, spent but for the waves of relief that tingle throughout my muscles, ultra-sensitive to the breeze coming past the curtains. I hear her laugh softly and turn my head to see her, squirming herself into the bed covers as she looks at me.

"How did I live without that for so long?" she says.

I roll toward her, brush a lock of hair from her forehead and kiss her.

"You didn't."

For hours I lay awake, looking down the length of our bodies out at the night. Ash sleeps against my chest, squirming occasionally in comfort, until she starts hunching a little and I draw a thin sheet over her. It's quiet enough that I can hear her breathe, and I stay still, in case a rustling movement might wake her up and spoil this perfection.

It feels pure. Good. An end—a happy ever after. A perfection that makes sense when I think about all the suffering and turns that brought us both here, to this night. The top of a mountain we both spent a lifetime climbing. For the first time in my life I don't want anything else—couldn't think of anything that would make me happier. Her slow breath running across my chest, her sleepy hums when I stroke her messy hair—this is it. This is everything.

But life doesn't stop when you get what you want—and getting it means that I've got something to lose now. My thoughts turn dark, even as the moon sinks and the pitch black of night turns almost imperceptibly blue, warning for dawn. I can sense it, like a sudden drop in temperature preceding a storm. Nothing this good comes easy, without a fight, without earning it.

I tell myself I'm being paranoid. That years of looking over my shoulder, of thinking about tomorrow, have made me unable to relax and enjoy this. I tell myself I just need to get used to this new normal, to let myself be 'open to everything that's going right' like Esther said a few weeks back, but it feels like a lie.

My cell rings, vibrating against the side table like a jackhammer in the silence. Ash groans and lifts her head.

"Shh," I say, stroking her head to coax her back to sleep as I reach over to grab my phone and answer it. She sinks back into my chest, shifts her naked body a little and is out almost before I get the phone to my ear.

"Teo?"

It's Ginger.

"Yeah," I mutter, quietly.

"Did I wake you up?"

"No," I say, putting a little urgency in my voice to show I don't want to talk. "What is it?"

"Damndest thing. See, I was crashing at the shop tonight, just me and that Rose there—you remember Rose? Big chick? One I had my eye on since the bike rally last month?"

"Get on with it," I say, looking down to check that Ash can't hear.

"Well," Ginger says, his voice slowing to an even more southern drawl. More serious, his tone a warning. "'Bout half an hour ago somebody starts slamming on the shutters like they think they're congas, so I get up—half-naked, so you—"

"Faster, Ginger."

This time Ginger takes a few seconds before he speaks, mentally editing to get to the point.

"Your dad was here, Teo. Looking for you. And it seemed like he wasn't about to give up until he finds you." He waits a few breaths for my response, gets none. "Teo?"

"I gotta go."

I hang up and look down at Ash, hoping that she can't feel the coursing heat of frustration that's growing inside of me. I sensed right.

And something tells me my dad is just the beginning of my problems.

15

ASH

Teo picks me up from work the next afternoon, waiting on his motorcycle that's so clean the chrome glistens and sparkles in the sun. It's been a couple of days since I first slept over—or rather, a couple of nights, because we've slept at each other's places each one. Every moment together feels like it's filled with something, a sense of meaning and purpose—even when we're just hanging out in the back of his tattoo shop eating takeout and listening to Ginger tell stories behind his worst tattoos. I spend quite a bit of my free time (limited though it is) at Mandala now, waiting for him to finish working, or just passing time until we head home.

Even when he's not there, spending time at Mandala makes me understand so much more about him. The way they never seem to judge anyone or anything, the way they can hear the wildest, craziest stories and not bat an eyelid. The general atmosphere of non-judgmental, easygoing acceptance of life's problems and strangeness, and the self-assurance that comes from finally overcoming so much of it. The way Kayla treats Teo like an older brother, and the way customers treat him like some kind of rock star. I feel like I get it, finally. I get why Teo finally stopped running, now that he has this.

Everyone around him so fiercely loyal, everything he does so passionately dedicated—as if anything less than this wouldn't be worth sticking around for.

In a funny kind of way, my own life seems to start making sense, too. Like Teo was some final piece of the puzzle, and I can look at the bigger picture now. I don't get off work and spend hours twisting myself in knots about it still. I don't have that insidious sense of resentment for myself when I realize I'm not quite where I want to be in my career. The bills and responsibilities, Candace holding me back and Carlos treating me like his PA, they don't take the spotlight in my thoughts anymore, they're no longer the center of my life. And when they do start to get under my skin, a little time with Teo is all I need to forget it all.

Even with everything going so well, though, I still feel the weight of some nagging thought, like a chore that needs to be done. That question I know Teo is afraid I'll ask again. It looms sometimes, in the silences, and even though I'm quick to change the mood, the subject—to let him know I'm in no rush to ask—there's a sense of inevitability about it. Despite what he said that night in the alley, about the truth hurting us and doing irreparable damage. Because if we're going to be together, he needs to tell me. No matter how bad it is, how hurt I might feel, I know we can get through it. He just needs to come clean.

Not now, though. For now this is too good to risk, too good to ruin.

He takes me down to Long Beach, and we barely say a word as we get off the bike, slipping off our shoes and taking each other's hand to draw a slow path of scuffed steps across the sand, lazily gazing out to take in the ocean and each other. There's always plenty to talk about, but we know we have plenty of time.

Eventually, Teo asks, "How's work? You still filming stuff on your own?"

"Yeah, I am," I sigh.

"Is there a problem?"

"No... Well...you remember it was about that yoga studio that all the celebrities love, right?"

"Of course. You told me all about it last week."

She bites her lip before continuing. "Well, I was supposed to get some interviews with some of the celebs—you know, really make the segment sensational. It's great as it is, but to *really* get the guys at *Hollywood Night* to sit up and take notice, I need some big names. The problem is, they've all fallen through. Dylan Marlowe and Gwen Rubens are filming up in Canada for the next few months. Michael Deore's publicist is advising him not to do it, and Kristy Monte keeps saying she's unsure until I get other confirmations. The only celebrity I have now is Sam Jennings."

"Who's Sam Jennings?"

I look up at him with dismay.

"Exactly."

"Damn," Teo says, putting an arm around me and pulling me to him sympathetically.

"Yeah," I say. "At the end of the day, it just means I have to wait a little longer for the schedules to sync up. And I know it'll come together. I just...want to get it going, you know?"

"Yeah. But I'm sure it'll pay off in the end. Maybe you can film some of your other ideas in the meantime."

"I'm going to," I say, nodding with determination. "For sure."

We walk on a little further, between the shrieking kids playing in the surf and the lazy chatter from the sunbathers. Feet covered in sand now, Teo takes my hand and leads me to where the waves push and pull, so our toes sink into the wet sand, water massaging our calves beneath our rolled-up jeans.

"Oh, hey," I say, suddenly remembering. "Are you free this Saturday?"

Teo squints at the sun as he thinks for a moment.

"Yeah. I think I am. Gotta put in a few hours at the shop, but I'll be done by four."

"You like barbecue, right?"

Teo spins me around to face him, his hands pushing back hair from the side of my face.

"The word alone makes me wanna bite something," he says, playfully swooping on my neck as I try to fend him off.

"Good," I say, wrapping my arms around his waist and looking up at him. "My sister is having a get-together at her place this weekend and I thought we could go. It'll be fun."

Teo's playfulness disappears almost instantly, turning into a wincing withdrawal as he pulls away from me.

"Aah...I'm not so sure about that," he says, reluctantly.

"What? It's just a barbecue, Teo."

"I know...but..."

"Come *on*! It's just my sister—well, and some of my family."

He grimaces. "Your dad?"

I shake my head and try to smile reassuringly. I understand Teo's reservations, but this is really important to me. "No, he's in NYC this month, helping some senator with a bill or something."

"I never really knew your sister," he muses.

"Right, so there's no weird history between you. Nothing to be afraid of. It'd be a good first step for you...for us."

"Eh..."

"She's celebrating the third-year anniversary of being elected mayor. It'll be fun. Food, booze," I stroke his arm and smile mischievously, "a big house with lots of empty rooms if we wanna get away for a bit..."

Teo's smile looks like it's pasted on, and he rubs the back of his neck like he's trying to remove a shackle from it.

"Politicians and all that...I wouldn't even know what to talk about. It just doesn't really sound like my kind of scene, Ash. I'd only draw attention to myself—and away from you having a good time with your family."

I glare at him for a few seconds, then exhale.

"You think Mandala was my kind of scene?" I say, sounding more annoyed than I want to. "Tattoo artists and rock stars? Runaways and transplants? Where all the stories involve brushes with the law and living broke? Christ, I don't even *have* a tattoo myself! You think I didn't feel like an outsider when I first met your friends?"

Love & Ink   131

"That's different."

"How? Because they were *your* friends?"

"Because they're open-minded, they're cool with everyone," Teo says, then frowns a little. "I thought you liked hanging out there, with them?"

"I *do*—that's the point. I gave your 'world' a chance, and I liked it. It made me feel closer to you. Why can't you do the same for me?"

His jaw tightens. "I came to your work drinks, didn't I?"

"For all of about two minutes. During which you got in a fight with my boss and probably made my relationship with her go from bad to worse."

"It's not my fault your boss pounced on me like a cougar in heat."

Teo shakes his head, his hands clenching a little with the anxiety of what I'm asking him. I look away, the happy kids playing in the waves now seeming a little farther away, the waves brushing against our ankles now a little irritating.

"Is this what it's always going to be like, Teo? You want me to keep you a secret? Hide you away from my family just like we used to?"

"Of course not."

"Then what is it?"

Teo heaves a big breath that puffs his chest out, then shrugs a little.

"I just figured we'd spend a little more time like this, enjoying each other, before we start doing the whole 'family' thing. This is good, right now—why risk putting all this weight on it?"

I laugh sadly, shaking my head as I turn away, unable to look at him as he says these things.

"My mistake," I say to the ocean. "Maybe I got a little ahead of myself—maybe I'm a little more into this than you are. I thought we were a couple. Adults in an *actual* relationship."

"Ash," Teo says, stepping in front of me and putting his hands on my arms. "How can you even say that? We're *in* this. Together."

"How can we be when all it takes is a barbecue at my sister's for you to start pulling back? Is that how fragile all of this really is?"

"Come on, Ash. This is ridiculous. It's no big deal. I just don't wanna go to some dumb barbecue."

My eyes narrow in anger, and I see in Teo's shifting gaze that he regrets saying that.

"Dumb?"

"Sorry, I didn't mean that."

"Dumb," I say, nodding.

"I shouldn't have said it. You've backed me into a corner—"

"No. It's good to know where you're at."

"Ash..."

"You know what this feels like, Teo?" I say, slowing down to make sure he hears me. "It feels like you making sure you don't get in too deep. Like you're keeping the exit doors open. You know, ever since that first night I spent at your place, I thought there was something...I don't know, something you were holding back."

"That's nothing to do with you. That's just...just another problem on my mind."

I nod.

"Another problem you won't tell me about. Another problem that you want to keep all boxed up in your separate little world."

"Ash," Teo says, moving closer now with determination, putting his hands on the sides of my face so he can look me straight in the eyes, forcing me to see the honesty in his own, "this is crazy. I'll come. I didn't know it meant this much to you, that's all. I'll come, I'll wear a nice shirt, I'll drink my beer out of a glass and eat my burger with a fork for you. Ok?"

I look at him and smile politely, but I wonder whether he can really brush it off so easily. It was always so simple for me and Teo to just be together, hanging out, doing things together, being intimate... but through all those years of high school I would sometimes wonder how it would be when we faced the world, actually existing in public as a couple. I'd struggle to imagine introducing Teo to my friends, my family, and having him fit in well. Too much of a loner, too comfortable playing by his own rules.

And what if he can't?

"You know...maybe you shouldn't..." I say, then stop myself. "Never mind."

"What?"

"Nothing," I say, nodding slowly. "I'm sure it'll be great."

But as he takes me in his arms again, I can't help praying I'm not horribly wrong.

16

TEO

We take Ash's car to her sister's—partly because I don't want to ride my bike there and partly because Ash couldn't wear the tight, yellow dress that drives me wild. So wild that I fuck her in it twice before we finally get going—the first time 'cause she looks so good, the second because I still don't feel great about going.

I feel like I'm being driven to jail as the imposing white structure looms up at the end of the long road.

"There it is," Ash says.

"I thought you said it was a house?"

"It is."

"That's not a house. That's a mansion."

Ash laughs, then looks from the road to me.

"Relax," she says, reaching over to squeeze my thigh. "It's gonna be fun. Just think about barbecue. We don't have to stay for the whole thing."

I shrug and look back at the large entrance, intricate wrought iron gates wide open. We pass through and Ash guides the car down a driveway long and wide enough to land a small passenger jet. She stops in front and before I can open my door, the dark-suited valet has it open for me.

Love & Ink

"Good day, sir," he says as I get out, feeling awkward for not opening my own door, and for being called 'sir' for the first time in my life.

"Cheers, buddy," I say, feeling suddenly like I'm in a movie, surrounded by people acting parts, reading from scripts.

I'm still taking in the giant mansion, as white as bedsheets, when the car spins away and Ash comes up behind me to lock her arm in mine.

"Impressive, huh?" she says.

"Yeah," I mutter. "Does anyone actually live here?"

Ash laughs and pats my chest.

"Only my sister, her husband, their three kids, and the help."

"The help?" I say, turning a shocked face to her.

"Yeah. The nanny, the housekeeper. A chef—though he doesn't actually live there."

I stare at her, waiting for her nonchalant face to break into a smile and for her to tell me it's a joke, that she's just playing on my preconceptions. Except she doesn't, and I feel some part of me sink even lower.

A guy in a white suit gestures for us to walk around the building toward the back, and I struggle to find some sense of reality in the clusters of well-dressed people around us. This is nothing at all like the laid-back, casual backyard barbecues I'm used to.

The men are all stiff and upright—even the portly ones. There's not a t-shirt in sight, and I'm glad I listened to Ash when she suggested I wear a button down shirt. They carry themselves with confidence, the arrogance of money and power. Not so much swagger, but a stiff, raised head as if looking down their noses at everything in front of them. Listening to each other's stories with a deadness behind the eyes, a distant judgment of everything around them. The weirdest thing is how they all look the same, no matter how old or young, like the same man at different stages of his life.

The women are the only color around, and as if compensating for the blandness of the men, they seem to make themselves look larger than life. Ruffles on skirts, wide-brimmed hats, unnecessarily flashy jewelry. Dressed in lurid pinks and greens, voices articulate and assured enough to ring like crystal, flinty, forced laughs that pierce the atmosphere like sirens. Faces made up to look constantly emotive, constantly engaged, even though their eyes scrutinize everything as if it's happening a million miles away.

"Oh my God. There's like a million people here," Ash gasps beside me. I just nod.

I overhear conversations filled with small talk, short and brief, as if people are exchanging headlines, name dropping people I've never heard of, words that mean things I don't know, a secret code as tight and exclusive as street slang.

Unconsciously, I start to roll down my shirt-sleeves.

"What are you doing?" Ash asks, noticing.

I look down at my arm as if surprised myself.

"I'm the only guy here with tattoos..." I say.

"So? Your arms are great. You don't have to hide."

I shrug half-heartedly and continue to pull the sleeves down.

"I know...I just don't want it to be the first thing people talk to me about," I say, as if I'm even considering entering into a conversation with any of these people.

Finally, we get around the house, stepping onto a gigantic lawn that feels like it's the size of a football field, grass as perfectly clean and deep as a fine rug. A gigantic stone fountain stands in the middle, a string quartet playing in front of it. There must be a hundred people here, mingling in tight groups, between a couple of long tables filled with food. Waiters in white gliding between them effortlessly, offering giant silver trays to guests.

One approaches us with a tray stacked with wine glasses, and we both take one. Ash smiles at me questioningly.

"Wine?"

"I'll take whatever they're handing out right now," I say, downing the glass like it's a shot of cheap vodka.

We move into the crowd, and I start thinking about switching to Plan B. Plan A was to find another schmuck who would rather be anywhere but here, another poor guy dragged here by a girlfriend or

Love & Ink

wife, and then use each other to fend off conversation with anyone else while we get hammered enough to forget the whole thing. But the more I look around me, the more I realize that everyone except me *wants* to be here. Plan B is to find the grill and be one of the 'grill guys,' watching whoever's turn it is to flip the burgers and sausages. Grill guys don't need to talk much. Entranced by the meat, hooked by the smell, there's little room for thinking of anything else. It won't last, but if I can get to the grill, it'll be like touching base for now.

Except I don't see it. All I see are long tables with pastries as detailed and delicate as ornaments, tiny cuts of cheese and meat, sushi and elaborately sculpted vegetables.

"Hey," I say, getting Ash's attention from scanning the crowd, "I thought you said this was a barbecue? Where's the grill?"

"It's here," Ash says, looking around, then pointing at a plume of smoke in the distance. "Over there. Grace likes to put the grill far from the guests—you know, so they don't end up smelling like smoke."

I look over at the two guys in white chef hats working the grill, so far away it'd take a minute to walk there.

Shit. I didn't come up with a Plan C.

Suddenly, there's a scream so shrill it makes me wince, and a stunning woman in a white pantsuit comes barreling toward us like a linebacker for a tackle.

"Ash!" she shouts, arms wide.

"Grace!" Ash screams in reply, as they smash into each other happily, Grace's wide-brimmed hat flopping about.

Her outfit has a silvery, glittering pattern all across it—to me it looks like the kind of thing a middle-eastern dictator would use for curtains, but then again, this whole place feels like another planet to me.

"I'm so glad you came!" Grace says.

They pull apart, and suddenly Ash's older sister turns her beaming, political smile to me, offering her hand.

"And you must be..."

Her eyes go straight to my neck, where my fire tattoo is.

"Teo," I say.

"Teo," she repeats, looking thoughtful. "Such an odd name...but it sounds sort of familiar."

Ash glances from me to her, then quickly says, "We went to school together."

"Oh, I see," Grace says. "Well, I'm eight years older than my sister, so forgive me if I don't exactly remember you."

"It's fine," I say, trying my own version of a political smile.

"So what do you do?" Grace asks.

I open my mouth, but stop myself before saying 'tattoo artist,' seeing a whole load of awkwardness, of stupid questions, of uncomfortable smiles ahead that way.

"I own a business," I say, then quickly add, in my best impression of the other clowns here, "Congratulations on three years. Very impressive."

"Well thank you," Grace says, satisfied enough to turn back to Ash. "How long have you two been..."

"A few weeks," Ash says, after glancing at me.

"Well, it's good to see you out with somebody for once," Grace says. "Nice to meet you, Teo."

"And you."

"I've got some great news, Ash," she goes on, beaming.

"Yeah?"

"Daddy's here!"

The words drop like an anvil, making me freeze.

"Really?" Ash says, her smile faltering. "That's...a surprise."

Grace nods.

"Apparently the bill got pushed back, so he took an early flight home this morning. Come on," Grace says, stepping away already. "You can introduce your new 'Teo.'"

Ash looks at me, half a step away already.

"Um," I say, pointing in the other direction toward the buffet table, "I'd like to get something to eat first, before we start mingling and...you know. I didn't eat all morning so..."

"Oh," Grace says, looking both disappointed and confused. "Sure.

Well, we're over here, by the fountain. Just come over when you're ready."

I nod. "We will."

I move toward the buffet, mind racing, chastising myself for the stupidity of even coming here in the first place.

"Teo...*Teo*," Ash hisses beside me, as she struggles to catch up. "Is something wrong?"

I stop to grab another wine glass from a passing waiter and look at her.

"It's nothing. I'm fine," I say, wishing I could sound a little more convincing than I do. "I just want to ease in, you know? A little more slowly."

Ash gazes up at me, searching my face for clues.

"You could have just said hello to my dad first. Gotten it out of the way? He doesn't bite. And I'll be right by your side. I know we didn't plan it this way, but..."

I sigh a little and try to keep myself from downing the wine in one gulp again.

"Look, why don't you go ahead. I'll just hang back for a few," I say. "Take all of this in a little. I'll find you, don't worry."

"*Teo*...I'm not going to go off on my own. We're here together. I'm not going to just abandon you."

Another waiter passes, this one with glasses of gin, and I down the wine to quickly grab one.

"Look," she says, "I know this is a little more...*fancy* than you expected, probably."

"Fancy? I feel like I just stumbled into a period drama."

She looks at me with bemused, almost pleading eyes, and I realize I'm stuck. "An hour, maybe two max, is that too much to ask?"

I nod.

"I can manage that. It's just, I thought it would be your sister, her family...you know, informal. Now I'm suddenly meeting your dad? I didn't think I was biting off this much."

She laughs and hooks an arm in mine.

"My dad'll love you," she says. "He's been nagging me to settle down for years."

"What if he recognizes me?"

Now she turns that smile into a confused frown.

"Recognize you? Why would he recognize you?"

"Well, we did grow up in the same town, remember?" I say, covering my concern with sarcasm, but it lands flat. She only twists that perplexed frown a little harder. I look at her and realize the full extent of her obliviousness, the full extent of the truths I didn't tell, building into a wall that's bearing down on me now.

"My dad barely had time to pay attention to his own kids—let alone every random teenager in town," she says, as if I'm being silly.

To Ash, her father was just a strict, overprotective patriarch who wouldn't like a teenage dropout dating her daughter. And now that that's all in the past, and we're both grown up, she can't see the problem anymore. She can't see how much more there was to it. Why would she? I never told her.

She breaks that frown into another relaxed smile, stroking my arm like I'm a horse she's trying to stop from bolting.

"We're not teenagers anymore, Teo, and you're not a dropout," she says, mirroring my thoughts back to me. "There's no need to hide anymore. Trust me, my dad's not as overbearing as he used to be. He knows I date—and you're far from the worst guy he's met, anyway. You're a business owner, he'll love that."

"I don't know..."

"Just come and say hi. Give him five minutes. And once you do, we can grab something to eat and leave—I'll say I have a migraine or something."

"Ok," I say.

"Ok?" Ash asks, to be sure.

"Ok," I say, easing up a little. "Let's go."

She takes my arm and leads me to the fountain, as if instinctively knowing where her father will be. When we get there the group reshuffles automatically, so it's just me, Ash, Grace, a guy who looks like every other mid-forties male here, and her father standing with

Love & Ink

one another. He eyes me with a relaxed smile, but his eyes can't hide their shock and distaste.

Ash's father's a big guy, a little bigger than me, even, though he's less muscle and more just big. Dyed black hair swept back, a youthful face betrayed by a droopy jowl that makes him look permanently angry. He looks exactly as I remember—like he's always posing for some expensive portrait he's planning to hang above the fireplace.

"Hey again," Ash says to Grace, laughing gently and then looking at her dad. "This is Grace—whom you already met—Jared, Grace's husband, and...this is Edward, my dad. Guys, this is—"

"Matteo," Ash's dad says, offering a hand.

"Mr. Carter," I say as I take it, shaking while Ash and Grace look confusedly at each other. He doesn't tell me to call him Edward, not that I would anyway.

"You know him?" Grace asks her father, while I exchange another little shake and a nod with Jared.

"Sure," Mr. Carter says. "You went to school with my daughter, didn't you?"

It sounds like an accusation.

"Yes I did," I say, firmly.

"My daughter's told me nothing about you. How long have you two been together?" he says, darting a suspicious glance at Ash, and I can almost hear him leaving out the word 'again.'

"A few weeks," an unperturbed Ash replies, happily clutching my arm and pressing herself against my side. "We bumped into each other again—really funny coincidence."

"I'll bet it was," her father says, still staring daggers at me.

There's a soft silence for a moment, probably caused by the fact that Ash's father and I are staring at each other like cowboys at the OK Corral, suddenly aware of the guns at their sides.

"So..." Grace interjects, "Teo, you mentioned that you owned a—"

"Do you like whiskey?" her father interrupts Grace to ask me, as if not even hearing his daughter.

I shrug nonchalantly.

"Absolutely."

"Good," he says, stepping forward. "I brought a single malt I wanted to share. Why don't you join me in the study."

It's a command, not an invitation, and I nod. He steps away, and I move to follow him. Jared makes a move too but is stopped by Ash's dad gripping his shoulder.

"Not you, Jared. Just me and the new boy—talk man to man," he says, slapping me a bit too hard on the back before moving away to stride toward the house.

I swap a quick glance with Ash, who's making an apologetic face, and then take a deep breath and follow. I'm never one to back down from a challenge, and I might as well get this over with as long as I'm here anyway.

We step inside the house, into an echoing, marble-floored hallway too big for anything but a rock concert, even the groups of guests and waiters moving around not enough to make it feel small. Ash's father leads me off to a closed door and I step through, slightly surprised at how the old man can treat Grace and Jared's home like his own—then realizing that he probably bought it for them.

"Shut the door," he says, moving to an old mahogany cabinet between the large windows with drawn curtains.

I oblige, reminded once again that I'm in completely foreign territory. The room is cast in dark, aged wood. Bookshelves line the walls all the way up to high ceilings, high enough to require a ladder. Bear rug, oversized desk, the smell of a million forgotten cigars, a landscape painting that makes nature look as tamed and ordered as the uniform of the soldiers in it. I'm a long way from Ginger slapping his belly and belching Lynyrd Skynyrd songs.

"I thought you left," he says, putting the cap back on the bottle.

"I did. Sir."

He turns in my direction and eyes me for an uncomfortably long beat. "And yet here you are."

I don't break eye contact. "Here I am."

He slowly comes close, as if he thinks I'm about to run, and then hands me a whiskey glass, though I can tell it pains him to make even this small friendly gesture toward me.

I take a slow sip of the drink.

"What do you think?" he says.

"A little too smooth for me."

He laughs, a low, mean cackle.

"That's four hundred dollar scotch."

"You must know it's not that good either, if you have to tell me the price."

His smile turns meaner, dismissive, and he turns away to move behind the large desk. He flips a box open and pulls out a cigar, offering me one. I shake my head and he lights it as he stands behind the desk, me standing in the middle of the room like I was brought here to be judged.

He waves the flame away from the match and looks at me like I'm a stain, cruel eyes burrowing their way into me.

"So is this your idea of revenge?" he says. "Did you plan this day for all those years? That you'd come into one of my family's houses on a day of joy, and stink the place up like some unflushable piece of shit?"

I sip a little more of the whiskey, if only to ease the tension caused by being in his presence without the option of putting my hands around his neck.

"I'm not a kid anymore," I say, after enough time has passed to let his anger fester. "You can't scare me with the 'power broker' routine. You did it once, and it was the biggest mistake I ever made."

"Mistake?" he says, poking his head forward, then turning down to gaze at the end of his cigar. "You know, I wonder if it was a mistake myself, sometimes. Then again, you'd probably have knocked her up eventually—and then we'd *really* have a problem."

I down the rest of the whiskey and slam the empty glass hard on the desk.

"Thanks for the drink," I say. "I should really get going, though—I hate to keep Ash waiting."

I walk back to the door but stop halfway when he says, "I kept tabs on you, you know." My blood runs cold. I turn back around. "After you left. Wanted to make sure you wouldn't come back like this." He turns his eyes up at the ceiling. "Last I heard you were involved in some shady business down in Florida. Had to leave the country. Funny—how you always end up having to leave things behind, how you always run away from your problems, isn't it?"

"Don't get your hopes up," I say. "This time I'm staying. This time I'm not letting Ash go."

That laugh again, harder, louder, uglier.

"Oh I don't doubt it! You must feel like you've hit the jackpot with her, am I right? Certainly a cut above the usual low-life trash that you must feel comfortable among, yes?" He wags his finger at me as he steps around the desk. "The question you need to ask yourself, Teo, is how long until Ash gets bored of you? How long until she finds out who you really are?"

"Ash knows all about my past," I shoot back through gritted teeth.

He shrugs, gestures out at the curtained windows. "You've seen all this, haven't you? There isn't a person on these grounds who isn't incredibly successful at what they do. Politics, entertainment, finance —it's all there, out there on the lawn. People who've gone to the finest institutions, who make the decisions that keep the world ticking over. *Fine* people.

"And then there's you," he says, looking me up and down as he shakes his head, "with your neck tattoos and your caveman build. Your lack of basic politeness and appreciation for anything fine. A dropout. Trailer trash. Look, I don't blame you, Teo. You were fucked from the start—growing up with that criminal of a father, what else could you be? But you've got to at least know your place—and it isn't here. It isn't with Ash. You can't do anything but bring her down."

Now I'm the one laughing at how ridiculous this all is.

"You don't even know your own daughter," I say, starting to look at him with a strange sense of pity at his cluelessness.

"Oh yes I do," he says, with that smug self-assuredness that makes me want to slap him humble. "I know exactly what she's doing with you. See, you're a cliché, Teo. A 'rough and ready bad boy.' Nothing but a little adventure for her, a rebellious 'walk on the wild side.' A little vacation from the pressures of the responsibility and demands of the kind of life she's meant to lead. A taboo, a way to get back at me. Let me guess, you still ride that motorcycle, right? See, that's what my mistake was, Teo. I should have let her get you out of her system. It would have saved all of us a lot of trouble.

"Ask yourself, Teo, why would she want to be with you when there are men right here with fantastic careers, who know how to present themselves, who know how to treat a girl from a good background? Then ask yourself, how long until she gets bored, until she wants more than you're capable of giving her? You're just a novelty."

I let the silence linger, wondering if it's even worth the reply. Then, half knowing it's a lost cause, I say, "You should really give your daughter a little more credit. Maybe try actually listening to her once in a while. Maybe you'd understand why she rejected all of your 'fine' suggestions up until this point and decided to go her own way."

That riles him up, and this time he starts poking his cigar at me as he speaks.

"You think Ash would be fucking around on some third-rate gossip show if she didn't have me? If she wasn't sure that when it all goes to shit and she's had her fun, daddy will swoop in to pick up the pieces? What can *you* give my daughter? Apart from a sense of danger and excitement?"

Through gritted teeth I say, "I will give Ash whatever she wants."

"Oh, please! Tell me, what do you do now? Are you still driving trucks? Is that what brought you back to L.A., wheedling your way back into Ash's life?"

"I own my own tattoo shop," I say, angry at myself for even feeling that I need to justify myself.

He looks at me for a second, then breaks into the loudest, nastiest laugh yet. Stopping to say, "Tattoo shop?" and laugh even harder at the words. I say nothing, just stare him down.

"God! Are you serious? A tattoo shop? Well, I suppose there are plenty of morons like you, so there must be *some* money in it."

"I make good money doing something I love. So does Ash. If you weren't such a self-important, control freak excuse for a father you might understand."

He straightens up a little, smirk gone and replaced by a sneer.

"I want to know something: Where do you see yourself in ten years, huh?" He lets the question hang there just long enough to confirm that I don't have a ready answer. "You don't know, do you? You don't think that far ahead at all—you never have, and never will. As far as you're concerned, you could be down and out in Alabama again, or hiding in the mountains of Colombia, right? Do you have plans to expand your business? Of course not.

"I'll bet you hire people you regard as your 'friends,' and it's all chummy-chummy. And I'd also wager that your little enterprise will be dead and gone in five years." He leans close so that I can smell the evil on his breath. "What happens when your business fails, Teo? What if...let's say...something should happen to it? A little fire, perhaps? A lost business license, a small mix-up with the tax board? Think you could overcome that? Or would you be back on an illegal construction crew? And who's gonna take care of Ash if I cut her off?"

The restraint I've been maintaining for this long snaps hard and fast. I step forward, close enough to see every wrinkle in his face, close enough for him to see the anger in my eyes.

"Fuck you," I snarl. "And don't you ever threaten Ash or my business again."

He squirms a little, backing up against the bookcase, but beneath the bravado of his hard, disgusted face I can sense his fear.

"You know I'm right, Teo," he says, a little quiver in his voice, but his arrogance too pervasive to stop himself. "That's why you're angry. You got lucky, with her, with whatever this business is. But the truth is, when all's said and done, you can't give Ash *anything*. You're a parasite, a loser destined for a correctional facility—just like your father. You stay with her, she'll end up with nothing. From me or from you, you lowlife piece of—"

I grab his shirt and pull my fist back, breath steaming from my nostrils, body poised and ready to sink my anger into his skull.

"That's it!" he says, his voice desperate once again, grasping at words as if to save himself. His eyes focus on my fist with heavy panic.

"Do it. Hit me! Show everyone who you really are. Show Ash the *truth*."

My heart pounds, every fiber of my being arguing against rationality, urging me to hit him. I close my eyes, and only then can I pull back, let him go and turn around to walk away.

That's when I see Ash standing there. Right in the doorway. Her hands over her mouth, her eyes large, deep brown pools of shock.

"Ash," I say, suddenly feeling like I'm running out of air. How much of that did she hear?

I step toward her and she backs away as if frightened. Hands going in front of her, showing me her palms. My heart breaks as with every step I take, Ash flinches back.

"Don't come near me!" she says, looking at me like I'm some kind of monster.

"Ash! Listen! If you'd heard what he said just a minute ago you'd understand! He was threatening my business! Threatening us!"

"Stay away from me, please," Ash says, through hitched breath, tears welling up in her eyes.

"Listen to her, Teo," her father says. I try to stop myself from gritting my teeth and flashing hatred at his voice, but my emotions are too close to the skin now.

"He's the reason we're not together, Ash! It's because of him! The thing that—"

"Just go!" Ash screams suddenly, loud enough to be heard throughout the house, to bring others peeking in beyond the open door.

The hurt and distress in her voice is too unbearable. It hits me too deep to even try and explain. I don't ever want to be the man who makes her sound like that—and if that means leaving her like she's asking me to, I'll do it. It wouldn't be the first time.

"I'm going," I say, stepping toward the door.

I step outside and push through the crowd that's gathered, glancing back despite myself one more time. Ash is crying into her father's chest, his arm wrapped protectively around her. His eyes look straight at me, his gaze hard and victorious. Again.

17

ASH

Work is the last place I need to be right now, but it's where I am. When I turned up this morning I kinda hoped that the dull routine and formulaic segments would numb the turmoil and shock inside, but they don't. My nerves are brittle, my patience shorter than a grenade pin, and I keep having to take bathroom breaks where I breathe deep in order to get through the next hour-long chunk of time. I end up working through lunch, gritting my teeth through Carlos' request for his 'lucky' red shirt, and order a double-helping of tacos to the office.

Jenny steps inside as I'm wiping up my crumbs, and it's the first bright spot in my day. So much so that I want to clutch at her like a life raft. I smile, but when I see her miserable expression my heart sinks again.

"Just in time," I say, pushing the leftover tacos across my desk. "You hungry? They're still hot."

Jenny steps to the desk, all slumped shoulders and downturned lips, then drops herself in the chair as if her strings have been cut.

"I didn't pass the audition."

"Oh, Jenny," I say, getting up to move around and hug her in the chair.

"They said I gave off too much of an 'intellectual' vibe. Said they wanted something a little more fun and smiley. Probably just wanted a girl who showed more skin."

"Intellectual is great," I say meekly, grasping.

Jenny rolls her eyes at me and then spots the chips and guac, digging in and holding the chip in front of her mouth.

"They're casting agents—they're good at letting you down gently," she says, then crunches mercilessly on the guacamole-laden tortilla chip.

"It's just one audition," I say. "It always takes a little time."

"No," Jenny says, pausing to swallow. "They're right. Look at me. Unless there's a shortage of 'hipster schoolteacher' roles, I'm not getting anything anytime soon. That's what spending half your life in the writers' room gets you."

"Bullshit," I say adamantly, lowering my face to catch her eye. "You look like—and *are*—a creative, witty, charismatic woman. And there aren't so many casting agents you can see before you find one with half a brain to appreciate what you've got."

Jenny chomps on another handful of chips and then allows herself the tiniest of smiles.

"Thanks," she says. "You mind recording that so I can play it back to myself later?"

I shove her playfully and go back around to my side of the desk.

"How are things with you?" Jenny asks, the taco box in her lap now. "I saw you stomping around in the studio earlier looking like you were going to murder someone. Carlos winding you up again?"

I nod slowly, then sigh.

"Part Carlos, part finding out my boyfriend is a psycho."

Jenny stops mid-bite, frozen with the steak taco halfway in her mouth to glare at me over it. I decide to tell her the details rather than have her mess up that knitted shawl.

"I took him to a barbecue at my sister's place. Kind of fancy, and he didn't want to go. My dad was there, and he wanted to talk to Teo, so they went back into the study—you know, a little 'boys' time.' After a while I went to go get him, but when I get there...God, Jenny. Teo was standing there in my father's face, grabbing his shirt, fist pulled back like he's about to punch him. I've never seen him like that before."

Jenny struggles to drop her jaw and not spill food at the same time. She hurriedly swallows and wipes her mouth before setting the taco down—more interested in asking questions than a second bite now.

"What the hell?"

"Yep."

"What happened? Why would he do that?"

I shake my head. "I don't know. My dad said he was asking Teo some questions about his business, and Teo flipped the fuck out."

Jenny exhales and scrunches her face incredulously.

"You believe him? I mean, you think he told you the whole story?"

"My *dad?*" I say, looking at Jenny with shock for asking. "Of course I believe him. I know what I saw. And yeah, I mean, he can be a little pushy sometimes, and maybe he said something shitty, but even so—who the hell does that? Assault the parent of a girl you're dating as soon as you meet them? It's just insane. I can't even process it. There's no excuse."

Jenny gives me a pained expression, and I know she can barely think of what to say.

"I'm sorry, Ash."

"Yeah," I sigh. "Me too."

"I guess it's over then."

I nod.

"Absolutely. Though I wouldn't be surprised if Teo doesn't think so."

When I finish work, Teo proves me right. He's waiting for me outside in the parking lot. I step through the exit, see him, and immediately harden my expression, redirect myself toward my car and around him.

"Ash! Wait, please," he says, jogging up beside me, but smartly keeping a little distance between us.

"If I wanted to talk to you I would have answered one of the many phone calls, or responded to one of the many, many texts." I glance at him across my shoulder, if only to emphasize my point with the firmness of my eyes. "I don't want to talk."

"I understand," he says, backing up to stay a little in front of me, in my field of vision, "but if you'd just let me explain—"

"There's nothing to explain," I say, stopping suddenly to direct the full force of my frustration at him. "Raising a fist to my father? What was that? Some kind of 'macho alpha male' crap? I don't even want to hear it. Some things are beyond excuses, Teo. I'm done."

I start walking again, and he continues trying to stay in my field of view.

"Your father isn't everything he seems, Ash. If we could just sit down somewhere, if you could give me five minutes—"

I stop again to glare at him.

"Are you seriously trying to blame this on my father?"

"He threatened my business! And us. He threatened to cut you off if—"

"My father isn't perfect," I interrupt. "Yes, he's overprotective. Yes he can be a little too controlling at times. And yes he's a little hard on my boyfriends. But none of those things—I repeat, *none*—justify being physically assaulted like that in his own home!"

I continue walking, even faster this time. I click my car lock paces away.

"I know it was stupid of me, and I'm sorry, Ash," Teo pleads. "I lost my shit, let my temper get the best of me, and I shouldn't have. But he was trying to come between us, he always was—"

"Bullshit," I say, as I yank my door open. "Actions speak louder than words, Teo. And the truth is that every time I think I actually know you, every time I think we have something steady together, you go ahead and do the one thing I thought you never could. Disappearing overnight without a word, refusing to show up for me the way I show up for you, and then threatening my family—"

"I love you, Ash," he interrupts.

For a moment I just stare at him, and then I shake my head. "I know you do. But this isn't gonna work, Teo. Nothing you can do, or say, will fix this."

I slide into the driver's seat and close the door just as he calls my name one more time, a desperate plea drowned out by the slam.

I don't look back as I drive away. I don't need to. I've got enough practice seeing him for what I think is the last time.

18

TEO

The ride home might be the loneliest I've felt in a life of almost complete loneliness. Ash haunts me all the way, my mind blank, my body feeling twisted and sick. I feel her hands on my chest, her face against my back, as if my body is yearning for it now that I know I'll never feel it again.

I take a long route home, so I can ride fast enough to feel like I'm leaving it all behind, so I don't have to go back to the condo that'll just remind me of her. A place I'll forever think of as missing her. An empty, barely-furnished home that needed someone like her, that someone like Ash could've turned into a place that meant something. A place that'll never be a home now.

Along the freeways and the winding canyon roads I see her still, suspended before me. That confused, upset face. Those beautiful features I saw a future in, the face that gave meaning to everything, set a purpose in my chest and a fire in my blood. My last memory of it will be warped, tainted, by how disappointed and angrily it looked at me. I see my future now. A million nights dreaming of her like that, a thousand evenings of wondering how I could have done better, regretting what she saw in that one awful moment.

It hurt to leave things between us like that, to talk to her like that.

Her mind so made up I couldn't explain anything. I've spent a lifetime running from explanations, and now that I finally realize that only the *truth* could fix something—my chance is gone.

Maybe it's for the best. A small part of me still thinks her father was right. Sure, I have a business and a house now—but what if something happened? What if he actually took it all away from me, or if bad luck or fate destroyed everything I've built? Then what? Would I go back to doing day labor? Would I turn into dead weight that Ash had to struggle even harder at her job to support? Maybe my 'bad genes' would pull me back to the other side of the law, for the quick and easy money. That same instinct that raised a fist when I should have stayed calm and steady. Maybe I'd have to start skipping state lines again, sniffing out work, some cash, the next oasis of brief security, like some stray dog—only this time, Ash would be dragged down right alongside me. Maybe that big, complicated past would start emerging from the swamp to pull me back under. Maybe the world is right, and a guy like me is destined for just one thing: Trouble.

I love Ash. And I'm sure she loves me. But one of us had to make a sacrifice. Either she gave up her family, her safety net, the certainty of knowing life will never get too hard, or I give her up and go back to the way my life used to be. There's no contest. Ash is the better of the two of us, and she deserves so much more than I can give her.

I tell myself all of these things, knowing that I'll tell them to myself over and over for the rest of my life, staring into empty whiskey glasses. By the time I get home I'm ready to order the biggest pizza I can, draw the curtains, put on the saddest records I can find and start drinking everything in the house.

I bring the bike to a stop outside my garage door and kill the engine, then pause for a second. Something's wrong. Something beyond the aching hole inside of me.

I concentrate for a while, listening out for the sound again, then move slowly toward the door of my place. The door's misaligned, ever so slightly ajar. I step carefully, until I can see the wood splintered around the lock, the lock itself jutting inward. This close, I can hear the blare of the TV inside—immediately realizing that whoever's in there (or was in there) was drowning out the noise of their breaking and entering.

Within seconds I've gone back to my bike, quietly pulled out the large wrench I keep in the pack, and then returned to the door, back against the wall as I peer between the crack, looking for movement.

I take my time, listening for anything that isn't the TV, then slowly push the door open, wrench held up in my other hand, muscles tensed and ready to fight. Soon I've got the door open enough to see inside to the living room, the TV screen, and the head of someone sitting on my couch. As slow as I can, my boots not making a sound, I step inside, and then...the tenseness drains out of me when I realize.

It's my dad.

"Hey, Son!" he says, as I step inside his field of view. "About Goddamned time!"

My dad's a big guy. Some people used to call him 'Monster.' Two hundred and fifty pounds of gnarled muscle wrapped in scar-hardened skin. A grey beard rough enough to sweep floors and lank, grey hair frame his permanently scowling eyes, as blue as mine but twice as cold. Over his dirty white tee he's wearing a black biker jacket with the arms ripped off that looks like it's seen as much hell as he has. Scuffed and grimy jeans over his combat boots, perched up on my coffee table. Several empty beers sit on the floor beside the couch, and a bulging green sports bag kept close under his legs.

"The hell are you doing here?" I blurt out, stunned.

"Where else am I gonna go? I must have been to that tattoo place three Goddamned times looking for you, but you weren't there. You ever work these days?"

"So you come here? You break my fucking door? How did you even find my place?"

"Don't be like that, Teo. I've been sleeping rough the past few days." His mood changes on a dime, eyes going angry like he's ready to strangle me. "Where the fuck were you, anyway? What kind of son doesn't pick up his old man after a four-year stretch?"

The whole thing is so surreal I feel almost woozy, half drunk from the sheer insanity of how shitty this day is turning out. Belatedly, I toss the wrench onto the couch beside him and drop my tired body down onto the chair. I grab the remote and turn down the TV, then settle back and breathe a little.

"I never said I'd pick you up," I say. "I was busy, anyway."

"Sure, sure..." my dad says, his voice knowing.

"You can't stay here," I say, as he empties his fifth beer.

"Why not? You got roommates?"

"No. This isn't a rental. I own it."

He's surprised now, putting the beer down and leaning forward to look around at the apartment anew.

"Well Goddamn...if I'd known that, I'd have been real gentle on the door. Pretty nice." He turns to look at me with a kind of vindictive blame. "You've done alright for yourself all around, it looks like."

"What do you know about it?" I say, dismissively.

"That tattoo place—real nice. Looks legit." He moves his head toward me, eyes conspiratorial. "What you using it for? Drugs, right? Got to be, kind of money you need for a place like this."

"It's not a front," I say, rubbing my eyes, already tired of his bullshit, but anticipating a whole load more before I get rid of him. "It's a legit business."

He laughs and shakes his head.

"Sure, sure..."

After a minute, I pull my wallet out and start counting bills.

"I'll give you some money," I say. "Go stay at a hotel. If you're sober in a week, maybe we can talk."

He doesn't even look at the money.

"You want me outta here, huh?" he says, smiling darkly, then tilting his head. "Your girlfriend coming over tonight?" He sees the tension in my eyes and seizes on it. "Running around with that Carter girl again. What was her name again, Ashley?"

"How the fuck do you know that?"

He sits back as if relaxed now.

"I saw you, picking her up outside your 'legit business.' She grew up real nice. Don't blame you for looking her up again."

I toss the bills on the coffee table beside his feet.

"Take the money and get out."

He ignores the money though, his eyes continuing to scrutinize me.

"What are you doing with a girl like that, Son? She'll chew you up and spit you out the second she's done having fun. Find herself one of those New York bankers and before you know it she'll have you out on your ass."

"Ten minutes out of jail and you're already taking the high ground, huh?"

He laughs and searches around the couch for another unopened beer, raising it to me in a mock toast before cracking it open.

"Listen to me, Teo. People like that don't give a fuck about people like us. The sooner you get that through your thick skull, the better off you'll be."

"What do you mean, 'people like us'?"

He looks at me with narrowed eyes, as if trying to figure out whether it's a serious question.

"Shit..." he says, shaking his head. "You're really full of it now, ain't you, Son? You got you a little place and a little money putting gang tags on people and now you think you're a member of 'high society.' System don't work like that, take it from your old man."

"You ain't ever given advice worth taking."

"Sure, sure..." he says, laughing again. "That's why you're out here thinking you're something you're not. Trying to build something, thinking about how high you can go—but that's for other folk, folk like the Carters. People like us only got to ask one question: How low can you survive?"

"I'm surviving just fine."

"Sure, sure...but time's gonna come when you lose it all. And that girl's gonna be the one to cause it, mark my words."

I don't answer, knowing that he can go all night like this. Around in circles as long as he has some alcohol in his hand and his body. It's an old pattern, one I know too well. He keeps going until I get fed up and go silent, then he'll say something to get me riled up, get my attention.

He gives it a couple of minutes, then says, "Prissy little rich girl like that, I'll bet she don't even suck dick properly."

I stand up suddenly.

"That's it, get your shit and get the fuck out of here!"

"Whoa, loverboy!" he says, standing up as well. "I only just got here. Ain't even given you your present yet."

I roll a hand roughly across my forehead, half crazy and half drained from his bullshit, knowing that anything I say or do, he'll have something to come back at me with, something that'll make everything worse, that'll get me even more wound up. Interactions with my father end only two ways: With him drunk enough to pass out, or in blows.

He lifts the green sports bag and dumps it on the coffee table, grinning at me through his beard.

"You're gonna love this," he says, unzipping it quickly.

It's cash. Thick wads of bills stuffed randomly in the bag, filling it to the top.

"What the fuck's all this?" I say, looking at him accusingly.

"That's my cut," he says, pausing to nonchalantly pick at his teeth. "Didn't think I'd stick four years without something good waiting for me at the end of it, did you?"

"I don't want this shit in my house. I told you, take it and get the hell out of here. We'll talk in a week."

"Easy, easy..." he says, holding his palms up like I'm acting irrationally. "Some of that's yours."

He pats me on the shoulder and I shove his arm away.

"You heard me. Get out."

He laughs easily.

"The only problem," he continues, as if not hearing me, "is that it's dirty. Need to run it through something. A legitimate business."

"I'm not laundering your cash—I don't even want it in my house."

"Ten per cent. That's more than fair."

I fight back a wave of disgust. "I wouldn't care if you gave me all of it. I don't *need* the money. I'm not risking my business and everything I have to break the law as a fucking favor to my deadbeat dad. Now get out or I'll call the cops."

His eyes change again, and I can tell he's about to raise his voice, I can tell we're about to get into it, that this isn't ending with him getting drunk and passing out.

"That bitch really did a number on you, son."

I grab the sports bag and lift it, glaring at him.

"You're done," I say, then march to the broken door.

"Whoa! Careful with that!" he calls out behind me, leaping off the couch now to chase.

I open the limp door and toss the bag outside, a few wads spilling out onto the street.

"You fucking crazy?" he says, torn between saving the bag and being angry with me.

"Go pick it up," I say, firmly. "You bring it in here again and I'm gonna burn it."

We stand, face-to-face for a few seconds, my dad's expression flickering through various stages of anger, until the pull of the money and the realization I'm for real compels him outside. I watch him crouch and scan the road like some desperate stray, looking for any fallen wads, then slam the broken door behind him and jam a side table in front of it to keep it closed.

I wish I could say I expected better of him.

19

ASH

When the anger starts to clear, and the emotions around every thought and memory start to fade a little, I start wondering what Teo's explanation would be. I start asking myself what could make him act like that, and I start struggling to find any pattern that fits.

And finally, against my better judgment, I start making excuses for him. I start to wonder if maybe meeting my dad brought up old issues with his own father, if maybe the party made him feel inferior, or insecure in some way, if perhaps my dad had touched a nerve... But then I remember the sight of him raising a fist, and it all resets to zero.

The pain of Teo leaving will linger—it lingered seven years before, and this time maybe it'll be longer. A question without an answer. The imagination is the worst kind of monster, and without the 'why,' I know I'll spend the rest of my life going through the infinite possibilities of what it could be. The answers I come up with will get even worse, even bigger, amplified with time, until it nearly tears me apart, until I start seeing these self-made conclusions in everything I do. But I'll find my way through it. I have to. It's the only way I'll survive.

My body goes through the motions of driving to work, picking up coffee, several meetings with the crew and the writers, but in my mind I'm back in that alley outside Isabel's show, listening to Teo tell me the truth would tear us apart, or at the beach that day, hearing him say that I don't understand. Dying a little more each time I remember our last fight, reliving all the best and worst memories like a wound I can't stop touching.

It's only when lunchtime comes and I go with Jenny to the bar around the corner that I feel some sense of myself being in the present moment—though only because I finally tell her all about it, spitting it out like a bad taste I can't get rid of.

"He was waiting for you outside?" she asks, once I've laid it all out in excruciating detail. "Like, stalker status?"

"Yeah. I mean, no. He said he just wanted a chance to explain"

Sensing the uncertainty in my voice, Jenny says, "You think he had a legitimate reason now?"

I shrug, feeling my eyes start to sting. "I don't know...maybe. No...I don't know."

"You said nothing can justify what he did, right? I mean, I wasn't there to see it myself, but you seemed pretty convinced afterward."

"Yeah," I say, nodding solemnly, reaching for my second martini and discovering the glass is already empty.

"I'm so sorry I had a hand in this. I never should have pushed you to—"

I wave away her apology. "It's not your fault, Jenny. And maybe it's better this way. Now I know for sure. It just wasn't meant to be."

I feel my lower lip start to quiver and Jenny gestures frantically to the bartender, who hotfoots it over to our end of the bar to replace my martini.

Jenny looks at me sympathetically as I gulp it down, and then says, "What are you gonna do now?"

"What *can* I do? This is it. Can't go back from this."

"Do you think you can really leave it at that?" Jenny says. "Maybe I'm wrong, but you don't really sound like it. And you still deserve some kind of answer from him, no?"

I take another long sip of my martini, allowing the alcohol to make my thoughts blurry—but they just come back even clearer.

"It's not easy to let it go, I'm not saying that...but maybe it's for the best."

I stare down into my drink, unable to look at Jenny. I know she'll be looking at me with pity, even more helpless to do anything about this than I am.

After a while she says, "Maybe you should take some time off work. Go be with yourself a while, or take a vacation somewhere."

"The last thing I need right now is more time alone."

"Ugh, I hate seeing you like this, Ash."

"Try seeing it when you look in the mirror. Try *feeling* like this."

Jenny reaches across and puts a hand on my arm.

"Fuck him, ok?" she says, with a little force in her voice now. "So he's your childhood sweetheart who you really, really loved—fuck him. You're twenty-five, incredibly talented, super smart, with a banging body—Teo can't take that away from you. There's probably a whole army of guys out there who'd put on their best cologne if they knew they'd see a girl like you that day."

I lift my head limply and shoot Jenny a meek smile.

"Thanks."

"Don't thank me," she says, still carrying momentum. "Everything I'm saying is a fact. Take it from me, ok? I could write the book on getting your heart broken. You have to kiss a lot of frogs before you find a prince—most of the time when you kiss one, it just stares at you blankly and you realize you've made a terrible mistake."

I laugh a little, putting my hand on hers to show I appreciate it.

"In your case," she continues, "you kissed a prince who turned back into a frog. It happens."

"I suppose."

"No suppose about it," Jenny says. "I mean, Christ, if you think breaking up is hard, try being single for four years. At this point I just go on dates to see how far the universe is willing to go—it's *got* to be running out of ways to disappoint me at this point."

"Come on," I say, feeling at least good enough to offer my own sympathies now, "it's not that bad."

"No," Jenny says adamantly, "it's not. You know why it's not that bad? Because I don't mind being single. I know who I am, I know what I want. I'm a bookish thirty-year-old who's extremely picky and who is confident enough to tell a guy he's an asshole—and I'm happy with that. I don't need a guy to feel good about myself, and I definitely don't need to define myself by his flaws. You shouldn't either. You're stronger than that."

"You know what?" I say, straightening up a little. "You're right."

"Of course I am."

"I don't know why I always end up like this," I say, feeling like I'm having some kind of revelation. "But it's like my whole life I'm being pushed and pulled in all these different directions. Like everybody has this way they want me to be, and I can never quite be good enough to match it. But why should I care what anyone else wants?"

"That's it."

"Whether it's being told I should take on some really major job, or having my ideas at work crushed, or Teo disappointing me like this for the second time—it's like I'm always having to understand everyone else, always having to accommodate them, and I never got a chance to just really be me, to focus on myself, you know?"

"Absolutely!"

"It's like...I don't know...sometimes I wish I could just tell the entire world to kiss my ass, you know?"

"Now *that's* something I could drink to," Jenny says, lifting her cocktail and putting it forward.

I take my martini and we clink, smiling and relaxed for the first time since yesterday.

Before I've taken the drink from my lips, though, my phone buzzes on the bar table. A message from Candace:

CLOTHES. CONDOMS. BURNER PHONE. BEVERLY HILLS FOUR SEASONS SUITE 237. NOW!!!!

I slam the phone down on the bar and close my eyes to breathe deeply, feeling a hardness at the center of my being, all of my frustrations catalyzing into a single, stubborn feeling.

"What?" Jenny says. "What's wrong? Was it him?"

I shake my head and rub my temples. After three deep, difficult breaths, I stuff my phone into my bag, slap a twenty on the bar top, and get off my stool to leave.

"Wait, Ash," Jenny calls. "Where are you going?"

I stop, just long enough to look back at her and say, "I'm about to start telling the world to kiss my ass."

I make my way to the hotel feeling ready to burn the world down. Several martinis and the breakup mixing inside of me to produce a kind of motivational jet fuel, a blind determination that—no matter the consequences—I'm going to start being honest, I'm going to start taking control.

I march into the hotel feeling seven feet tall, shoulders back and chin up, unsure of what's going to happen, but sure of myself at the very least. The receptionist calls up to the suite and gets the ok for me to go up. Then I march into the elevator car, stab the button for the second floor, and brace myself for a confrontation.

When I get to the hotel room I knock loudly on the door which is slightly ajar.

"Ash?! Jesus Christ, finally," I hear Candace cry haughtily from the other side.

I push the door open and step inside. The suite is a mess, as I expected. Once again the pungent smell of make-up, sex, and alcohol hits the back of my throat like tear gas. The door to the bathroom is open, and I can see Carlos preening in the mirror, a bath towel around his waist. Candace is sitting at the breakfast table, typing something out on her phone.

She laughs at something on the screen and then, without looking up, orders, "Put the stuff on the bed and leave. That will be all."

I don't move, glaring at her until she senses my lack of movement. She notices that I'm not carrying anything but my bag.

After looking at me with indignant confusion, she looks around as if there's somebody else to confirm what she suspects.

"Where's the stuff?" she says. "The clothes, the phone, the

condoms?"

"I didn't bring them," I say calmly.

"Well, where are they? Aren't you going to get them? Do you need cash?"

"No."

Candace is staring at me like I just stepped off a spaceship now, even the Botox unable to hide how much she's struggling to understand.

"Excuse me?" she says, face twisted with perplexity.

"Hey," Carlos says, stamping out of the bathroom to step in front of me, his palm already out anxiously. "You got that phone? I got to make some calls, cover my tracks—I think my wife's started searching my messages."

I turn to him and say, "I didn't bring the phone, I didn't bring the clothes," and turning back to Candace, "and I *definitely* didn't bring you condoms."

Carlos mirrors Candace's confusion now. He glances back at her, searching for an explanation, but finds only an equally clueless glare.

"Well what the fuck are you doing here then?" he says, suddenly frustrated. "Go get them!"

"Get them yourself," I parry, forcefully. "I'm not your personal assistant, or your errand girl. I'm a producer on the show—and it's about time you start treating me with the respect that commands."

Candace and Carlos exchange a quick, menacing look, as if checking to make sure they've got each other's backs, before looking back at me.

"Outgrowing your boots there a little, don't you think, sweetie? You might be a producer, but I'm still your boss, remember?" Candace hisses.

"In name only," I reply quickly. "When was the last time you coordinated a shooting schedule? Or edited a segment? You don't even turn up to the writers' meetings. The only time you seem to care about the show is when you're crushing my ideas or begging me to fix problems you can't handle."

Candace laughs as she stands up, crossing the room to stand

beside Carlos.

"So *that's* what this is about—you're upset because I won't allow you to use *Hollywood Night* as a showcase for your little pet projects. Because I won't let you turn it into some dull, hipster-baiting garbage. Because you're dumb enough to believe our audience wants more than entertainment, and I'm smart enough to realize they're morons."

"No," I say, pausing to take a deep breath and gather my thoughts. "It's not just that, it's this whole thing. This ridiculous situation you think you can just get away with over and over again. The emergency texts ordering me to random hotels in the city, getting everyone to pretend that they don't know what's going on. *Hitting on my boyfriend* so that you can make Carlos feel jealous. It's insane! And I'm sick of covering for you."

"Now hold up," Carlos says, in a tone that makes it sound like he wants to take control of the situation, "that's no way to talk to—"

"And you're just as bad!" I interrupt. "With your constant hissy fits over your hair or your shirt colors and tantrums over lighting. Do you know how long it takes me to edit your segments because you don't care enough to do something in one take? Or how difficult it is to write a script that doesn't have long words you'll complain about in it? You're both the most egotistical, selfish, lazy people I've ever met— let alone had to work with."

They look at each other for a little longer this time, as if telepathically exchanging ideas about how to respond to this.

Candace turns back to me, her expression droll.

"And?" she says, dismissively.

"And I'm sick of it! I'm sick of doing all the work, getting none of the credit and no support or freedom despite it—and I'm *especially* sick of the fact that I also have to cover up this gross affair. I don't want any part of this."

"Wait a minute," Carlos says, suddenly. "Is this a blackmail attempt? You saying you'll go to the media if you don't get more freedom at work?"

I sigh heavily and shake my head.

"I'm not interested in blackmailing you."

Candace groans and rolls her eyes.

"Then what, exactly, is the point of this obnoxious display? Why come all the way here just to stamp your little feet and scream a little, huh?"

"I came to tell you I'm not covering for you guys anymore. You're on your own."

"I see," Candace says, nodding confidently. "But the thing is, sweetie, I'm still your boss. That means when I tell you to do something—you do it."

I fold my arms and smile grimly at her.

"Or what?"

"Do you think you're indispensable? You think I won't fire you? Right here, right now."

"I'd love to see you try to run *Hollywood Night* without me," I say, feeling both exhilarated and terrified of what I'm saying. "You couldn't put a single segment together if I wasn't there."

Candace's face is hard and impervious, a face that only mean, spiteful things could come from.

"I suppose we'll just have to see, then, won't we?" she says. "Consider this your two weeks' notice, Ash. You're fired. *Good rid.*"

I freeze, even as Carlos shoots an alarmed look at Candace, though he isn't brave enough to say anything. I knew it was coming, flirted with it even, but to actually hear it, to be forced to think about what it means now, overwhelms me in the immediate aftermath. But I feel something other than panic and devastation right now—something I never expected: Freedom. An utter lightness of my entire being.

And it feels fucking amazing.

"Fine," I say with a coy smile of my own, then turn on my heel and head for the door.

I leave, whipping the hotel door shut behind me with a satisfying slam, then stride toward the elevator feeling like the whole building is about to come crashing down around me. Liberated, terrified, euphoric.

My new life is about to begin.

20

TEO

It's torture, losing her. Like wolves tearing at my heart every second of the day, like the world turning flimsy and distant, monochrome and meaningless. As if the rest of my life is just going through the motions, a perfunctory imitation of what everything should have been, *could* have been. No amount of slammed punching bags, commiseration chats with Kayla and Ginger, runs with my dog or bouts of intoxication are going to fix these dark clouds inside me.

I throw myself into my work, my art—the only thing I feel like I have any control over anymore. It's late evening, and I'm hunched over the toned leg of a dancer, finishing up an elaborate rose with detailed thorns running down her thigh. Through the open curtain I can half see Kayla at the front desk, checking schedules. Ginger comes back in after giving some final advice to a guy he's just finished a tattoo on, sitting on the tattoo chair next to me to try his hand at sweet-talking the girl—which I'm semi-grateful for, considering the girl's been hitting on me for the past two hours, and doesn't seem any closer to taking the hint.

"So let me guess," Ginger says, putting some of that good old southern musicality into his voice, "you're a dancer?"

The girl laughs a little.

"Don't move," I warn her, too close to finishing to slow down.

"Yeah, I am. *Burlesque*," she says, though I can hear she's looking at me as she says it. "You wanna come to a show? I can get you guys on the list."

"Don't mind if I do," Ginger says.

"How about you?" the girl says in my direction.

"Aw, forget about him," Ginger says, "he ain't no fun these days."

"Why's that?" the girl says, through a smile.

"Let me finish this, would you?" I growl, without looking up.

Ginger's about to say something, but we're distracted for a moment by somebody coming into the shop. A tall, scrawny kid with plenty of tattoos and gaged-out ears beneath a wide-brim baseball cap. I turn back to my work and Ginger laughs.

"God," he says, "this kid don't quit."

"Who is he?" the girl says, glancing over.

"Comes in twice a day to see Kayla. You'd think he would get it by now. I mean, it's not like she ain't blunt enough with him."

As sure as he says it, we all notice the slightly raised voices. Kayla laughs, though it sounds more like she's forcing it in order to navigate being put on the spot by this guy. I stare at them for a few moments, but the kid doesn't notice, too focused on Kayla, and I turn back to the tattoo—desperate to finish it now.

"Anyway," Ginger says, settling his eyes back on the girl, "you were saying? Burlesque? Tell me about that..."

The girl giggles, and then a second later I hear Kayla again. This time she's a little louder, a little clearer.

"No. I'm sorry. But no. You need to leave."

"Come on!" the boy says, in a tone of voice that aggravates my already discordant nerves.

I put the needle down on the tray and get up. At the front desk I move to stand beside Kayla and glare at the kid, who looks at me like I'm a bad smell.

"What does this guy want?" I ask Kayla, without taking my eyes off him.

He points at Kayla, as if indignant that I'm interrupting.

"We're just talking."

"About what?"

"Teo," Kayla says, soothingly, "I can handle it."

"I asked you a question. What you two talking about?" I repeat.

The kid snorts, as if finding me too strange to understand.

"Relax, buddy. Ok?"

"If there's one thing I hate," I say, already moving around the counter toward him, "it's people telling me to relax."

He makes a feeble attempt to plant his feet, raise his hands and get into punching position, but before he's even done that I've got a hand around his collar, fingers twisting his shirt. I drag him to the door, shouts swelling behind me.

I yank the door open and toss him outside like a bag of trash. He lands with thump, a strangled wail of pain. I see red, blood hot and pumping as if some pressure valve has been let off inside of me. Some aimless, charged manifestation of all the shit I've been stacking there for days.

I step toward him, ready for more, ready to pound him into a pulp, but before I can take a second step my arms are grabbed, and I'm being pulled back toward the shouts, back into the tattoo shop.

"Holy shit, Teo," Kayla scolds.

"You wanna get your ass involved in a damned lawsuit or something?" Ginger says.

"Take him in back," Kayla shouts, moving toward the dancer, who's clutching the chair like she's just heard an air raid siren. "I'll finish up in here."

Ginger pushes me into the back room and shoves me down onto the sofa, where I suddenly feel how fast my heart's racing, how hard I'm breathing.

"The hell was that about, Teo?" Ginger says, pacing in front of me. "Damn near lost your shit!"

"I can't have people abusing my employees," I say, though it's a feeble excuse.

"Just some dumb kid with a crush, for God's sake. You only needed to scare the shitkicker."

Love & Ink   171

I put a hand over my eyes, Ginger's words making the wave of regret come quicker, harder.

More than Ginger, though, I think of Ash's father, as if he were right there, watching it. I think about how he'd probably smile in victory. He'd probably say something about my 'violent tendencies,' about me being 'criminal minded,' an 'animal with no refinement.' And I wouldn't have anything to say back, because the bottom line is that he would be right.

Ginger drops to sit beside me, the weight of his body making the couch bounce a little.

"I know it's been rough," he says, slapping a hand on my shoulder, "but you gotta keep it together a little more than that. Especially during business hours."

"I know," I say, still rubbing a fist across my forehead.

"I ain't gonna give you some speech or anything—I ain't no psychologist, and I sure as shit have done worse things than get tough on a punk over a woman—but one thing I *do* know is that when you're acting like that, it's probably 'cause you know you should be doing something else."

"I'm just stressed," I say quickly, leaning forward, elbows on knees to stare at the ground. "Losing Ash, and my dad getting out of jail— it's a little too much for one week."

"I hear ya," Ginger says.

We hear the door to the shop bang open, and immediately look at each other, thinking the same thing. Maybe the kid's back.

"Stay here," Ginger says cautiously, as he gets to his feet and goes to see who it is. I hear him from the back. "Well hey... Sure he is... Come on back—maybe you can get through to him better than I can..."

When he emerges into the back room again, Isabel is close behind.

"Teo, there you are," she says brightly.

"I'm gonna go handle this lovely redhead that you've just scared seven shades of purple out of," Ginger says, leaving us alone.

"Hey, Isabel," I say, forcing as much happiness into my voice as possible—which isn't very much, despite my best efforts.

"I've been trying to reach you for days," she says, leaning back on a counter, folding her arms, and directing a concerned look at me. "Messages, calls—"

"Uh, yeah," I say, apologetically. "Guess I've been a little...out of it."

"No shit," she says. "I'm leaving in a few days—going to New York to finish off the album, and I'm not sure we'll even be back for a while. I figured we could meet up—you, me, and Ash. Except both of you seem...I don't know. What *happened* with you guys?"

"You spoke to Ash?" I ask, with more interest than I've had in anything for days.

Isabel notices, and nods slowly.

"Just a phone call. She sounded...a little strange, to be honest. I asked about you and she just told me she had no idea—told me to talk to you if I wanted to know anything."

I sigh heavily.

"Yeah," I say, looking down at the ground again.

"She lost her job," Isabel says, sorrowfully.

I snap to attention. "What? How?"

She just shrugs her shoulders.

"I don't know. She said she got fired, but that she didn't care. Honestly, she didn't sound that upset about it. Like I said—she sounded strange. And to be honest, looking at you now I'm getting the same vibe."

I don't answer, my mind too full of new questions, new angles to think about the conversation at hand. Ash losing her job and not being cut up about it could only mean one thing. Perhaps she finally decided to bite the bullet and take her father up on his offer. Deciding at last to take that big executive producer job he had lined up for her, instead of continuing to struggle and 'earn it' the way she had wanted to.

I remembered the way she had spoken about it before, how sure she had been about cutting her own path, the enthusiasm she had for bringing her own ideas to the table. Then I remember how frustrated she sounded when she found herself coming up against walls, bosses who didn't appreciate her, who held her down and kept her from flourishing. That would be enough to make anyone fall back on their connections, their 'safety net.' And I can't blame her.

Maybe I had been the one to push her. Maybe I made her realize that her best future didn't lie with me, in the unfurnished apartments and outcast-ridden tattoo shops of the world, but the manicured lawns and stale conversations of success, of people who had all the breaks, who put the barbecue grill far away so their clothes wouldn't smell.

I feel my heart sink and my tensions dissolve, leaving only misery, a sense of bitter vindication. I was right, but about all the things that I didn't want to be right about. Ash was better off without me...and I would just have to suffer without her...

"Teo? Are you ok?"

Isabel's voice draws me back to the present moment, as if I'm waking up.

"Huh?"

"You ok?"

"Yeah. I'm fine."

Isabel looks at me like I'm a terminal patient.

"I'm going to see her again before I leave town. Do you want to come?"

"No," I say, resolutely. "I can't."

"Well, do you want me to tell her anything, at least?"

"No," I repeat. "Nothing. Just tell her that—" for a moment I hesitate, but then my resolve hardens. "Tell her that when you came to talk to me, I didn't care."

The words hurt, the lie of it twisting ugly and deep in my soul, but deep down I know—it's better this way.

21

ASH

A giant tub of ice cream—eaten with a big spoon. An old romantic comedy I've seen so many times I know all the words—more like an audio-visual comforter than entertainment at this point. A blue hoodie with paint stains all over it that should have been thrown out three years ago, pajama bottoms that are worn thin enough to see my skin color through.

This is my life now.

I have an idea for a segment: Hollywood breakups. Interviewing major stars on how and why their breakups with other major stars happened, how it affected them, how they got over it. I could tag it 'Celebs reveal the hardest part of breaking up.' I'd have no problem getting approval for it.

Then I remember I've only got my job for another week, and after that there won't be any more segments, no more ideas to manifest (or have crushed by Candace). My stomach sinks to an even lower state, and I shovel another spoonful of melting, sugary, chocolate fudge brownie ice cream inside of me to numb the sensation for a few more minutes.

The hardest part of breaking up is how much more difficult the rest of your life gets. It's like pulling that final Jenga piece, wavering on a tightrope. Flickering back and forth between that moment of believing it might just hold up, and the utter hopelessness of realizing it won't.

It's not just work seeming so pointless and insignificant, or the giant spaces of time that would have otherwise been filled with spending time together—it's the smaller things, the details you only notice in terms of absence. No late-night phone calls where you lower voices and raise the volume on your phone, only realizing by the cramp in your hand and the dying battery level how many hours you've been talking. It's the way the world suddenly seems full of couples, and everything seems like it's about love. Commercials, music, every single TV show—relationships everywhere, only now they seem so gloating and envy-baiting. It's the way seemingly random things always draw your mind back to him, how anything you see or hear is just three degrees of separation away from thinking about him. The Santa Monica Pier. Motorcycles. Germany. Any tattoo anywhere.

Actually, maybe the hardest part is knowing that you've only got yourself to blame, and beating yourself up over it. Finally seeing the things that you ignored so easily, and kicking yourself for being so blinded. Teo had literally done this exact same thing to me already. Nothing from him in seven years. Then as soon as he pops up again I let him back in without a real explanation, without guarding myself, without any restraint. How could I blame anyone but myself for that? Fool me once...

My phone rings and I jump a little. Partly because I'm so locked in my own bubble of self-pity that even the sudden blare of my phone feels like an intrusion, and partly because there's a shameful, lingering hope that it might be Teo.

I see that it's Grace, and take a deep, steadying breath before I answer.

"Hey sis," she says.

"Hey."

"You ok?"

I take a moment to actually consider it.

"Not really. But I'm getting there."

"I'm sorry. I can't imagine what this must be like for you."

"Did Dad say anything?"

Grace pauses on the phone, and I can sense she's biting her lip.

"Um..."

"I'll take that as a yes," I say.

"He's just glad that you found out before Teo did anything worse... To be honest, I think he's drawing up a list of replacements for you."

"Oh, God," I say, facepalming with my phone.

"How's work? Any better?"

"Um..." Now I'm the one biting my lip. "About as good as my relationship status."

"What's wrong?"

"I kind of lost my job."

"*Ash!*" Grace says, as if I'm falling off a cliff.

"It's kind of my own doing," I say. "I just got tired of being everybody's lapdog."

"I'm so sorry," she says, sounding even more sympathetic than she did about Teo. "So you're just sitting at home alone?"

"No. I've got my ice cream."

"Listen," she says, her voice renewed with a decisive edge. "I know you're gonna want to say no, but we're having a fundraiser—"

"Oh, Grace, I can't—"

"Shh, just hear me out," she interrupts, with political firmness. "I want you to be there. It would be great for me to have my whole family at this thing, and—"

"And I suppose it'll be a great opportunity for you and Dad to set me up with some 'appropriate suitors'?"

"Well..." Grace says, drawing the word out. "I mean, there *will* be a lot of eligible men there. And if you're not interested in that, fine, but at least come for the chance at networking with people who could help you get a new job."

I sigh heavily, trying to consider whether I'm actually above this anymore, whether everything blowing up in my face the past week is a sign I should just bite the bullet and start following my family's advice.

"There will be cameras there," she says. "It's going to be on the news. Big networks, anchors, maybe a few producers. You'll probably struggle *not* to come away with a promising job lead or two."

"Ugh...I don't know."

"Do it for me," Grace says, as if sensing my hesitation. "I want to see you. I can't bear the thought of you sitting at home alone in such a state."

"Ok," I say, unable to resist her tone. I would like to see her, and I know that she barely has time for a simple coffee or brunch these days—a fundraiser is about as intimate as it gets when your sister is the mayor of a small town.

"Wonderful. I'll text you the details."

"Sure."

"See you then. Take care, sis."

I hang up and grab my ice cream spoon. Maybe this *will* be good for me. A new start, a clean slate. Maybe it's what I've needed for a long time. Maybe my father was right all along. I mean, it makes a kind of sense. I just wish it didn't feel so wrong.

22

TEO

Work consumes me. I take on all the appointments I can in order to push my real life into the background, so that I can go home late enough that there's no time for me to mope before crashing out, so that every second of the day is filled with images and art and the narrowing, almost zen-like focus of needle on skin.

The customers are happy for it, especially those who thought they'd spend months waiting for an opening. I'm doing three, four, five tattoos a day, my phone is blowing up with the comments and likes on our Instagram page, and I've drawn almost an entire book's worth of new designs.

But I still can't sleep well.

So here I am, sitting at the drawing desk in the back of Mandala at close to midnight, sketching with a focus even Buddhist monks would be impressed with. I hear Kayla and Ginger step into the back.

"You guys still here?" I ask, without looking up. "Go home. I'll close up."

They don't answer, and instead I hear Kayla close the curtain, Ginger pour a deep whiskey and plant it on the table beside me. Kayla comes up on my other side and puts a hand on my drawing arm. I glance up, frustrated that I've been interrupted.

Love & Ink

"What's going on?" I ask.

"We just want to talk," Ginger say.

I grab the whiskey and spin around in my chair to face them.

"You sound like the cops," I smile, then gulp down a burning mouthful. They look at each other seriously, then back at me. "Tough crowd."

"How are you feeling?" Kayla asks me like I'm laid out in a hospital.

"What is this, an intervention? I feel fucking fantastic," I say. "I kicked my dad out, business is booming, and I'm drawing some of the best designs of my life. Yeah. Fucking fantastic."

"You *have* been pulling a lot of overtime," Ginger says, as if it's a bad thing. "Working real hard..."

"Maybe a little *too* hard?" Kayla suggests cautiously.

I exhale deeply so they know this isn't the time. I can tell where this is going, and I'm not in the mood to go there.

"Look: If you came by to tell me you're worried about me, or to try and get me to talk about Ash—forget it. Everything's fine."

I gulp more from the whiskey, then spin back around to the drawing desk. Ginger grabs my shoulder and spins me back to face them, though.

"This isn't healthy," Kayla says. "You can't leave it like this."

"What's not healthy?" I say. "I've never worked this good."

"The fact that you're working so hard shows there's a problem," Ginger says. "You ain't hardly eaten or slept, I can tell, and outside of the tattooing you've just been walking around this place like a zombie. When you gonna relax? When you burn out?"

"If I burn out."

"And you're just gonna give up on Ash?" Kayla jumps in.

I sigh and check my glass to see if there's anything left, but I've downed it all. Ginger pours a little more in there.

"She doesn't want to talk," I say, taking a sip. "What am I supposed to do? Bust down her door? Demand she hear me out? I've done enough damage already."

"You've got to try, Teo," Kayla says. "At least give her your side. Maybe she's calmed down a little, now. Maybe she's willing to listen."

I take a few moments to think, to sip again and let the alcohol burn that emptiness inside.

"She's better off without me."

"Maybe she is," Ginger says, and Kayla glares at him like that was the wrong thing to say. "What? I'm not gonna lie," he tells her, then turns to me and slaps a heavy hand on my shoulder. "You fucked up, buddy. And you're gonna have to make up for it. She probably thinks you're a crazy, uncontrollable asshole right now. So you've got to show her how sorry you are, try to convince her you're not the asshole you acted like, prove to her that you deserve her despite all that—because if you don't, then that's proof she thought right."

I look up at them, feeling a wave of gratitude and compassion pass over me. Friends I'm lucky to have—a family that chose me.

"Maybe you're right," I admit.

"You bet your granny's biscuits I am," Ginger proclaims with a grin.

Kayla pats my arm and I break into a smile, put the whiskey glass on the desk behind me, and stand to wrap my arms around both their necks, walking them back through the curtain.

"Ok," I say. "I'll give it one more shot. But you guys are gonna have to help me figure out how."

23

ASH

Grace and my father call me throughout the day, at work and after, all the way up to the point at which I actually confirm that I'm getting ready to leave the house. They tell me they're just checking in on me, but I can tell they're anxious I'm going to back out at the last moment.

To be honest, the fact that they're so intent on having me there is what's making me feel even more uneasy about going in the first place—they've obviously got some big plans for me, some well-meaning (but probably unwelcome) tricks up their sleeves.

Anticipating the hungry-eyed bachelors they're inevitably going to introduce me to, I decide against a dress, and wear instead a pair of stylish burgundy pants, leather Chelsea boots, and a tucked-in loose white blouse. A 'don't talk to me unless you want to be judged' outfit. It'll probably take more than an outfit for them to get the message though.

I pull up outside the address Grace texted me for the fundraiser location and immediately wonder if she made a typo, feeling like I might have taken a wrong turn somewhere and ended up in nineteen thirties-era New York. The place is a vast, sculpted structure with neo-classical columns and stone steps leading up to a gigantic arched doorway. It's *grand*—ball gown, old Hollywood, Fred Astaire grand.

Less like the location of a fundraiser, and more like a palace or a museum transported to the hills above Los Angeles.

The stream of tuxedos and elegant dresses emerging from chauffeur-driven vehicles in front of the place let me know it's exactly where I'm supposed to be, though, so with a knot in my stomach I pull up to a valet standing at the curb. As I step out I suddenly feel very underdressed—and very overwhelmed.

I try not to notice that I'm the only one walking in alone as I hand my keys over, and head up the steps to that huge entrance feeling like I'm sneaking in somewhere I don't belong.

"Name?" a woman with a clipboard and headset asks me.

"Um...Ash Carter. It probably says Ashley on that list."

The woman raises a suspicious eyebrow, just about bordering on polite.

"Hey sis!" Grace squeals as she glides out from the hall, steering me away from the woman with the headset and past the crowd of guests waiting to be checked in.

"Hey, Grace," I say, then pull back to study her incredible blue gown. "You look amazing."

"Oh, thanks!" she says, glancing at my outfit and then looking at me quizzically.

"I know," I say, almost apologetically. "I suck. But when you said 'dress up,' you could have mentioned it was going to be this...elaborate."

Grace just laughs and guides me down an echoing hallway.

"Ash, you could turn up in a boiler suit and still make it work. Don't worry about it."

I laugh, trying to sound relaxed. Grace must hear the apprehension in it, though, because she stops and pulls me aside, reaching behind her neck to unclasp the glittering statement necklace she's wearing. Then she motions for me to lean forward and puts it on me.

"I can't wear this!" I hiss. "Are these real diamonds?"

"Relax, they're Swarovski crystals," Grace says, leaning back to look me over. "Hmm. Almost there."

She reaches out to pop my collar and then spins me around to

Love & Ink

twist my hair up, transporting me back to when I was a gangly little kid and she was my cool older sister trying out the latest hairstyles from her *Seventeen* magazine on me. I get stabbed in the back of the head with a few bobby pins in the process. "Ouch, Grace! You're pulling too hard."

"Hush," she scolds, whipping me back around. A satisfied grin lights her face. "You look perfect now. As elegant as Grace Kelly."

I know she's exaggerating for my benefit, but I smile anyway. "Thanks, sis."

"Welcome. Now come on. You're gonna have so much fun," she says, and then links her arm through mine to usher me through the corridor toward the main hall. "We'll have dinner first, sit through a few boring speeches—and then we'll really let our hair down."

I smile politely, and refrain from expressing how I doubt anybody here is willing to let their expensively-fashioned hair down for anything.

When we step into the hall I find it hard to speak, anyway. The place is huge, an actual honest-to-God ballroom with gleaming, inlaid wood floors, even more breathtaking than the place is on the outside. From a domed ceiling elaborate chandeliers hang low, sparkling in their own soft light. We move through it toward the large glass doors that lead outside, onto the grounds at the back of the building. Despite the beauty of the hall, it's a warm and colorful enough evening that the events of the night will take place outside.

There's a large stage at one end of the grounds, and an empty area of elegant stone patio laid out in front of it. Around this are numerous large tables that look like art installations, filled with impossibly beautiful tropical flowers, origami-like folded napkins, silver cutlery and crystal stemware. All of it glowing beneath the paper lamps that make the night beyond look mysterious and magical. People are already taking seats, searching for their places, and I suddenly feel like there are hundreds of pairs of eyes on me.

"Far too nice out for us to be cooped up inside," Grace explains, as if reading my thoughts. I nod in agreement.

That's when I see my father split away from a group of men to come and greet me.

"Ashley," he calls warmly, embracing me. "I'm glad you made it."

"I wouldn't miss it for the world," I say meekly, the sarcasm only for my own benefit.

"I'll catch you two later," Grace says, smiling graciously as she darts off to greet some other newcomer.

"There's somebody I'd like you to meet," my dad says, already angling himself to bring me over somewhere else.

"Uh...I'd maybe like to get a drink first."

"Oh, it'll only take a second," he brushes me off, already scanning the room.

Within a few minutes he has me standing in front of a tall man with slim shoulders and a tuxedo that's at least half a size too big. His small, dark eyes are glued to my father, reverently, and his smooth face looks like a polished egg with chocolate frosting for hair.

"Ashley, this is Tim Bellos. Tim, this is my daughter Ashley."

"Nice to meet you," Tim says, though he seems more tuned in to my father than me.

"You too," I say, shaking his hand on autopilot while trying to see if there are any waiters with drinks close by.

"Tell her what you do, Tim," my father says, in a self-satisfied tone.

"Well, I work with my father—he owns an independent film studio and production company just south of the city."

"*Very* successful," my dad adds, like an elderly hype man.

"Impressive," I say, struggling to make it sound genuine.

"Presumably," Tim continues, "you work in politics as well?"

"Actually, no," my father says, practically rubbing his hands together. "Ashley decided to go her own way and become a producer. She's very talented—and just recently left a very successful television series where she practically ran the entire show herself—"

"*Dad...*" I say, trying to make my annoyance sound like humility.

"I see," Tim says.

I notice him size me up again, as if recalibrating his opinion with this new information, and then my dad pats both of our shoulders, looking at us like we're shy children.

"Well," he says, "I'll leave you two to get acquainted. I'm sure you've got plenty of 'inside baseball' to talk about regarding movie-making. See you at dinner, Ash."

"*Dad*—" I say quickly, but he's already turning, and Tim is already closing the gap so he can stand closer to me.

It takes a wealth of effort not to let the mental groan of despair reach my face.

"So," Tim says, smiling like he's just been given a gift, "what show were you on? Your father didn't specify..."

"He tends to over-embellish, to be honest. I've worked on a few things, a handful of artsy indie films and a few episodes of a web series for the Science Channel before I landed my latest gig, which was a celebrity gossip show," I say, keeping my tone clipped and looking around to let him know I'm eager to move on. "Nothing all that thrilling."

He nods, and his glazed expression says he could care less about anything I just said.

"Well, things are going a bit more exciting on *my* end," he brags. "We're actually working on this amazing new superhero movie right now. Gonna make it really dark and gritty—very urban, lots of character arc. It's gonna be huge. Do you like superhero films?"

"Um...sure. Nothing wrong with a good popcorn movie every now and again."

"*Popcorn movie?*" His eyes narrow. "Superhero films are so much more than mindless entertainment for the masses. I don't know why they get so disrespected—they're brilliant! Good vs. evil, you know? It's so...timeless. These films are about culture, politics, society. They're the best thing to happen to Hollywood! And the international markets gobble them up. Why wouldn't they? These movies have the power to unite the whole world!"

I've already subconsciously taken a step back from the near-panting, zealous frenzy he's worked himself up into, and as I glance at the fists he's clenched at his sides I help myself to another few steps.

"Oh, um," I say, waving at the corner of the room as if I've just noticed somebody, "I'll have to catch up with you later. It was nice to meet you."

I'm already walking away when he calls after me, losing myself in the now-thick stream of people coming in from outside. But my escape is short-lived. Within minutes my dad finds me on my own and steers me over to a pasty-looking guy with an unfortunate avant-garde haircut and bizarre, doll-like eyes.

"Ashley," my father says, barely able to contain his excitement, "this is Guy Greene."

"Nice to meet you," I say, taking the guy's limp hand.

"Hey," he says, his voice nasal and fluttery.

"Guy is a startup king—his latest company just went public for twenty billion dollars."

"Oh, wow," I say, trying to sound enthusiastic, but the way he's staring at me is making me feel like he's malfunctioning.

I wait to see if he's going to stop staring and start speaking, but he doesn't.

"Um...what kind of company is it?" I ask politely, if only to break the silence.

"*Lifer*—spelled without the 'e,'" he says, with a grin that looks stolen from a third-grader being offered ice cream. "You've probably heard of it."

"Actually," I reply, "I haven't. I'm not that into tech."

"*Lifr*," Guy begins, his hands grabbing an imaginary ball in front of him, "is all about connecting people, and allowing them to achieve their goals by giving them a clearer understanding and self-awareness."

"Impressive, huh?" my dad says, smiling. I shoot him a confused look, perplexed by the fact that the guy's explanation seems to make any kind of sense to him—though he's probably still thinking about the twenty billion dollar figure.

"Sure," I say, still struggling to be polite, but I follow it up quickly with, "what exactly does it do, though?"

"Our latest venture," Guy says, as if reading from a script, and still tumbling his imaginary ball, "tracks your activities throughout the day, your work history, your medical information, your sleep patterns, and your appearance—then uses advanced machine learning algorithms to suggest key areas and actions where you could improve to better achieve your goals. For example, if influential people within your sphere of work prefer a certain style of dress, *Lifr* will suggest stores and outfits for you to try. It might tell you what you should be eating, or what time to go to bed, or what computer you should buy."

"Very clever," my dad say, happily.

Guy turns his doll-face to me expectantly, as if telling me it's my turn to compliment him.

Instead I feel my face screwing up into an expression of skepticism. "So essentially, it tells you how to live your life so you can be just like everyone else? Don't you think that's a little creepy? I guess you've never watched any sci-fi films—'cause that sounds like the premise of one where things go *really wrong*," I say, laughing before I take a sip of my drink.

As if in sync, my father and Guy drop their smiles and stare at me like I just flashed them. Even outside, the silence between us suddenly feels heavy and uncomfortable.

"We'll catch you later, Guy—great to see you here," my father says suddenly, slapping him on the shoulder lightly, though he still almost stumbles. Then he puts a hand on my back and leads me away, leaning over to reprove me quietly. "What the hell was that all about?"

"What?" I say, alarmed by his change of tone. "I was just making a little joke."

"You don't tell a guy that his twenty billion dollar business is 'creepy.'"

"Even if I think it absolutely is?"

"*Especially* if you think it is. You're not in some downtown bar now, these people need to be treated with respect—*deserve* to be treated with respect."

"Nobody deserves that—you've got to earn it."

He looks at me the same way he did when I failed a math test in ninth grade, then shakes his head and walks off in something of a huff.

Thankfully I find some more alcohol quickly, and a spot on a bench shrouded in darkness that allows me to play wallflower. I almost fall to my knees and thank the Lord when the dinner call finally comes and it's time for everyone to seat themselves.

Yet even here, I find that I'm not safe from my father's intentions. He sits me across from both him and Grace at the table—too far to really carry on a conversation with them—but between two more 'eligible' bachelors.

The guy on my right keeps reaching for something whenever I grab my glass, forcing our hands to brush so he can shoot me a slightly-creepy smile. The guy on my left cracks jokes about everything from the flower arrangements to the folded napkins, even putting on an obnoxious show of getting a 'cleaner' set of silverware from the poor server for the purpose of what he thinks is my amusement. When I tell him he's being a dick he seems to interpret it as flirting.

My father watches from the other side of the table with a proud smile, completely oblivious to the torture, and seeming to interpret the exchanges and looks I'm having with these two men as some kind of segue to intimacy.

I make it through dinner by chewing every bite so long I can't respond to either of them, and then make it through the series of speeches by keeping stony faced despite left-guy's constant leaning into me to whisper rude jokes about the speakers.

When the speeches are done, a live 4-piece orchestra assembles on stage and starts to play. The diners get up and take to the floor to dance, or begin mingling around the tables. Left-guy and right-guy must have gotten the message by now, because when I turn down their offers to dance they actually leave me at the table, finally alone and in peace.

I sit there in a posttraumatic haze, pushing food around my plate until the caterers come to clear the tables and take even that diversion away from me. Sipping my martini, I watch the others dance—too drained to get up and leave, too wary to actually speak to anyone. The songs are fun, surprisingly. Orchestral versions of upbeat hits from my teenage years—no doubt Grace chose most of the playlist. But it gets harder and harder not to think about the past...about him...

They say you're never lonelier than when you're in a crowd, but I'd add to that being out of a job, recently-single, and surrounded by men not even your family could convince you to like.

Suddenly I sense the air change, some shift in the energy of the room. I notice a few people turning their heads around, as if searching for something. I scan the flower beds and manicured trees, straining a little to grasp at some strange sawing sound in the distance. I notice some of the waiters looking panicked, talking hurriedly with each other and running off. Some of the other guests notice too, and in the still air I can sense the rising tension that's suddenly coming from everybody.

Before anyone can figure out what's going on, however, the sound grows loud enough to be unmistakable, and from a far corner of the outside area some gleaming beast draws everybody's attention. Some of the mingling crowd parts and I look at where the other people are focused, the motorcycle's chrome reflecting the millions of twinkling lights, the black-suited figure with just enough cool restraint in his movements to quell the panic in the air.

I can hardly believe what I'm seeing right now.

It's Teo.

Everything stills in shock and awe, and for a moment the only thing moving is the bike as it revs up and starts to weave between the rose bushes, manicured hedges, and flower beds. Finally it comes to an abrupt stop beside the stage, Teo manipulating his motorcycle like a stuntman. In an elegant, single move that feels like a flourish, he steps off the bike and pulls his helmet off, tossing his head to shake out his hair just for good measure. With a wry smile, he straightens a crease in his tuxedo blazer, and there's a sense of giggling relief among the guests. Trickles of laughter and claps, even a few whistles, as if they half-believe this was part of the night's entertainment.

It's not that they remember him—most of the crowd is completely different from the one at the barbecue—but there's something magnificent about him. The confident ease with which he now stands, as if gatecrashing a fancy fundraiser on the back of a Harley is just another Friday night for him. An ease that seems to compel all the waiters and guests to just laugh it off. I almost believe for a second that it's not actually him standing there, that this is all just a daydream, the effect of too many martinis and too much self-pity, but there he is.

In a tuxedo, no less—something I never thought I'd see him wear —and now carrying a small bouquet of flowers as tenderly as if it were a delicate bird. I see him whisper something to a waiter, who hurries off. As Teo scans the guests, I drink in the sight of him.

"Hey," left-guy's voice says behind me, "you still sitting here all by yourself? You don't want to—"

"Beat it," I say without looking at him, finally finding the tone and firmness that gets him to leave me alone.

Teo's eyes find mine, and we both smile. He moves toward me between the dancers, who seem to part for him. His large frame in that well-fitted tux seeming to emit some charismatic force field that clears the path between us.

I push my chair back as he rounds the table and stands in front of me, looking as impressed with me as I feel about him. We look at each for a few moments, as if adjusting once again to the energy between us, the intensity of the connection that always seems to exist —no matter how far apart we get.

"You're beautiful," he says.

I can feel myself blushing, and my eyes drop to the small bouquet in his hand. "What is that?"

"A corsage," he says. "For you."

"For me? What for?"

He takes a second to gaze at me again, now that I'm a little closer, and then brings the corsage to my hand, slipping the elastic over my wrist carefully. It's small and delicate, the colors complementing each other—it reminds me of one of his tattoos, and I have no doubt he chose every flower himself.

"Look, Ash. I didn't come here to fight or argue or force you to listen to excuses—I came here for the dance you still owe me."

I let out a small, surprised laugh.

"The dance I owe *you*?"

"Prom. I wanted it as much as you did."

He holds out his hand.

"Just this dance," he says.

I look from his eyes, to his hand, and take it. I lift out of my chair as if light as air, the fatigued loneliness of a few minutes ago gone now, replaced by a sense I'm the most elegant, beautiful woman in the room, convinced by his eyes.

He leads me toward the dance area, and I feel almost frightened at how easy it is to forget everything that went wrong between us when that face is so close, near enough to kiss. But then again, it doesn't even seem like the same Teo in that tux, holding my hand so gently, his hair neatly combed to one side.

The music stops, and then a few seconds later starts up again, and I let out that surprised little laugh once more.

We never really had a 'song,' but the one that's playing now is as close to one as we could get. A slow guitar ballad we'd listened to on repeat the months before prom, sitting at the lake with my head on his shoulder. I'm sure he asked them to play it, but I can almost believe the universe is willing things into place now.

"Shall we?" he says, and I nod, letting him lead me to the center of the patio.

There's a brief crackle of electricity between us, a single moment of dizziness as I recognize what's happening, that I'm dancing with the guy I left so determinedly, and at an event I wish I wasn't at, but it fades as soon as he clutches me to his body, and as soon as we start swaying in sync to the gentle beat.

It's just a dance, just my head on his chest, his arms around my waist, but it feels like a revelation. As if we could actually rewrite the past and make all of it never happen, as if this dance we never got to have might be the start of the future we always wanted.

I look up at him, and he kisses me, as softly as the first time. A fragile, lingering kiss the makes my entire body swell, the entire world contained in that meeting of the lips. I'm eighteen again, with my whole life ahead of me. A life with Teo.

But the song is over too quickly, the chords fading sadly. We sway a little longer and then Teo pulls back, my hands trailing down his arms as he separates his body from mine.

"Thank you," he says.

"What are you doing?" I say, as he steps back.

"I'm leaving."

"Why?"

"I don't want to ruin this moment."

I take a second to look at him, to see that he means it. A pain in his eyes. A guilt and shame behind the happiness of the dance.

"So take me with you," I say, and grab his hand to leave.

"Ash?" I hear Grace's tense voice call behind me.

I turn around and see my sister there, a question in her eyes. She glances from me to Teo, concerned and slightly confused.

"It's ok," I say, seeing my father begin to storm toward us from inside the hall. I plant a quick kiss on her cheek. "I'll explain later."

"Be safe," she calls after me.

We move quickly away, toward the motorcycle, and I mount it after him—grateful that I wore pants tonight instead of a dress. Teo buckles the helmet under my chin and then I grab onto him as he makes the bike rumble between our legs, then launches us forward, back into the dark flowers and trees. I think I almost hear my sister call behind me again, but I just want to be away from the hall now, away from all those people.

I squeeze his front, press my face into his shoulder, shielded from the wind by his broad back, watching the world turn into a blur, dream-like. We sweep through the city as if it were our playground, leaving cars and shops and palm trees behind, out onto the winding

Love & Ink

roads, up into the canyons. I start to wonder if Teo just wants to ride forever now—and I start to wonder if I would even mind.

We ride where the roads are empty, away from the oncoming evening lights, until the city sprawls out beside us, off into the distance and down below. The sky streaked with golden-lined clouds, the disappearing sun making the air around us cool and still.

24

ASH

Eventually, Teo slows down at a spot where there's nobody else, by the fence behind the Hollywood sign up in the hills. He slows to a stop, then kills the engine—making the silence around us suddenly intimate.

We get off the bike, but he barely lets me get away from him, pulling me close once again to kiss me long and slow.

This time, when we break apart, his face looks at me with devotion, eyes darkened with guilt, lips parted as if he's searching for the right words to express something so deep.

"You won't like what I have to tell you. But I owe you the truth," he says. "And you owe it to yourself to listen."

"Teo," I say, tensely. I can sense this isn't going to be good, and though I want to head it off, to bury it again, I know neither of us can bury anything anymore. "If this is about what happened at the barbecue—"

"It's about way more than that," Teo says, with a seriousness that grabs my attention.

I take a deep breath, bracing myself. I can see he's feeling that abstract pain that always rolled close to the surface, the pain that always threatened to eat him alive.

"I'm gonna tell you why I left that night," he says. "I'm gonna tell you everything. But I need you to trust me."

My body shudders at the words, at the prospect of finally hearing this. I can barely speak, careful not to say or do anything that might stop this moment from happening.

I nod.

"That night, prom," he begins, "I always meant to come. Always. Picked up the rental tux that afternoon, had a corsage waiting in the fridge. But something happened. I was putting that tux on—the one you helped me pick out. I remember it like yesterday. I ain't gonna lie, I was scared. Going back and seeing all those guys from school, with you on my arm. Scared in a good way, though. Scared like you when you're doing something awesome for the first time. Shit—I never tied a bowtie in my life, and I sure as shit wasn't getting it right then. But I was going anyway. I never considered backing out."

He stops himself and takes a deep breath.

"Then my dad came home drunk, hours before he said he'd be there. I wasn't expecting that—him coming home early, not the drunk part. Soon as he saw me he went wild, baiting me into a big argument."

"Why?"

Teo laughs sadly.

"Not like it was out of character. But...something about seeing me in that tux...I don't know. I thought about it a lot, and I think...I think he didn't like seeing me try to do something better. Didn't like the idea that I was trying to dress nice, to get a good girl, to live life a little better than him. Jealous, maybe. Or scared that he was gonna lose me —as weird as that sounds for a dad who treated me like shit.

"Anyway, he was spoiling for a fight, and I was already pent-up from all the shit going through my head that night, and we ended up getting into it. Bad. A real big one, maybe the biggest. Trashed half the trailer, blood all over us. He lost a tooth, I had a black eye for a month. Only reason we stopped was the police showed up and hauled our asses to jail. Some neighbor called the cops on us."

He pauses, as if to swallow down the bad memory. I put my hand on his arm, rub his tricep to let him know he's not alone.

"Maybe you remember, maybe you don't—but I was on probation at the time for all those graffiti and traffic tickets the cops loved giving me. It's not like my dad was gonna press charges, but still—it wasn't good. I was eighteen—no problem tossing me in for a long sentence now that I was an adult.

"So I sat there in that cell, thinking of what a fuck-up I was. How dumb I was to get into that fight, how I should have just walked away, got my ass out of that trailer and over to you. I thought about how I only ever seemed to realize my mistakes once I'd made them, and it was too late. That's when your dad showed up."

"My *dad*? At the station?"

Teo looks at me, then nods slowly.

I feel my confusion creasing my brow. "What was he doing there?"

"He knew about us, Ash. I don't know how, or when he found out, but he knew. And he didn't like it. He came into the cell and gave me this long speech about how I was going to fuck up your whole family. About how well Grace was doing on the city council, and how you were capable of doing great things in your future, but I was going to ruin everything."

I gasp, needing to look away and take a moment. My *dad*... And yet as much as I want to think there's something Teo got wrong, that maybe he misunderstood, I know—from both the look in Teo's eyes, and the things I've always tried to ignore about my father—that Teo's telling the truth.

"You ok?" he asks.

I nod and take a breath. "Yeah...yeah. Go on."

"He offered me a deal. Five grand to leave the city and never speak to you again." Teo pauses. "I told him to stick it up his ass. He said he could give me more, I asked him how much he could fit there. Then he got nasty. Told me if I didn't leave he'd make sure I did a full bid—ten years, no parole. I wanted to think he couldn't do that, that there was at least some justice in the system. But I know it would have been easy for him. Shit, he walked into that station like he owned it—and the chief treated him like a king.

"I told him that even if I did time, you'd wait for me. That he'd have a daughter visiting prison two times a week. He laughed at that, and said you wouldn't be his daughter anymore if that happened. He'd pull everything, he said. The scholarship, your car, your savings, everything he ever bought you. Said he'd rather you weren't his daughter at all than watch you become trailer trash like me."

"Fuck," I say, feeling like I'm about to vomit, shaking so much I have to lean back on the bike. I hold my head, trying to stop the feeling of being spun around.

Teo pushes some hair behind my ear, his cool hands the only thing that soothe some of the tension, his touch the only thing I can orient myself on.

"Go on," I say, determinedly.

Teo hesitates, just to be sure, before he continues.

"He gave me a few minutes to think about it. Left the cell. I was about as fucked up as I'd ever been, sitting there on that hard bunk, holding a blood-soaked tissue to my nose. I thought about you waiting there, on the corner like we planned. I never saw your dress, but I could imagine how beautiful you looked. In the moonlight, smiling as you waited. A person so perfect all the shit in the world couldn't touch them—shouldn't touch them.

"And there I was, in a dirty police cell. Blood all over my tux, bowtie choking me, barely able to look out of one eye, staring down a decade of prison time. Broken. It was pretty damned hard to deny what your dad was telling me—that I didn't deserve you, that I'd only drag you down. And that was that.

"I didn't take the money. But I let him bail me out so I could leave that night—just like he wanted. I thought it was what I wanted, too. To save you. I stopped home to change my clothes, pack a bag, and then rode out of there so fast the tears didn't leave tracks."

I grab him, hold him tight, as if afraid he's about to leave me again. Anger swirls through me, anger at my father, enough to wring his neck. It's drowned out only by the waves of shame, all the times I hated Teo, presumed and doubted him.

"I'm so sorry, Teo," I splutter desperately into his shoulder. "I'm sorry."

Teo laughs sadly again and rubs my back, firm and deep.

"*I'm* sorry," he says, pulling me away so he can look in my eyes again. "I never should have left you. I've regretted that night ever since."

"What choice did you have?"

"I could have told you. We could have kept it to ourselves again. Or I could have come back, written a letter, waited until you left home and got back in touch with you—but I did nothing. The longer I stayed away, the more I believed that I'd done right by you. I told myself that I didn't have a choice anyway, but not doing anything is sometimes the worst choice you can make."

"Teo, I—"

"I fucked up, Ash," he says, looking torn up. "Every second of those seven years that I didn't get back in touch...I just let the time pass. Hating your father, my father. Hating the world. Sometimes I even told myself it was your fault for not running away with me when I asked...but there's nobody to blame but myself. I fucked up—I'm still fucking up—and maybe that's proof that I still don't deserve you."

I let my head drop against his chest, feeling overwhelmed and dizzy again. I let myself catch my breath, let my thoughts settle. Teo strokes my hair, as if knowing I need a minute, patiently waiting.

"Hold up," I say, looking up at him suddenly. "Is that why you were arguing with my dad at the barbecue? Did he give you another ultimatum?"

Teo says nothing, just clenches his jaw, but it's all the affirmation I need.

"Fuck!" I shout, pulling away from Teo, my hands on my head. "Are you *kidding* me?"

"Ash..."

"Take me back there right now," I say, standing by the bike. "I need to talk to him."

"Ash, no. Wait a second."

I fumble in my pocket, so pissed that I drop my phone as I pull it out. I pick it up with shaking hands but before I can find my dad's number, Teo comes close and puts a hand on my arm, pushing it gently away. His other hand goes to my chin, lifting it so that I face him.

"That's not going to fix anything," he says calmly.

"The hell it will! My dad is the reason I suffered all those years. And he's *still* trying to control my life?"

"What are you gonna do?"

"I'm gonna tell him exactly what he made me go through!" I say, lifting the phone back up. "I'm gonna tell him to stay the hell out of my life!"

Teo pushes my arm down again.

"And then what? You fight and you fight. You end up hating each other, and nobody gets anywhere. Trust me, Ash, I know what I'm talking about."

Something about his eyes now holds me, keeps me from lifting my phone again.

"You can't fix your parents. You can spend your whole life blaming them, hating them, fighting them—but you'll never be happy."

I shake my head. "So what exactly am I supposed to do?"

Teo shrugs nonchalantly, smiling a little like we're just talking about a bad roll of dice.

"At some point you've just got to accept them the way they are. Even if they never really accepted you."

I stare at him for a few seconds, then breathe, nowhere else for the nerves to go. His answer diffusing the anger inside of me somehow, none of it mattering anyway now that we're together.

"You ok?" Teo asks.

I nod slowly.

"I think. My whole world just turned upside down, but...I think I am."

Teo looks at me like he's trying to decide between hugging me, comforting me, or kissing me. Then he makes up his mind.

"You can put the world right later," he says, as he grabs my hips and yanks them against his, half-smiling as he moves in for another kiss. "Let's put us right first."

Minutes later and we're back on his bike, our bodies throbbing and growling like the engine between us. My fingers tease between his shirt buttons, and I squeeze my thighs around his. Even the whip of the wind at this high speed not enough to stop my body from burning for him now, for that physical confirmation of us being one again. As if my body needs to learn what my mind already understands—that he's mine.

He takes us to my apartment because it's closer, and from the moment we get off the bike until we reach my door we can't keep off of each other. He takes my hand and spins me back up against a wall in the hallway so he can sink his tongue into my mouth, grind that thick cock into my hip, press those heavy pecs into my melting body. I moan loudly, my knees weak, not caring if the neighbors hear. When the elevator doors open I shove him back into it, hands desperate to unbutton his crisp white shirt, thighs sliding up against his legs until the hands cupping my ass are so frantic they're carrying me against him. An entirely different kind of prom dance, less a waltz and more like some red-blooded South American tango.

Half-drunk on the taste of each other's mouths, bodies twisting with desire for skin-on-skin, we stumble out of the elevator toward my apartment. I turn my back to him to get the door open and he wraps his arms around my front, hands rolling over my stomach, kneading my breasts through my shirt as he bites hungrily at the nape of my neck. Somehow I manage to fumble the keys out and unlock the door, pushing through as soon as it's open.

I turn around to see him watching me with eyes narrowed and on fire, trapping me in their intensity. He slams the door behind him without looking, then roughly tears off his tuxedo jacket and tosses it aside.

"Nobody drives me as wild as you do," he growls, as his eyes flick

Love & Ink 201

possessively down the length of my body, eyes so intense I can feel them, can read the intent, all the lustful thoughts behind them.

I smile a little and step toward him, then hook my fingers in the top of his belt.

"Good. Because I like it wild," I say, as I pull him by the belt backwards into the bedroom.

I sit back on the bed, his body broad and powerful before me. My eyes go from the bulge in his black tux trousers up to the hungry look on his face, and he responds by tearing his shirt the rest of the way off. It hangs loose, framing the taut muscles underneath. I'm thirsty for him, my nails scratching down the indentations of his abs like I'm deciphering them, feeling his hard muscles tremble beneath my touch. I need my mouth on him.

His fingers bury themselves in my hair as I tug off his belt, whipping it off and working his pants open. His cock is already stiff and thick in front of me, the veins pulsing with need. All I can think about is sucking it. I trail my fingertips along him softly as I drop to the floor and get on my knees, my mouth watering, ready for him. I lick the drop of pre-cum off the tip, enjoying his sharp intake of breath, the way his eyes narrow even more, the determined, muted groan that he can't help letting out.

"Ooh, you like that," I tease. "You want more?"

Instead of waiting for an answer, I lick him again as his hand grabs a fistful of my hair, as he fucks my mouth. I almost choke on the length of him, he's so big, the head ramming the back of my throat for a few short, quick thrusts, before he pulls out with a gasp. I remember this Teo. Aching for me but doing everything in his power to hold back, stay in control. I grin and lick my lips, making eye contact as I let the head of his cock roll over my tongue, taking my time as I slowly trace the underside of his shaft. Then I open wide and take all of him into my mouth. He groans, his body already swaying a little to the rhythm of my sucks and the pulse of his desire. I start to work him faster, increasing the pace, but he pushes hard into my throat again, impatient for me to deep throat him.

"Nuh-uh," I hum with my mouth around his cock. I ease up now, just to punish him for rushing, and then start back at the beginning with just the tip of my tongue lapping his head. I lick him all the way down to his balls and then back up again, keeping him there on the edge. Sucking softly and then harder, letting him thrust shallow and then deep into my mouth, alternating the pressure as I bob my head back and forth. He's pulling my hair hard now in his fist, sending tingles through my scalp and a wet throb through my pussy. I could do this for hours.

"Fuck...Ash..." he growls, like some powerful prayer. I smile with my eyes, then moan, long and low so he can feel the vibrations against his cock. He lets out a half-laugh half-sigh, his body too under my control for him to do anything else.

With one hand rolling up and down his wet shaft, making him pant with tense frustration, I use my other hand to undo my blouse. Then I let go of him just long enough to shrug out of my shirt and bra, listening to him sigh with pleasure.

"God, you're good," he gasps at the ceiling, before looking down at me again.

I sit back on the bed, smiling devilishly as I cup my breasts in my hands, knowing it drives him crazy, and then pull him toward me. I give his cock one last suck, then roll it from my lower lip, down my throat, down between my tits, listening to the way he murmurs and hums between his clenched jaw. I squeeze him between my tits, pushing them together to give the friction we both want.

"You like that?" I tease.

"Fuck yes," he groans, and he starts to thrust harder.

I arch my back and roll my soft tits around him.

"*Fuck yes,*" he repeats, locking eyes with me now.

He glares down at me with grim determination, his icy blue eyes boring into me as hard as the cock against my chest. Eyes that can't hide the unbearable longing in his body, the lust that goes almost soul-deep. I can hardly control myself.

"Fuck!" he roars, unable to bear it, unable to let me toy with him anymore.

In seconds Teo is straddling me, teasing my slit with his cock.

Love & Ink

"Fuck, you're wet," he groans. "I need to be inside you."

He pulls away from me, sucking my tits one at a time before trailing his mouth down my body. When he laps at my pussy, I'm already on the edge. He slips inside me, filling me up.

He thrusts into me and in no time, I'm so turned on I can feel myself clenching around him. He sucks my nipple into his mouth and I feel an electric pulse in my clit.

"Fuck," I moan.

He slams into me, so deep, hitting all the right spots. I'm grinding against him, faster, losing control, until I come so hard I see stars. Teo hugs me closer to him.

"Ash, you're so tight," he whispers, slowly pulling out of me.

I need him in my mouth.

"Come back," I say, motioning to my tits, and he moves back over me.

I open my mouth and let my tongue drop, lapping at the head of his cock. It tastes like us together. I knead my breasts around him as he slams forward and back, faster and harder, until I can feel the beating closeness of his orgasm.

So close I feel even the moment of hesitation, the second he starts pulling himself back like he's reining in some wild beast.

"Don't stop. I want you to come all over me," I say, almost a whisper, but it's enough.

His head thrown back, his front like some glorious statue of a Greek god above me, he comes over my tits, my chest, my neck. All that mental frustration, those days of pain, that longing for me, turned physical and exploded out of him. I watch the hard, beast-like tension of his body turn back into his normal relaxed swagger.

He leans down, elbows on either side of me, bringing his face to mine to kiss me softly and then pull back just to look at me. I bring my hand up to that sharp cheek, feeling the sweat under my palm, and he smiles back.

"You're mine," he tells me.

"I am."

25

TEO

I wake up in a strange place, with a sudden burst of dark, heart-sinking fear as I wonder if I just dreamt everything. Then the sound of clinking glasses draws me a little further awake. I realize I'm at Ash's place, and the fear disappears, replaced by the feeling of everything being right, balanced, peacefully blissful.

She comes into the room carrying a cup of coffee, and smiles when she sees me.

"Morning. I was just about to wake you," she says, putting the coffee on the stand beside me and sitting on the bed.

"Morning," I groan sleepily. "Where you going?"

She puts a hand on my naked chest, and I put my hand on hers, bringing it to my mouth to kiss her palm.

"Work," she says, smiling from the sensation, but her eyes down-turned at the subject. "Well, sort of. Pretty much the only reason I'm going in is to pack up all my things."

"Seriously?" I say. "We've barely had a chance to just...I don't know...*be* together."

"Yeah," she sighs. "Well, that's life. There's always something more important than the thing you actually *want* to do."

"I'm sure it won't take long," I soothe.

She laughs. "I'm sure it will. I've got plants there, ornaments, tons of giant art books I was using for inspiration. Paintings, photographs, this old camera collection I was starting—" She stops to laugh at herself cutely. "I've got this really bad habit of over-decorating, you know? Trying to make wherever I am feel interesting and comfortable."

"I noticed," I say, planting another kiss on her palm. "Look, I'll come and help. I can borrow Ginger's truck."

"What? No. I'll manage with my car."

"I'll take the truck," I insist. "We'll have it done in no time."

She looks at me, smiling at the gesture, but still unconvinced. Then she sighs regretfully.

"I don't know..." she says. "Thanks... But it might be weird, you being there...you know? Everybody seeing my boyfriend, Candace stomping around..."

"Who cares? You don't work there anymore. You think I could just laze around all day knowing that you're struggling to fit a bunch of potted plants in that tiny car of yours? Forget it."

She laughs easily now, looking at me with a sense of appreciation that compels me to draw her near and bury her in my embrace, under the covers, despite her laughing shrieks about how she'll be late.

After meeting Ginger at Mandala, where he hands over the truck with a big grin and a fist bump, we head on over to Ash's workplace on the studio lot and go on up to her office. She's a little on edge, glancing around her, shying away a little when she exchanges some hellos in the lobby. No amount of subversive ass pats or whispered assurances seems to relax her. I wonder if it's having me there, the possibility of facing Candace or Carlos again, or just the general unease of leaving all this behind, her job, her colleagues. A confirmation that she's finally giving it all up for an unknown.

"Don't look so worried," I tell her in the elevator, rubbing a hand across her back, folded boxes under my other arm, "we'll be done before you know it."

She nods and purses her lips, trying to smile for me.

We step through her sleek office, past desks where well-dressed, stressed-looking women and conversely laid-back looking guys hunch over laptops, then go into her office.

"You weren't kidding," I say, as I look around the small room. Glass figurines and old cameras line bookshelves of books big and heavy enough to tile a patio, the potted plants are more like small trees, and there are several large posters up on the walls. It makes the rest of the office seem like a call center by comparison.

Ash shrugs and shoots me an apologetic look. I half-smile back and start unfolding the boxes to show I don't mind.

As we slowly get into the rhythm of filling the boxes up, Ash directing me on what to put inside, there's a knock at the door.

"Ash? Oh, God, it's really happening..." the girl with the grey-blue hair says as she steps inside, looking tangibly sad.

She notices me suddenly. "Oh, hey," she says.

"Jenny? Is it?" I say.

"Yeah," she says, looking pretty happy I remembered her name, then turning back to Ash.

They embrace warmly, then break apart with sad, longing looks on their faces.

"Don't..." Ash says, as she gets back to packing. "I don't want to cry or anything."

Jenny laughs, but I can hear in it that she's close to tears as well.

"This place is going to fall apart without you," she says. "We've already had to rerun a bunch of old segments the past few days. Ugh...don't leave me."

Ash crumples up some newspaper to wrap a glass figurine in.

"We'll still be seeing plenty of each other, you can be sure of that," she says, placing it carefully in a box. "And you know what? Soon enough they'll hire somebody else to come in here and do way more work than their salary's worth. Everything's going to be fine."

"Yeah," Jenny says, rolling her eyes, "I'm sure Candace has an equally obnoxious nephew somewhere, or a young meathead that she's got a crush on. Anyway, I wish I could help, but I've got a script to write—Carlos needs something to butcher for the big interview tonight."

We say our goodbyes, Ash and Jenny arranging to go for drinks over the weekend, and then Jenny leaves.

"What's this 'big interview'?" I ask Ash.

"The show's going out on a really great slot tomorrow—minutes after some big season finale of a TV show. We usually put a big segment up when we know we'll get a lot of viewers like that, and Candace managed to arrange an interview with some actor. Though Carlos isn't that great at interviews—it'll basically be a fifteen minute advertisement for his new B-movie."

"I see."

We continue packing for a while, and I start bringing some of those gigantic potted plants down to the car, tying them up with bungee cords in the back and covering them with plastic so they don't make a mess. When I get back upstairs for the next few boxes, Ash is talking with a meek-looking bald guy who looks like Santa Claus if he worked in the tech industry.

"Teo," she says, spotting me over his shoulder, "this is Sean. He's an executive producer on the show."

"Hey," I say, shaking his hand and quietly judging his expression, trying to determine if he's one of the bad ones.

"I was just telling Ash," he says, looking a little frightened of me, "that we're really going to miss her. I've been keeping my ears open for anything else she might be good for—" he turns back toward Ash "and if you're still available, I might be able to—"

"Thanks, Sean," Ash says, seeming genuine. "I appreciate it. And yes, go ahead and let me know if you hear anything—for now at least, I'm still unemployed."

Sean looks sad for a moment, before perking up and pulling something from his blazer pocket.

"I got you something. Nothing big—I'm not very good at gifts, but I wanted to at least try."

He hands Ash the envelope and she flashes him a smile before opening it. She pulls out the card, reads it, then examines the small slip of paper inside with a growing smile.

Sean looks pleased. "It's a VIP certificate for *Knife*. I remember you saying you wanted to go when they changed up the menu but you thought it was too expensive, and you couldn't get reservations anyway."

"Oh Sean, this is fantastic, thank you."

"It's for two, so you can take Teo," he says, looking at me. "I mean, whatever you want, it's up to you."

Ash sees his awkwardness and side-hugs him warmly, like he's a favorite uncle, and then there's another knock on the open door.

"Hi," the man says, grinning from ear to ear. "Just wanted to say goodbye."

I recognize him from TV, but it's still a little weird to see him in real life. There's a glossy smarminess to him, an aura of smug superiority, that on television just seems to go with the territory, but which I always assumed was just for the camera. Seeing him in front of me, though, only seems to exaggerate it to unbearable levels. The guy looks at me like I'm a camera, talks as if he's reading from a script, and acts like all eyes are on him.

"Hey," Ash says, and I can hear in the low pitch of her voice she feels the same way I do. "Um, Carlos, this is Teo. My boyfriend."

"Nice to meet you," he says, offering his hand and standing up straighter, as if feeling a little threatened.

I take his hand firmly, staring blankly at his smile. When he winces and tries to pull his hand back, I just grip it even tighter.

"You're the reason Ash is getting fired, right?" I say.

He lets out a snorted laugh of shock, a quick glance around to see if anyone else is surprised, but still I don't let go, staring at his face as if trying to see behind it.

"Teo..." Ash says, sounding concerned, and finally I let go of the guy's hand.

He laughs, shaking out his hand a little, and though he tries to act casual I can see that he's rattled.

Love & Ink 209

"Well, I should go prepare for the big interview. Hopefully we'll speak again before you go," he says insincerely, then disappears quickly.

I look at Ash, who glares at me reproachfully.

"What? I was just being friendly," I say, spreading my hands.

Sean's phone rings and he gains an air of urgency as soon as he looks at it.

"Excuse me," he says, already marching out of the office. "I have to take this."

"Sure thing," Ash says.

I look to her and shrug.

"Seems like a nice enough guy."

"Yeah, he is," she says, glancing down at the gift. "Maybe *too* nice, actually."

We continue packing for a few more minutes until Jenny runs into the doorway, having to stop herself by grabbing onto the frame. She looks a little flustered and panicked.

"What's wrong?" Ash asks quickly, while the writer catches her breath.

Jenny glances back over the bullpen, sees something, then comes inside.

"Brace yourself," she says, in a tense voice.

"What?"

The explanation comes in the form of Candace, her face twisted with rage, the glowing screen of her giant smartphone held out in front of her like some crucifix ward. She steps inside the office looking like she's ready to explode and kill us all.

"So *this* is your idea of not telling anybody, is it?" she hisses at Ash. "Couldn't resist getting a little revenge, could you?"

"Hey!" I snarl bristling at the way she's speaking to Ash, but apart from casting a brief, disgusted scowl in my direction, Candace loses none of her anger.

"If you think for one second there won't be consequences for this—"

"For what?" Ash asks.

Candace seethes. "Oh, please! Let's skip the 'playing dumb' part, shall we?"

"I'm serious," Ash says, with a look of sincere confusion that nobody could mistake for an act. "I honestly don't know what you're talking about."

Candace thrusts her phone screen at Ash, but before Ash can even read it she pulls it back to read aloud herself.

"Hollywood Night *goes from reporting on sensational affairs to engaging in them, as details emerge of the married host, Carlos King, having a long-term affair with an executive producer on the show.*"

Ash's jaw drops open, but Candace doesn't take the hint, and snorts scornfully.

"You couldn't help yourself, could you?" Candace says. "Do you know what you've just done?"

"I swear to you, Candace. I didn't say anything to the press."

I see Carlos rush past the door, scanning the office, then notice us all inside. He comes in and covers his mouth, realizing even further that the cat's out of the bag.

"*Really*?" Candace says, still spoiling for a fight. "You expect me to believe that? If it wasn't you, who was it then? You're retaliating because you got fired! And this is all *lies*. So if you think I'm not gonna have the company lawyers so far up your ass that you—"

"Honestly, Candace," Jenny interrupts, "it could have been *anyone*. It's not like it was a secret. The whole office knows—anyone who's had anything to do with the show must have known. It could be any one of the actors or celebrities who we've reported on in the past, who holds a grudge, maybe, or..."

"Maybe it was your wife," I say, looking at Carlos, but the guy's too stunned to do more than stare at me with shock.

There are a few moments of tension, focused on the space between Candace and Ash, as if waiting for one of them to break. It's only when Sean comes in, shoving his phone in his pocket and looking about as authoritative as he ever could, that it breaks.

"You're all here?" he says, suddenly noticing the group that's gathered in Ash's old office. "I take it you all know, then?"

Love & Ink

"It's on fucking *TrendBlend*," Candace jeers. "Everybody knows."

"Well," Sean continues, "I just got off the phone with the network. I'm afraid they want to let go of both of you." He looks from Candace to Carlos. "Immediately. They want to release a statement within the next few hours, so. I'm really sorry, Candace. Carlos. It's been a good run."

Sean offers his hand to Candace but she slaps it away petulantly.

"You are all absolute amateurs," she says, scanning all of us. "I should be glad I'm done here."

She spins on her heel and marches out of the office, shoving past Carlos, who still has a hand to his mouth. His typically-tanned face so pale now that he looks almost monochrome.

He breathes deeply, casting desperate eyes over all of us, then reaches for his phone.

"I need to call my agent," he says, his voice quivering. "And my wife. Lord have mercy." Already typing frantically on his phone as he rushes away.

For a few moments we stand there in silence, nothing moving but our eyes as we look at each other for what's coming next. It feels like the eye of the storm.

"Ash," Sean says, pulling her attention away from the open door. "I know this is rather sudden...but...well—"

"You want me to stay?"

Sean nods like a begging dog.

"Very much so. If you'll consider it, we can discuss a pay raise, giving you more control—"

"What kind of control?" she says. "Will I only have control over certain segments, or the whole show? And what about the scripts? Hiring?"

"Well," Sean stammers, "with Candace gone, I'd like to promote you to EP, pass all her duties over to you. I spoke to the network already and they seemed open to you taking her position, so if you still want to shake things up a bit, now seems like the right time..."

Ash glances at me once again, then back at Sean. She offers her hand.

"Deal," she says.

Sean shakes it, but he doesn't seem quite that relaxed yet.

"I suppose it's just you and me as producers now," Sean says, sounding adrift.

Ash smiles reassuringly. "It always was, in a sense."

Sean looks around the floor, wringing his hands a little.

"Well, I suppose there's a lot to go through...but the most pressing thing is that we've just lost our headline segment for one of the best slots we've had in months."

"Can't we still conduct the interview with Ray Bell?" Jenny asks.

Sean shakes his head.

"I doubt it. We only got him because he's friends with Candace—and I would put money on her telling him to stay clear of us."

"So we're screwed now?" Jenny says.

"What about the stuff you've been filming?" I ask, turning toward Ash.

She sighs heavily and says, "No. Nothing's ready. I'm still waiting to hear back from the celebrities. Without them I don't have anything good enough for the slot."

Another few seconds of silence pass, and then I say, "I can get you someone."

"You?" Sean says.

"Uh-huh. You guys familiar with Eli Compton?"

Jenny makes a sound like she just got punched in the gut.

"*Eli Compton*? *The* Eli Compton? There are probably isolationist monks in Tibet who've heard of him."

I shrug. "Well anyway, I can probably get you an interview with him."

"No chance," Jenny scoffs. "Eli Compton doesn't talk to anyone."

"He talks to me," I say. "He's coming in for a tattoo tomorrow—private one, but I can get him to do it tonight, no problem."

"But," Sean says, "how would you get him to actually *talk* to us? For an interview."

"Eli trusts me," I assure him. "We go way back. I can get him to do an interview."

Love & Ink

"Even if you could," Sean says, "we've lost Carlos. And we don't have a backup."

"Sure we do," Ash says, turning toward her friend. "Jenny could do it."

Jenny straightens her back like she's up against a wall.

"Jenny?" Sean says, looking at her as if seeing her for the first time. "Staff writer Jenny?"

Ash grins. "Trust me on this, Sean. It's my first decision as EP. You're up for it, aren't you?"

Jenny gulps, and her chest visibly starts to rise and fall deeply.

"Sure," she says slowly. "Everything else is going crazy today, so why not?"

"Ok." Sean nods grimly. "Trial by fire, then. Let's get you to hair and makeup."

Jenny lets out an excited little squeal and throws her arms around Ash before they both run out the door, leaving me to follow behind them with an amused smile on my face. Guess today's gonna turn out alright after all.

26

ASH

Teo makes the call and gets the ok from Eli for the interview. Even though I don't really believe it, and fully expect Eli to back out or kick us out of the shop when he realizes what he's actually agreed to, I start putting everything in place, directing the whole office and the production department to prepare.

Teo loads the stuff from Ginger's truck back into my office, and then starts taking down some of the equipment to bring to Mandala for the filming. Since Mandala isn't big, I decide to take just a single light kit, a skeleton crew, and one trusty cameraman (Vince) with me (as well as Jenny, of course), and then settle in for a brief meeting with Jenny and the other writers in order to go over some of the stories buzzing around about Eli, and potential questions to throw at him.

Time flies, and before I realize it the work day has gone by in a blur of fast meetings and logistical preparations. Even though the tattoo is arranged for shortly before midnight, when Mandala is closed to the public and the last drifters will probably be gone, the decisive moment speeds toward us with a sense of forceful inevitability.

At around ten in the evening, with Vince and Teo already waiting at Mandala, the crew setting up light, sound, and camera equipment,

Love & Ink   215

I finally head downstairs with Jenny to get in my car. As we sit at some lights, I watch her stare ahead with a dazed look on her face, arms folded, lip-biting and jogging her heels.

"Don't be nervous," I say, putting a hand on her shoulder.

Jenny looks at me like I surprised her and exhales loudly.

"I feel like I'm tripping balls right now. This is a crazy way to start a new career."

"He's just a guy, and this is just a conversation. And I can do amazing things in the edit bay, so don't worry about screwing up. Just be your usual badass self, ok?"

Jenny exhales heavily again.

"I just can't help thinking...this is such a scoop. There are, like, a thousand ways this could end in disaster. What if I ask something too personal and he walks out? Or I piss him off and he won't let us air the interview? Or if I just can't get anything interesting out of him?"

"Just relax and start talking—you have time. The tattoo will take hours. Think of it like meeting someone new, someone interesting."

Jenny tries to smile, but it looks more like a puppy dog face, and I laugh.

"You've got way too much confidence in someone who's never done an interview before," she says.

"I've got a lot of confidence in *you*."

Eli Compton came from Australia in his twenties, and began his career in action movies. Tall, muscular, absurdly good looking, and with a powerful, gravelly voice that only emphasized his powerful stare. Typecast as the strong, silent type, his name became synonymous with brutal heroes bordering on the psychopathic. He looked and sounded tough enough for audiences to actually believe he could kick several asses without getting hit. You knew what you were getting with an Eli Compton movie. War films, ex-cops dragged back into the fray, astronauts who risked their own lives to save the crew, and TV interviews where he'd scowl and smirk at the interviewer like he knew something they didn't.

While his blockbuster action flicks were guaranteed hits, Eli began working with some more esoteric directors on the side.

Quirkier, more subdued films in which he displayed a range of emotion that was almost an affront to the audiences who loved him as the emotionally-stunted ass kicker they secretly wished they could be. In response, he grew reclusive, started making films fewer and farther between, attaining cult status practically overnight and racking up critical acclaim and awards twice as fast.

But despite being one of the biggest stars around, Eli rarely sits for interviews—even for promotional purposes. And when he does, they're usually strict affairs. The only thing most people know about Eli is that despite his genius IQ and incredible talent, he has a temper, a short fuse, and is very low on patience. Stories abound of him walking off sets or disappearing midway through Hollywood meetings, or cursing at interviewers he deemed not up to scratch. So even though I'm encouraging Jenny as much as possible, I know her fears aren't unfounded.

As soon as we get to Mandala, we rush about in the cramped space to finalize the set-up. Vince and I go over camera angles while the crew finishes up the last touches on the sound and lighting. Meanwhile, Teo arranges his tattooing equipment and Jenny sits in a couch as a young hipster from the hair and make-up department puts a braid in her blue hair that reveals the line of studs running up the outline of her ear.

When Eli arrives, it isn't with the large entourage that we're expecting, but alone. Casually, he steps inside the back room and greets Teo warmly.

"Hey mate," he says, with his Melbourne drawl, clasping hands and pulling him in for a hug. "Long time no see."

He's bigger and more handsome than even the big screen makes him look, effusing a powerful charisma that makes the world around him seem like merely a stage.

"You good?" Teo asks him.

"Great," Eli says, then turns his eyes from Teo across to the rest of us, the way I've seen him do to a thousand bad guys in films.

"What the hell did I let you talk me into," he mutters, shaking his head.

Teo laughs, slaps Eli on the back, and gestures toward me. "This is Ash, who I've told you about. She's the one running this whole thing."

"Hi, Eli," I say, stepping forward decisively. "Thank you very much for agreeing to do this interview."

The actor shakes my hand, silent for a second as he holds my gaze.

"Yeah, well, I've got no problem talking. There's just usually nobody worth talking to. If Teo says you're cool though, I trust him." He scans the tattoo chair. "Anyway, doing it like this—kinda interesting. And who's gonna be grilling me, did you say?"

"Um. Me. I'm Jenny," she says, blushing a little as she steps forward to shake his hand. "I'll be doing the interview."

Once again Eli takes a second to look at her before speaking.

"I like your hair," he says, and they share a warm moment that I know everyone in the entire room can feel. It's in that instant that I know this is going to be sensational.

The interview goes like a dream, so good that I panic at several moments, making sure we're getting it on tape, making sure the mics are picking it all up, convinced a last minute Hail Mary couldn't actually be this good. Visually it's amazing, Teo etching the eagle onto Eli's chest while he tells the real story of why he walked off the set of his last blockbuster film and never looked back—something people have speculated about for years, but that he's never come close to opening up about. The close, intimate surroundings of the shop making it feel almost cinematic, Eli displaying both vulnerability and strength, a complexity that most directors spend a lifetime failing to capture.

It's difficult to even remember Jenny being nervous now, as she talks with Eli confidently, so that the interview feels less like one, and more like being a fly on the wall at a late-night conversation between two old friends. She makes him laugh, asks questions that he has to think about, trades quips, and compels all kinds of emotions and stories out of him.

We're a million miles from the PR-prepped, pre-scripted interview-cum-advertisements of *Hollywood Night*, now. There's something unique and magical in the air, and every single one of us can feel it, and just lets it happen. Almost everything Eli says feels like a secret—important and insightful.

Even Teo gets in on the act, bringing the whole crew to hysterics as he tells Jenny the story of how he and Eli first met while skiing in Germany, both of them falling down almost an entire black diamond trail after Eli tried to pull off some insane stunt turn, all the while cursing the air blue at each other the whole way down. They ended up spending the rest of the afternoon drinking the pain of their bruises away in a beer hall and finding out they actually had a lot in common.

Most of all, though, Eli opens up in a way that's rare for any actor —least of all the most infamously guarded one.

"Hollywood needs you to act off-screen just as much as on it... If you pretend to be someone long enough, you start to forget who you were in the first place..." This is gold.

The interview only ends when Teo finishes the tattoo, and even then Jenny and Eli continue on for another quarter-hour after Jenny's made her final remarks and the cameras have turned off.

At around four in the morning, Eli leaves, embracing all of us warmly, and taking his time over goodbyes. In particular Jenny, whom he pulls aside to have a private word with before leaving, whispering something in her ear that has her blushing all over again. Vince rounds up the crew and they break everything down and then take the equipment back to the studio, and Teo cleans up at Mandala, leaving Jenny and me outside, breathing in the cool air and trying to regain some sense of reality, still coming down from the high of what just happened.

"God..."

"I know..."

I turn to her with a sly smile. "What did Eli say to you? When he was leaving?"

"Oh, nothing..." she says casually. "He just invited me out for coffee."

"Seriously?!" I grab Jenny by the shoulders and we just laugh.

"What was that, two hours?" she asks.

"Nearly three."

"I don't know how you're going to edit that down to fifteen minutes."

"I'm not," I say. "I'm gonna run it for the whole hour of the show."

"What?" Jenny says, dubiously. "They'll never allow it."

"Who's 'they'? The show's mine now." I put my arm around her shoulder and pull her in for a buddy-hug. "Ours."

Three days after the interview airs, people are still talking about it. About Eli's charisma, about where the hell Jenny came from, about how *Hollywood Night* is so much better than they'd previously thought. The Candace-Carlos story is old news now—but it couldn't have come at a better time, the scandal bringing in even more new viewers for the show. The network decides to air the interview again at a primetime slot on the weekend, and numerous shows and blogs are now approaching Jenny herself for an interview. Teo half-jokingly complains about how many new people are now coming into his shop for tattoos, and I keep a running list of the dozen or so actors virtually begging me to be interviewed by *Hollywood Night*, hoping to emulate the organic, open charm that Eli gave off.

Jenny even meets Eli for drinks a few times before he jets off to Europe to do an indie film with a hot new avant-garde director, and she tells me that Eli said as soon as the interview aired, he was offered more roles than he had even before he first broke out.

Somehow I even find it in me to talk to Grace about what happened, about my father and Teo, about the past and all the things that still hurt to think about. We spend hours on the phone, Grace sympathizing, and struggling to believe it about our own father almost as much as I do. I tell her I'm done, that I don't ever want to see him again, but Grace resolves to fix things, to talk to him, to bring our family back together again. Ever the diplomat.

But even all of that seems unimportant, incidental. The real news happens on a Sunday morning, when Teo, Duke and I are finishing off a run at Runyon Canyon.

I rub Duke under his chin, making him waggle his tail and get a funny kind of loose-lipped, toothy smile when I do.

"Should we stop at a store on the way back and get some dog food?" I say, pulling faces at Duke. "Since you're both probably coming back to mine."

"I have some at my place," Teo says.

I glance up at him.

"No offense, but that's pretty much all you have. I don't think I can handle another lunch of beer and whatever frozen burritos you picked up at the mini-mart."

Teo laughs as I stand up in front of him.

"How would you feel about fixing that?"

"Fixing what?"

Teo looks away like he's struggling with something, then speaks slowly, as if having to reach for the words.

"I was just thinking... With you staying over all the time, you're hardly ever at the place you're renting...and me with this big, empty luxury condo that I don't even know what to do with... I mean...it kinda seems a little silly, right?"

I shoot him a playful look.

"You're asking me to move in with you?"

"What would you think if I was?"

I laugh gently.

"You sure? Think you can stand a woman's touch? Fresh flowers on the kitchen table, framed photos in the hallway, *throws*. I always kinda figured you liked having your own space. Lone wolf, fortress of solitude, all that."

Teo half-smiles but he puts his hands around my waist and pulls our sweaty, sun-soaked bodies together, and I know he's serious.

Love & Ink

"Yeah, fuck all that," he says. "I don't just want you—I want *you*. Everything. I want to live somewhere that feels like you even when you're not around. I wanna come home to you, have you come home to me. I wanna make a *home*." He pauses, but only to kiss me softly for a second. "I can't promise I'll be good at it—shit, I ain't had much practice—but I want it more than anything, and I want it with you. In fact, if you want, we can go shopping for throws together."

I gaze up at him, squinting a little in the sun.

"How can I refuse an offer like that?"

27

TEO

It's a kind of magic, what Ash does for me, and it makes everything that came before seem irrelevant, so long ago, as if it were only half a life, a preparation for her.

Even my dad can't get to me anymore. He calls me from a payphone in Arizona, and I almost don't recognize him for the fragility and humility in his voice. Even more so when I tell him about me and Ash. He doesn't say much, and I can tell he wants to ask for help but doesn't know how. Once we get off the phone I tell Ash, and she somehow convinces me to try and help him, repeating my own words back to me, *you can't fix your parents, and at some point you've just got to accept them.*

Before she even starts moving her things over, Ash has me painting the house with her, turning the anonymous grey siding different shades of duck blue, mint green, and pastel red. Then, after a lot of cute begging, I finally give in and allow her to convince me to put my artistic talent to good use and paint a couple of murals. Moonlit trees against one wall of the bedroom, a watercolor landscape in the breakfast nook, a flock of birds in the bathroom.

The place starts to fill up as she brings over her stuff, and buys plenty more. Furniture and ornaments, newer, more stylish appliances for the kitchen and lounge chairs in the yard. For a while I freak out a little, start getting uncomfortable, as if the place isn't mine anymore, as if a place this alive and stimulating couldn't possibly be my own. Then Ash does something amazing.

It's an off-hand suggestion. One I made while we were drifting away in bed, to the smell of paint and freshly bought flowers, the moon visible beyond the windows at the foot of the bed, beyond our heavy eyelids. I'd always wanted my own place to make art.

When I get home from work at the end of the week, the spare room has been transformed into an art studio. I'd almost forgotten the spare room—a locked door I never opened. But it's perfect, with those big windows facing the Pacific Ocean. Ash covers my eyes and leads me there, pulling her hands away so I can take in the canvases against the wall, the work bench stacked with paints and brushes. A chaise-lounge for portraits, stools and stands. She even got Ginger and Kayla in on it, to come and help tear up the carpet and put hard flooring down, with shelves along the walls for any other art supplies I want to add to the mix. I make love to her right then, up against the window, unable to express how much it means to me in words alone.

But it's not just the objects and colors—it's as if the place has a soul now. The record player always turning, spilling our favorite music through every room, the smell of pasta sauce simmering in the kitchen, and more than anything, the sound of other people stopping in, of family coming over to visit. Jenny starts dropping by for brunch on the weekends—bringing Eli with her every once in a while. Barbecues with Kayla, talking about how she's finally planning to go back to Seattle and start her own tattoo shop, where Ginger and I finally build Duke that kennel in the yard, taking way longer than we should over it because it's kinda fun. Isabel crashes when she's in L.A. for a weekend and plays some songs as Ash and I watch from the couch. It's almost perfect.

Almost...but there's still one thing we need to get around to.

"You ready?" I say, taking Ash's hand as I get off the bike and lead her through the back door of Mandala.

"No," she says. "I think waiting so long's just made me more nervous."

We move through the shop to the chairs and I turn to the table to get my equipment ready.

"What do I do?" Ash asks, as she settles in one of the chairs.

"Take your shirt off and try to relax," I say, then look back over my shoulder. "I can help with the shirt if you'd like."

Ash laughs.

"I can manage."

Gloves on, everything ready, I move the wheeled stool beside her and start preparing her arm. I glance up and find her looking at me with a little trepidation in her eyes, and surprise her by darting in for a kiss. Then I begin.

Ash and I have spent hours talking it over, and this time, this is what we've come up with: A blooming purple nightshade. Her mother's favorite flower—the one her garden had always been full of, the kind Ash would help her plant, the kind Ash *still* plants wherever she lives to remind her of her mother.

After completing the outline, the familiar soothing buzz of the needle cutting through the tracks of Ash's favorite album set up on my mp3 player, I take a break to let her see my work and to ask how she's feeling.

"It's looks amazing," she says, settling a little. "And I'm fine. Go on."

"Just tell me if you start getting uncomfortable."

She looks up at the ceiling again and I continue, filling in the details, finalizing lines, taking my time over the shading.

"You know," she says, when I'm pretty much done, adding a few last touches to set it off just right, "I didn't realize getting a tattoo was so intimate."

I laugh gently. Moving my head back to look at the tattoo and see if it needs anything else.

"Uh-huh. You've got to trust someone completely."

Love & Ink

"And I do," she says.

I kiss her slow and deep, then pull away and gesture to her arm. "You're done."

Comfortable enough to take her eyes from the ceiling now and look at the finished tattoo, adjusting her arm as I clean up my equipment and look for the ointment. She casts a smile in my direction and says, "Is that why you like them? You like feeling that trust?"

I lean back to her arm, dabbing a little. She hisses through her teeth gently.

"Not really."

"What is it then?" she asks.

I take off my gloves and look at her directly.

"I've thought about that a lot. It's the permanence. I think...you get a tattoo and it lasts forever. A single moment in time—a decision, a memory or a feeling, or some version of who you are or what you stand for—and you make it something eternal. You force yourself to live with it, to see it when you look in the mirror, to stick to you like a shadow." Ash smiles at me, and the air between us seems to cloud, dream-like and ethereal.

"Humans...there's not much about us that's permanent, you know? We break promises, we change our minds, life throws you curveballs... So the idea of taking something, something you weren't born with, an expression of yourself, something or someone you love, a decision you made, and turning it into something that endures...I think that's rare. Unique. Something only tattoos really do..."

She's glowing now, face soft as if exposing herself, a tenderness in both of us connecting. I reach into my pocket for the small box I've carried around for days.

"Well," I say, getting up off the stool and down on one knee in front of the chair, "tattoos, and maybe one other thing."

Ash gasps and sits upright on the end of the chair now, hands covering her mouth, eyes wide.

"Marry me, Ash. I want to make this happiness as permanent as anything. I want you in my life for eternity."

I flip the box open, revealing the white gold custom ring I

designed, inset with a halo of diamonds surrounding the shiniest, most light-catching version of her birthstone I could find in the city.

She lets out an involuntary sob behind her hands, then shrieks a 'yes,' and leaps off the chair at me. I stand up just enough to catch her embrace.

"Ow!" she wails, remembering the tattoo, then laughs.

"You ok?"

"Yeah," she says, voice still wavering with shock.

I take her hand and slowly slide the ring onto her finger as she watches in wonder.

"Always a little pain at the start of something beautiful," I say, and she raises her eyes from the ring to my face.

We kiss, and it feels as good as the first time, as good as any other, as good as it'll be until we're old together. A kind of perfection that was meant to be, that even the universe seems to want.

Me and Ash. A love so strong nothing could tear it apart. Not the mistakes I made, not the years we spent apart, the parents who didn't want us together, or the fact that we came from different sides of the tracks. All of it just obstacles, just a bumpy road that was always going to lead us here.

Us against the world.

EPILOGUE

ASH

It's a small, well-kept farmhouse in northern California. So clean and white it seems to glow in the sun, the walls broken by giant oak beams. Around it the fields are a verdant green, lilting softly, the hills undulating like a calm ocean. A few big, powerful horses grazing contentedly among them, and the smell of coastal pines and cedar and lavender intoxicating to the point where you really feel like it might all just be a dream.

I know the place as well as anyone—I picked it, and spent months preparing it, but here and now, in the back of my father's classic Rolls Royce, it feels like I'm heading into a place unknown.

I turn to look at him, and find that he's already looking at me with that subtle, proud smile he's had all morning.

"You look beautiful," he says, for the twentieth time today.

I look down bashfully at the bouquet in my hands.

It was rough at the start. Real bad. Knowing what my dad had done, and confronting him about it was hard and messy. I filled Grace's house with shouted rage, and though my father had some shame when I articulated how betrayed and disrespected I felt at what he had done, he still stood his ground firmly. He told me everything Teo had—that I was meant for so much more, that he couldn't in good faith accept Teo.

I was ready to cut the cord, to remove my father from my life entirely. And then Teo did something amazing. He told me not to blame my dad, that he was only doing what he thought was best for me, that it was from a place of love that my father had done all these terrible things to us. He came with me to see him once again, and as we spoke—Teo calm and confident, my dad sounding petulant and arrogant in comparison—we somehow managed to gain some peace, a first building block toward a proper relationship, toward where we are now.

"Here we are," my dad says, sounding about as anxious as I feel.

He steps out and comes to my side of the car, opening the door and offering his hand. I take it and step out onto the carpet, laid out on the grass, lavender and rose petals scattered across it. It goes all the way up between the rows of chairs, the guests turning to look at me, all the way up to the wooden, canopied arbor, decorated with sunflowers and orange marigolds, where the man I love stands nobly.

Isabel starts playing, plucking on the country guitar in her bridesmaid's dress. An old, soft ballad Teo and I had listened to in the woods, a song I used to play to remind me of him, a song he told me he played to remember me. I take my father's arm, and start to walk.

I hear some gasps and murmurs, and turn to look at faces I've never seen so earnestly kind. When I finally get to the arched arbor, I barely have time to acknowledge the others, Kayla, Grace, Ginger, Jenny—it's like I can't pull my eyes from Teo. In his suit, and with his face so free of sadness, it's almost like seeing him for the first time, and I can't bear even to look at the minister as he speaks. Teo takes my hands and we look at each other, frozen in perfection.

Duke barks from Ginger's side and there's good-natured laughter, then the minister continues, and finally asks the question.

"I do," Teo says, in that strong, confident voice, loud enough for everyone to hear.

Again.

Love & Ink 229

"I do," I say, whispering it meaningfully, just for Teo.

Teo's dad steps forward, bearing the rings on a small white cushion. He looks good now, since he's been going to the rehab Teo arranged for him. Clean shaven and nicely-dressed, you can see where Teo got his looks from. He sniffs a little, wipes an eye, then holds the rings toward us. We take them and place them on each other's fingers, then don't even wait for the minister to say it. Teo pulls me into his lips, into a kiss that feels like it could last a thousand years. I barely hear the whistles and applause, so lost in this moment with the man I love, will always love.

The reception passes by in a blur of happiness and excitement. Everything people say to me, to us, a compliment, a congratulation, a best wish. Praise for choosing this rustic farmhouse, filling it with candles in jars, fairy lights wound around the beams, fresh flowers tied to the chairs, the dark, triple-tiered gateaux. I almost feel guilty for accepting it, as if I wasn't the one who organized the wedding, as if I'm somebody else now.

And after the dancing and drinking, the joy and the elation, Teo emerges to take my hand, and I notice that everybody is looking at us, parting for us. He leads me to the door, almost running as petals cascade upon us, all the way outside, into the open door of the Rolls Royce, where we collapse into each other, kissing and laughing. We stop only to look back and wave at the disappearing crowd as the car pulls away.

In his arms I gaze up at him, smiling so hard I wonder if I'll ever manage to stop.

"I don't know how this could get any better," I say.

Teo pulls his hand from my waist and places it on my stomach, looking at it longingly.

"I can think of something."

He glances back up at me, noticing my look of surprise.

"Really?" I say. "You think you're ready to be a dad?"

He nods slowly.

"I think I can do anything with you beside me."

His eyes narrow, and I know that he means it. I know that he's going to be absolutely perfect.

Perfect.

THE END

ALSO BY JD HAWKINS

Insatiable Part 1

It's not cocky when you've got the goods to back it up.

Lust-maker. Pleasure giver. Fantasy creator. I can blow your mind in five seconds flat — but trust me, you'll want this to last all night.

There's not a woman in the city who can resist me. Except one.

Now she's got a proposition: Seven days. Every position. No strings attached.

She wants to know what she's been missing.

Who am I to say no?

BUY NOW!

Insatiable Part 2

It was supposed to be simple: I teach her a crash course in pleasure. No commitment. No strings.

Now she's found the perfect guy — and it's not me.

I should move on, but I need her. And I never back down from a fight.

Now I've got one last lesson for her:

I'm going to make her mine.

BUY NOW!

BOOTYCALL

"I'm going to show her just how good a bad boy can be..."

When you're the prince of Hollywood, and everyone wants a piece of the action. I've got paparazzi stalking my every move, and supermodels lined up to spread their legs for a shot at fame. But this girl is different. She's been hired by the studio to keep me in line. One wrong move, and my comeback is going up in smoke.

I should keep my distance, but I've never played by the rules.

BUY NOW!

BOOTYCALL Part 2

I'm going to show her just how good a bad boy can be...

Everything's riding on my comeback, but suddenly, Hollywood is the last thing on my mind.

Gemma Clark was supposed to keep me out of trouble, but now I'm in way over my head. What we have is real -- too real. It's just a matter of time before it all comes crashing down.

I need to face my demons, but what happens when she discovers the truth?

BUY NOW!

THE BET

What would you do if a famous producer approached you at a club and told you he wants to make you a star? Would you take the leap?

Brando Nash is a bad boy with a wall of platinum records and a line of girls just begging to work with him--and under him. And he wants to make me famous. Who could say no? But I'm not in this for cheap thrills, no matter how hard his body is, or how good he is at charming my panties off.

When we start working together, I fight to keep my heart in check. He's unbelievably hot, a musical genius and a dirty talking, arrogant playboy. There's no way I can resist.

But when I find out he's just in this for a bet, everything changes. I'm not just a dirty game. With my heart and career on the line, I have too much at stake. Can I risk it all and give him a second chance?

The Bet is a full length, stand-alone romance starring a dirty talking alpha male. If over the top sexual fantasy and out of control chemistry offend you, don't buy this bestselling book.

BUY NOW!

CONFESSIONS OF A BAD BOY

Confessions of a Bad Boy Episode 1: Never Commit I'm the internet's favorite Bad Boy - the guy who'll tell it to you straight. No bullshit charm. No excuses. Consider it a public service, letting women know the truth about what guys are really thinking and teaching guys how to get what they want. Yes, we were checking that girl out. No, you don't want to meet her parents. And no, ladies, we don't care what shoes you wear - as long as they're up around our neck by the end of the night. Life was simple, until fate brought me back together with Jessie. My best friend's younger sister, who I just happened to have the hottest one night stand of my life with four years ago. Who calls me at 3 AM to get bailed out of jail. Who I can't keep my hands off of. And who can never find out who I really am. She's off-limits, but I don't care. And when I need a fake girlfriend to help me out of a jam at work, she's the only one who can help. Now I'm stuck sharing a hotel room with her for the weekend. A long, sexy weekend. This is your Bad Boy, signing off.

BUY NOW!

SECRETS OF AN ALPHA MALE

What happens when a cocky bad boy falls for a good girl?

I'm Connor 'Alpha Male' Anderson. Pound for pound I'm the best MMA fighter in America, and I've got the brains, balls, and brawn to back it up - 230 pounds of pure muscle, infinite charm, and the stamina to last all night long. But with the biggest fight of my career coming up, I've got to keep my pants zipped and get my head in the game.

That's when Frankie Jones comes in. An amazingly hot yoga teacher, she drives me crazy with those booty shorts and sports bras. I'll hold downward dog as long as she wants so I can show her my cobra. She's a total bombshell, feisty, and challenges me every step of the way. She doesn't fall for my alpha game, and that only turns me on more. But how can I get myself into her skin-tight leggings, with the pressure of this title match coming up and my trainer's orders to keep it in my pants?

Before I met Frankie, all I wanted was to win this fight.

But now?

All I want is her.

Opposites attract in this Standalone Romance Novel with an HEA that will knock you out!

BUY NOW!

UNPROFESSIONAL

What happens when you fall in love with your best friend?

I have the best job in the world. Date beautiful women and write about it.

But I want to take it to the next level: instead of writing about my experiences make it into an online reality show.

But here is the catch. My boss wants me to share the show with a woman co-host. And he wants that woman to be my best friend and co-worker, Margo.

I'll date beautiful women and she'll date hot men. Sounds fair enough.

So now I have to watch her fake date hot men. I used to love going home with a different woman every night, but suddenly this isn't as fun. Seeing Margo with anyone else is driving me crazy.

And the more time I spend with her working on the show, the less I want to keep our relationship in the friends' zone. And the harder it is to stop myself from imagining her bent over the copier.

Things are about to get unprofessional.

BUY NOW!

COCKY CHEF

You can call me arrogant as much as you want. But when you're the best at what you do and have the hottest restaurant on the west coast, with enough Michelin stars to make Gordon Ramsay's head spin, you've earned the right to your confidence.

When I give an instruction in the kitchen, it's not a suggestion--it's an order. So when a new chef thinks she can do things her way, and dares to say so to my face, even her sharp wit and gorgeous pouty lips don't make it okay.

But I have to admit, she's got talent. She's creative in the kitchen and not even that double-breasted chef jacket can hide her perfect body. As I get to know her, I can't help wanting to know everything she thinks. I've never met a more talented chef. And I've never met a sassier and sexier woman in my life.

There's only one way this push and pull can end.

With her in my bed, begging for more.

BUY NOW!

ACKNOWLEDGMENTS

Thank you to my wife, my PR kick ass "I'm gonna cut you Chicagoan" Candi Kane, my editor B, and readers.

I love you long time.

ABOUT THE AUTHOR

JD grew up in Southern California and now lives with his wife in Venice, CA. JD loves to travel and enjoys surfing, training in MMA and riding motorcycles.

Join his newsletter where all the cool kids hang out.

When I'm not surfing or being my badass self at my local coffee shop, you can catch me on: